THE REBEL PRINCESS

Doris Leslie

SAPERE
BOOKS

THE REBEL
PRINCESS

Published by Sapere Books.

24 Trafalgar Road, Ilkley, LS29 8HH

saperebooks.com

ISBN: 978-0-85495-057-7

FOREWORD

In presenting this story of the ill-fated wife of George the First I have kept strictly to documentary evidence. All excerpts from letters are authentic; no character nor major incident is fictitious. This is no romanticised version of the tragic life of a sixteen-year-old bride forced into a merciless State marriage with a coarse libertine whose brutality and promiscuous adulteries caused her to seek consolation with one of whom Thackeray says, 'no greater scamp walks the pages of history'. Her all-absorbing passion for him and her reckless rebellion against autocratic and insupportable conditions resulted in the monstrously unjust penalty of lifelong imprisonment, deprived of her rightful rank and forbidden the sight of or communication with her children, nor with any from the outside world.

While I hold no brief for the Countess von Platen, whose maniacal jealousy brought about the final catastrophe, yet I think had she lived in our more enlightened age she almost certainly would have been a case for the psychiatrist. As for the rest of the characters, who feature in the life of this uncrowned Queen Consort of our first Hanoverian king, I write as I find them, typical of the licentious times in which they lived. But has human nature changed so very much during three centuries?

Among authorities quoted in the compilation of this book I am particularly indebted to: W. H. Wilkins, M.A., Fellow of the Royal Historical Society who, in 1900, first published from the originals the correspondence between Sophia Dorothea and

Philip Christopher, and Count Königsmarck, in *The Love of an Uncrowned Queen.*

Others to whom I have referred are:

Lewis Melville, *The First George;*

W. M. Thackeray, *The Four Georges;*

Winston Churchill, *Marlborough, His Life and Times;*

Macaulay's *History of England;*

National Dictionary of Biography,

State Papers, etc.

DORIS LESLIE

PART ONE (1682-1689)

ONE

'The sky,' she said, 'is in tears for my birthday.'

Her nose, whitened at its tilted tip, was pressed against the window-pane where, kneeling on the cushioned seat, she watched the raindrops trickle down. The lawns lay dreary, sodden, dark, under drenched trees nudging heavy clouds. So did it rain on her birthday four years since, when she had watched her father's page — cloaked, muffled, hatless, his long fair hair floating wet about his shoulders — mount his horse and, followed by his lackey, ride away. Dismissed.

'And all because,' she turned her head, continuing her thought aloud to tell Eleonore von dem Knesebeck, her lady-in-waiting and confidante — not a very wise one, but withal her closest friend — 'only because he wrote me a letter with some poetry in it which he said he had composed, but he hadn't. It was what Juliet said of Romeo, and he pretended he had made it up about my taking his heart and cutting it up in little stars. And Herr Bernstorff found it — I must have dropped the letter somewhere in the garden — you remember the fuss they made, thanks to that wart-hog Bernstorff always spying on me.'

'Perhaps,' said the confidante, who had heard all this a dozen times and would hear it all again, 'Count Philip read of Romeo and Juliet in a French or German translation and misconstrued it.'

'No, he didn't.' Sophia Dorothea wheeled sharply round. 'He read it in English. He was always saying or writing to me about Romeo and Juliet, because he said I reminded him of Juliet being of her age, but I wasn't. She was fourteen, and I was twelve on the day my father sent him away…' Her mind dwelled on their last meeting to bring a tingling recurrence of memory revived, and with a warm colour in her cheeks she was back at the window to divert Eleonore's attention from that tell-tale flush. 'Oh! I hear wheels and horses. Lennie, look! There's a great coach and six in the bend of the drive. It can't be my cousin of Wolfenbüttel — what hideous names they have! — come for me so early.'

'I expect it is,' answered 'Lennie', as familiarly called by her young lady. 'Since Your Highness's betrothal is to be announced tonight, he will want to be early in readiness.'

'He may be in readiness,' was the hot retort, 'but I am not in readiness to be handed out to him as if I were a parcel.'

'His Highness is so handsome,' Knesebeck sighingly ventured. She was full-bosomed, buxom, an incurable romantic and some three years older than Sophia Dorothea. 'From all accounts he is very much in love with you.'

'From whose account? Your own? You live in fairy tales. He has seen me but once in his life, and sat staring and sucking his thumb with nothing to say more than "yes" and "no", while our respective fathers discussed my marriage settlements in the ante-chamber. As for handsome, with a face like a cheese — if that's your idea of handsome you can have him, for I won't.'

Eleonore held her peace. Long custom had inured her to refrain from argument with the Princess of Celle were she in her 'moods', the confidante's synonym for tempers, in which this darling only child of her parents too frequently indulged. Instead, peering through the window in her turn, with Teutonic phlegm she remarked, 'Madame, I think it is not His Serene Highness, the Prince … it is…'

'*Sacré nom!*' was Madame's dismayed ejaculation, lapsing into French, her mother's native tongue, as always when unduly agitated. *Je crois ... évidemment! Bon dieu! Mais ...* so it is!'

And so it was: the castle's uninvited, most unwelcome, guest.

The Duchess Sophia, having travelled from Hanover to Celle over roads hock-deep in mud, could scarcely have been in worse humour. Stiff, cold, aching in every limb as the coach rattled and bumped along the cobbled streets of Celle, she surveyed with apprehension and disgust the errand that had brought her there to meet the woman whom for seventeen years she had shunned, humiliated and despised.

In letters outpoured to her niece, second wife of Philippe d'Orléans, brother of the King of France, she was wont to anathematise her sister-in-law, the Duchess of Celle, as 'that dot of dirt', and her daughter, Sophia Dorothea, as 'the little French bastard'.

Of all the duchess's aversions — and they were legion — she nurtured primarily the French. This particular animus may have had its origin when, in her late twenties, she might have been condemned to lifelong spinsterhood had not a betrothal been tardily arranged between herself and George William, Duke of Hanover, who was disinclined for marriage, least of all with Sophia, sister of the Elector Palatine.

Finding her less desirable than the infinitely more attractive young women he had encountered on his travels in Italy and France, George William — after many amorous encounters with ladies of the high world, the low world and the half-world — fell head over heels in love with Éléonore d'Olbreuse, daughter of an impoverished Huguenot Marquis, and married her — *ad morganaticum*!

Thus Sophia, granddaughter of England's James I, daughter of Elizabeth — Winter Queen of Bohemia, a Royal Stuart by descent, which none was allowed to forget — found herself jilted by a petty German Princeling. But it may have somewhat, lessened her humiliation when Ernest Augustus, Duke-Bishop of Osnabrück, youngest of the four orphaned brothers of the Duke of Brunswick-Lüneberg, declared himself willing to take to wife the discarded Sophia for a substantial reward: the solemn assurance of George William that he would never wed, since the State could not recognise a morganatic marriage. This being so, he agreed to surrender not only part of his revenue to his two younger brothers, but that at his death his valuable inheritance should pass to his brother Ernest or his issue.

Reparation enough for backing out of a betrothal, Sophia might have thought, when the first shock from that left-handed marriage had subsided. And she may have found some satisfaction in the sudden death without issue of the eldest of four brothers, the wealthy Duke Christian of Celle. The principality of Hanover had been allotted to a younger brother, John Frederick, by the simple-minded, over-generous George William, now Duke of Celle; and John, a bachelor, was likely to remain so — as also, in point of law, was William. Therefore Sophia's husband, Ernest Augustus — or his eldest son — would, in the fullness of time, reign not only at Osnabrück but at Celle and Hanover.

The birth of a daughter born to George William in September 1666 — named Sophia Dorothea in a somewhat tactless attempt to oil the turbulent Osnabrück waters — had served further to increase Sophia's resentment against the d'Olbreuse, whose bastard bore her name, which is possibly why the child has always been known by both her baptismal names. And when the christening was celebrated with much pomp and rejoicing at Celle, 'If the brat had been born a princess instead of his "Madame's" by-blow,' was Sophia's acrid comment to her Duke, 'they couldn't have made more fuss and palaver about it.'

But the fuss and palaver continued with the ensuing years, while mother and child were paid all homage and respect by the subjects of the Duke of Celle as though they were his legal wife and daughter.

One may well imagine the consternation and multiplied fury of Duchess Sophia to learn, from certain of her spies at Celle, that the 'clot of dirt' had exerted her influence with the Emperor Leopold of Germany — with whom it was said that she, in her past, had been on favourable terms — to grant legitimacy to the child, Sophia Dorothea. This was bad enough, but worse followed in the nature of a thunderbolt to cause a brainstorm to the duchess, vented in a series of tirades to her Duke. The title of Countess of Wilhelmsburg, and the island of that name — along with other vast estates — had been bestowed upon the child's mother by her infatuated 'husband' to revert to their daughter after her death. Was the woman aiming at a greater title yet?

Possibly. No tigress disturbed in the suckling of her young could have fought with more ferocity than did Éléonore to secure for Sophia Dorothea the royal rank that should now be hers.

'She and her brat are a menace to our honour and our House!' stormed the duchess. 'If my cousin, Charles of England, can foist young Monmouth, that strumpet Lucy Walter's son, on his people as second Duke in his kingdom to his brother York, God only knows what Celle is like to do for this by-blow of the d'Olbreuse, which may not be his at all but begot by one of d'Orléans' fancy boys. Who,' she grimacingly

12

added, 'will play the cat with two backs on anything, in petticoats or breeks!'

Duke Ernest blinked. Notwithstanding his own infidelities, coarse speech and ribaldry, he — even after almost twenty years of marriage with this scion of the Stuarts — could not stomach her outspokenness, sharp tongue and sharper temper, which ran riot when attacking the d'Olbreuse.

'And don't,' rampaged Sophia, 'sit there gaping like a sawney at a fair. Hearken here what Bernstorff has reported…'

Herr Bernstorff, Celle's chancellor, was a past master of intrigue to hunt with the hare, the Duke of Celle, and 'those two bitch-hounds at Hanover', as he privately designated the Duchess Sophia and one other: Clara von Platen, the mistress of Duke Ernest, whom she had successfully captured in his susceptible middle age.

Bernstorff had an eye to higher preferment, a tobacco factory and vineyards on the Rhine with a 'von' before his name — 'Baron von Bernstorff', as insinuated by the Platen — for news from Celle that might be of advantage to herself. The Platen's tastes were extravagant. Her husband, a minor official at the Court of Osnabrück and ex-tutor to the duke's eldest son, George Louis, had not the wherewithal to meet with her demands, and willingly renounced his wife's bed and board to the Reverend Father in God, Ernest, Duke-Bishop of Osnabrück. But the duke, more or less dependent on his brother's generosity, could not oblige his Clara with her own establishment, after which she hankered — at least not while the daughter of Celle and her mother were receiving the bounty that by rights should be Duke Ernest's.

These sentiments were shared by the Duchess Sophia, who voiced them, with invective, to her Duke.

'I tell you,' she vociferated, 'that while the Frenchwoman's daughter remains at Celle there will be no peace for us, and no more compensation from your brother for having broken his troth to me. We must get the bastard away, out of Germany. Marry her off to one of those foreign pages that Celle takes to train for military service, British, French, Swedes — yes! He has a Swede there now, young Königsmarck, and Bernstorff says…'

What Bernstorff said, respectively related to the duchess and the Platen, gave them both, hopefully, to think.

The page, Philip, son of Count Königsmarck of one of the wealthiest and most respected families in Sweden, had been caught playing truant from his studies and attendance on the duke to play with and attend on the duke's daughter. Heads together in an arbour, they had been seen by Bernstorff, reading, and heard reciting love poems in French and English. Letters from the page, 'full of nonsense', had been intercepted by Herr Bernstorff and brought to the Countess von Wilhelmsburg.

For Bernstorff had more than one diplomatic card hidden up his sleeve, and however much the two ladies at Hanover might wish to dispose of Sophia Dorothea by marrying her off to some foreigner and so get her out of the country, a marriage nearer home might benefit him better. He knew that the dearest wish of the Countess von Wilhelmsburg was to see her child take her rank and title as her father's daughter, a princess. Were she married to a Swede or any other foreigner, the countess's dearest wish could not be gratified. Moreover, he surmised that the wealthy Lady of Wilhelmsburg could offer greater reward for service rendered than lay within Duke Ernest's purse when rifled by the Platen.

Accordingly he came to Éléonore with his findings: the 'nonsense' letters and quotations from the poets, both French and English, which Bernstorff — who had but scantiest knowledge of either language — thought to have been the inspiration of the presumptuous young page.

'He might, dear Countess,' suggested the chancellor, 'be better employed at the Court of the King of England, or sent to Monsieur Foubert's famous military academy in London. Count Philip neglects his duties to attend on Fräulein von Wilhelmsburg. Far be it from me,' Bernstorff pietistically pursued, 'to believe that the Fräulein would take *au grand sérieux,*' pronounced in guttural German-French, 'the vapourings of a schoolboy, but she is very young and impressionable. Would it not be well to remove the young man from the Fräulein's vicinity?'

That suggestion met with the warmest approval of Éléonore and, when brought to her husband, led to the dismissal of Philip, the page.

So far so good; for 'the Fräulein', applied to Sophia Dorothea, rankled in the heart of her mother as Bernstorff intended it should. He saw the tobacco factory looming ever nearer, as did the crest of an eagle *couchant* inscribed upon his table silver and his lackeys' liveries, with a castle on the Rhine thrown in.

Well pleased with his manoeuvres, the chancellor had seen young Philip ride away, inly vowing to get even with 'that wart-hog Bernstorff' as he named him to his child sweetheart when he took farewell of her, with tears on her part and promises on his to come back and claim her for his own.

'And then we'll be married. I am sixteen. In four years' time *you* will be sixteen and I'll be twenty. I'll have fought many battles by then,' he bragged, 'to bring honour to my country and yours. I am going for a soldier. I'll be a general before I've done. My King of Sweden will confer on me great military honours. All my family are soldiers — and great lovers.'

Whereupon, to prove it, he kissed her long and skilfully. For his age he was precociously experienced to set her young blood ablaze with delicious undreamed-of sensations, and what might have come of it only the serpent in their Eden could have known, as — watching with one eye screwed to a crack in the woodwork of that rustic arbour — he saw the sensitive long fingers of the page exploring where they had no right to be, and heard delighted little squeals from her and sighs and gasps from him.

'Good heavens!' breathed Herr Bernstorff. The chancellor, in a sweat of vicarious pleasure at this infantile love-play, was loth to interrupt it until, with dust in his nostrils from his spidery peep-hole, he sneezed, halting the giggles of the shameless young lady, and bringing the page in a scramble to his feet, one hand sprung to his sword-hilt — a trifling toy capped with a jewelled crest, worn more from braggadocio than use.

'What in hell!' exploded this new-born Adam, his cracking boy's voice deepening in a moment from its juvenile croak to that of a man, steel-edged. 'What do you here? Who are you? Come out and show yourself and I'll slit your guts for trespass!'

And she, who had darted forward to see the chancellor beating a hasty retreat, called to him with sweetness, 'Herr Bernstorff! Do you have a cold?' And, inexcusably, she cocked a snook at him as he disappeared behind a hedge.

'The wart-hog, is it?' cried Philip. 'Spying as usual!' Apparently to no good effect, when Bernstorff went to Hanover full of a tale for the Duchess Sophia, told with much hum-ing and hah-ing, of how that the page, Königsmarck, had been dismissed from Celle. A boy-and-girl — um — *friendship* had been discovered by the countess. The two young persons had been seen — um — *misbehaving* in an arbour.

The duchess pounced on this. 'In what way misbehaving? Do you mean — what *do* you mean? Speak up, man. Did he rape her? If he didn't he's no Königsmarck.'

Said Bernstorff in reminiscent discomfort: 'To the best of my belief, Serene Highness, the girl is still a maiden.'

'How do *you* know?' cackled Her Highness. 'Unless *you* were misbehaving with her in an arbour.'

'Your Highness!' expostulated Bernstorff, hot beneath the fall of lace that hid his Adam's apple. He had further disquieting news to impart, were he given a chance to tell it.

But: 'It seems,' said the duchess, 'that you have not succeeded in finding a husband who must,' she emphasised, 'be a foreigner, to rid us of this girl still, doubtfully, a maiden, and who is a continuous menace and encumbrance upon Us.' She invariably used the royal plural when addressing an inferior. 'Which, being so…' She clawed a handful of bon-bons from a silver casket on an ornamental table at her elbow, crammed her mouth with them and handed a couple of the same to Bernstorff. 'Take them. You'll find them more tasty than I do your news.' And, her nose uplifted as if at a smell, she pointed to the door and said, 'Go!'

Bowing, backing out of the door flung open by two lackeys, went Bernstorff, mightily deflated; but no sooner was he out of eye- and earshot than he detached two brandied cherries from his palm, where they had stuck. Muttering: 'To hell with her!' he took himself to Madame Platen. He had gauged to a nicety her backstair methods that equalised his own, and, on reflection, saw in her a more rewarding instrument for his designs than the Duchess Sophia or the Lady of Celle.

Having been summarily disposed of by Her Highness before he had time to impart news far more calamitous than his failure to rid the duchess of her 'menace and encumbrance', he communicated to the ducal mistress his confidential gleanings from the council chamber; that Duke Ulrich of Brunswick-Wolfenbüttel, a cousin of the Duke of Celle, had in mind to effect a betrothal between his eldest son and Sophia Dorothea.

This intelligence was received with a shrug of the Platen's ample shoulders, and the reminder that no such marriage could possibly take place. The girl was a commoner and therefore could not marry royalty. But Bernstorff had more to tell than that: it seemed both dukes were agreeable to the marriage, and had petitioned the Emperor Leopold to permit that the title of Princess be granted to the now legitimate daughter of the Duke of Celle. Yet even this, did not unduly disturb Madame Platen. While George William of Celle and his brother John remained unwed, Celle's daughter could not inherit the Duchy; it must eventually revert to his brother of Osnabrück, and after him to his eldest son, George Louis.

Now Clara von Platen had no love for any living soul but herself and one other: her younger sister, Catherine-Marie. Having secured for her a husband, one Johann Busche, also former tutor to George Louis, she had seen to it that Catherine, a pliant tool in her hands, should annex Duke Ernest's heir as her protector. If Clara could have foretold that in giving her sister to the embraces of this princeling of Osnabrück she was offering her to a future King of England, she would doubtless — although some fifteen years his senior — have seized him for her own. However, as she could not have imagined so remote an improbability, she concentrated on the advantages that lay within her reach: the crumbs dropped from Celle's table for his brother Ernest to gobble and regurgitate for her adornment.

Certain of snatching her share of any bounty that might come to Hanover from Celle, the Platen sent Bernstorff away with a gold bejewelled snuff-box in token of her goodwill, should he have anything further to impart concerning Wolfenbüttel's proposition that, she made abundantly clear, the Duke-Bishop of Osnabrück would decidedly oppose.

Yet oppose it as he might, and did, Ulrich of Wolfenbüttel had his way. His petition, backed by his cousin of Celle, resulted in His August Majesty not only granting the title of Princess to Sophia Dorothea but — charmed by the beauty of his fair suppliant Éléonore, sent by the two dukes to plead her cause and theirs — gave permission, in fact commanded, that the Duke of Celle should 'enter into Holy Matrimony with the high-born lady, the Countess of Wilhelmsburg, and proclaim her throughout his principality as his lawful wife and duchess.'

The marriage, so long delayed, was celebrated with every pomp and solemnity befitting a royal wedding, and attended by all the dignitaries of the Courts of Celle and Hanover; but from these ceremonies the Duke and Duchess of Osnabrück were conspicuously absent.

It was these agonising memories on which Sophia brooded as she jolted and bumped on the seat of the coach during her journey to Celle. What torture had she suffered to know herself and her ducal bishop thwarted; all hope of attaining her Mecca, the Duchy of Celle, and of Hanover should John, the younger brother, die without issue … gone! Her castle in the air and the wealth of its coffers vanished as if it had never been. And to think that Ulrich of Wolfenbüttel's son should carry off the prize, the richest heiress of all the principalities, that 'French bastard'. For no marriage, however 'holy', could, in the sight of Sophia, make her anything else, since she had been born out of wedlock.

For these last seventeen years the duchess had nursed her hate of Éléonore until it became a malignant growth eating into her soul, a hate that only revenge could tear from her. And, as if in answer to her constant prayer, revenge was offered by the death of the 'bastard's' betrothed, killed in battle during the war between Louis, King of France, and the Emperor of Germany, in which so many of the young princes of military age were involved.

The announcement of the death of Wolfenbüttel's heir almost coincided with the death of John Frederick of Hanover, who although he had eventually married, died childless. So now Ernest Augustus reigned over Osnabrück *and* Hanover. What a lucky turn of fortune's wheel! And if George William should die — as Sophia prayed he would — before his brother Ernest, then their eldest son, George Louis, would succeed his father as Duke not only of Hanover but Celle! A just revenge, and punishment to the Frenchwoman for having got herself legally married by selling her wares to the emperor — who was known to have a sweet tooth for French pastry, ha, ha — and by the same token, to have made her misbegotten brat a princess!

Alas, Sophia's elation was short-lived. Barely had the months of official mourning ended than, with somewhat indecent haste, Duke Ulrich offered his second son for the gold-lined hand of Celle's daughter, and was accepted. The betrothal between the present heir of Wolfenbüttel and the Princess of Celle was to be publicly announced on her sixteenth birthday.

Once again were the hopes of the Duchess Sophia ground to dust, yet she too could fight for her young with as fierce determination as ever could Éléonore.

'No! Never! It shall never be, save over my dead body!' Up and down her salon in a ferment of rage stormed the duchess to her duke, who had taken this latest catastrophic news with much less disquiet than did his wife. His unexpected succession to the Duchy of Hanover had relieved him of much pecuniary anxiety, despite the fact that he had been unable to squeeze a further fifty thousand thalers out of his brother of Celle to meet the demands of his Clara. And now, endeavouring to calm his virago: 'Pray, my heart,' he bade her, 'do not waste your breath and energy on what cannot be helped. Ulrich of Wolfenbüttel holds Celle in his pocket. They have always, since their boyhood, been hand and glove.'

But this effort to make her see reason served only to make her see red.

'Fool! Idiot! Don't talk to me — wasting energy. If you had not wasted your energy in your woman's bed, the overspill of Wilhelmsburg and of Celle's coffers — which Ulrich's pup will come in for — might have been yours and —' She halted in her frenzied pacing to stand struck with a God-sent inspiration and the wondrous chance it envisaged for their eldest son. Pursuing that lightning flash of revelation: 'Why,' she demanded, 'should not Celle's girl yet be his — and ours!'

'His? Ours?' was the duke-bishop's not unreasonably befogged comment.

'Don't you see?' screamed Sophia. 'We can yet thwart Wolfenbüttel!'

She did some rapid thinking. Yes! And so achieve a double purpose: retributive punishment served to the Frenchwoman for the birth of Celle's daughter, and to give to their son

George Louis the 'bastard's' wealth, and that of her father's Duchy, at his much-desired death.

'Listen, jackass! Will you listen?' She stood over her husband where he sat hunched in his chair, fearful of assault, for in her tempers she had been known to come at him with her fists. One was now threateningly raised. In self-protection he ducked, and heard, 'You must go to Celle. Tell him we offer our son and heir to his daughter. Do you understand, sheep's head? George William would sooner take his brother's son of Hanover than Wolfenbüttel's whelp. Why should not George Louis have that which by right should be his? And *shall* be his!'

'B-but,' stammered Ernest, roused from his stunned apathy, 'my brother William and I are n-not on the best of terms since he refused me th-that fifty thousand thalers —'

'What are fifty thousand thalers compared to the millions of Wilhelmsburg and Celle? You —' A shaking finger was pointed at the shrinking duke. Her lips, foam-flecked, snarled back against her teeth. *Surely,* thought Ernest in terror, *the woman's run mad!*

'You,' she italicised repetitively, 'you must go to Celle! The betrothal is to be announced on her sixteenth birthday. We must forestall it and we will announce George Louis as — good God!' Another, more appalling thought had struck her. 'On her sixteenth birthday, which is the fifteenth of September — and today is the fourteenth! There's no time. There *must* be time. You must order the coach and go now!'

But in the end it was not the duke who ordered the coach to go then, it was the duchess. On further and calmer reflection, she decided that only she could undertake so delicate a mission, however odious it would be to meet again; after all these years, the loathly Éléonore and to offer her son, Hanover's heir, to the 'bastard' heiress of Celle. Yet the luscious cornucopia of Celle's fruitful millions, held before her yearning eyes, spurred her on…

And so we find her in her coach on that September morning, her thumbnail bitten to the quick — a habit, this, of all the Stuarts when *in extremis* — arrived at the end of her journey. *Pray God,* she appealed, *that I may be in time!*

Frantically she peered through the breath-misted windows for a sight of the Wolfenbüttel equipage. Had he come there before her? Was his coach in the coach-house, were his horses in the stables? Were he and his cub even now drinking toasts in celebration of the forthcoming announcement?

She heard the clock tower strike seven sonorous strokes, and shouted to the footman who had descended from his box to help her alight. 'Ask if another visitor has arrived before me. Ask! There are a dozen sentries standing there — so ask!'

No need to ask. The sentries were about to change guard and it was obvious no other vehicle had driven up to the drawbridge of the castle, which was being lowered for the entry of the coach.

Stiff and aching in every joint, Sophia, faint with fatigue, was handed out and, assisted by her lackeys, made her entrance.

Wakened from sonorous sleep by his valet, the Duke of Celle, when told of the duchess's arrival and her desire for immediate audience, was hurriedly got out of bed. But before he could be made ready to receive her, Sophia shoved aside a bowing, hand-washing gentleman-in-waiting who apologetically informed her that His Serene Highness was not yet dressed.

'Dressed or undressed, I will see His Highness *now*! My business is urgent and will brook no delay. Allow me to pass.'

The gentleman, in a flurry, allowed her to pass. He could scarcely have prevented her as she swept by him, her voluminous petticoats almost extinguishing two scared little pages. 'Conduct me,' she commanded, 'to His Serene Highness's bedchamber.'

She was conducted.

At the door of the ducal apartment she dismissed the gentleman-in-waiting, the lackeys in attendance and the pages, who had their ears cuffed by the gentleman for nervously giggling. 'Go, all of you.' Sophia waved them off. 'I will announce myself.'

Into George William's privacy she marched, and bore down upon the startled duke where he sat at his dressing-glass in the hands of his valet, who was shaving him.

'My dear Sophia!' When he could find voice to speak through the lather on his lip and his horrified astonishment at this untoward invasion. 'Welcome! De-delighted! I — I must beg you to excuse my *déshabillé*. A towel,' to the valet, 'wipe me.'

He was wiped. His chin, not yet shaved, showed the night's growth of fair beard, resembling a miniature stubble of corn. 'I trust,' babbled George William, 'that this — this unexpected — pleasure does not p-p-presage ill news.'

Had she come on behalf of Ernest Augustus to bleed him of those fifty thousand thalers, as if he had not been bled enough? Or, he hopefully wondered, was Ernest dead, or Hanover in revolt, or — what?

Sophia, who had seated herself and removed her gloves to chafe her numbed fingers, said, 'It has been a cold drive. I am chilled to the bone. Your roads are abominable. Ill news? Not at all. I bring good news, and am come to congratulate you and Sophia Dorothea on her sixteenth birthday with a gift —' she brought to her face a smile that resembled the grin of a skull — 'to rejoice the heart of your daughter and you, and your — er — your wife. Where is she, your — wife?'

George William, whose mouth had gone suddenly dry at sight of that skeletal smile, swallowed and, pointing to the door of the chamber communicating with his dressing room, muttered, 'Éléonore is — I think — still in bed.'

She was in bed, gazing at the ceiling realistically adorned with frescoes depicting amorous gods and goddesses at play and an intimate representation of Leda and the Swan, while her thoughts pleasurably reviewed the festivities for that evening's announcement of her darling's betrothal.

Hearing voices in the adjoining room, the door having been left ajar, she called to her husband to know who had come to disturb him at this unconscionable hour, whereupon, through the half-open door, Sophia was heard loudly to tell her: 'It is I, the Duchess of Hanover, come betimes to be the first to congratulate you and your — your husband.' She repeated the words she had just told George William: a sugared pill offered before the bitter physic with which the pair of them would presently be dosed.

Then, without waiting to hear Éléonore's reply to that, she drew a chair close to the duke and, after bidding him, 'Send your man away', she spoke to him in Low Dutch, well aware that the 'Frenchwoman' couldn't understand a word of it.

With vigorous intensity did she unfold to the apprehensive William the main purpose of her visit. She greatly deplored the family feud that had existed too long between Celle and Hanover. 'What a misfortune,' lamented Sophia, having heard of the impending betrothal of his daughter to Wolfenbüttel's son, 'that so fine a domain as Wilhelmsburg and the wealth of Celle should be lost to the House of Brunswick-Lüneberg and create even more ill-feeling between Hanover and Celle. We must bury the hatchet,' she declared, glancing at the half-open door with her skull-like grin that held in it an evident urge to bury the hatchet in the head of the listening Éléonore, 'let bygones be bygones and unite our two children. Your daughter and my beloved son —' whom she endowed with every deific grace, and inwardly prayed that William, who sat pop-eyed with amazement at this extraordinary change of front, had not learned that her beloved son had taken to himself the sister of his father's whore, and was even at that moment most likely in her bed. That affair, she swiftly decided, must be at once suppressed.

'And think,' moving her chair closer to the duke with a ghastly attempt at charmful persuasion, 'how such a union will be welcomed by my cousin of Orange, with whom my beloved George Louis is in highest favour.' A monstrous fabrication, since William of Orange, her Stuart mother's nephew whom Sophia beshrewed as 'that little yellow toad', detested George Louis and had resolutely refused his courtship of his young sister-in-law Anne, daughter of James, Duke of York. A courtship pre-arranged by Sophia — another wishful hope lost. 'And think,' she continued, perceiving the duke had swallowed the bait, 'how this connection with the Royal House of Stuart through my blood and descent will win the approval of my cousin, Charles of England. Who knows what the future may hold for your daughter as wife of one who is in the direct line of succession to the throne of that great power!'

This was the first time Sophia had voiced her secret dream. It had the desired effect, finally to land her gaping fish and secure him, hooked, to say with what breath he had left: 'Sophia, I — I am overwhelmed. No one could regret more than I the breach between my brother and myself. It has always been my — my hope to see that breach mended, and now —' his voice cracked, and tears, an ever-ready sentimental fount of the

Hanoverians, welled up in the gooseberry eyes — 'now that hope, too long deferred, is f-fulfilled.' Joyfully he wept.

'God be praised,' said Sophia briskly. 'And now all that remains for us to do is to dispose of Wolfenbüttel. Your Bernstorff, an admirable diplomat, must attend to this. But no need,' she added hastily, 'to offer Wolfenbüttel compensation more than your polite regrets for the severance of a betrothal that has never been announced and was only in the air. You must tell him the affections of Sophia Dorothea are engaged elsewhere and that you cannot oppose her heart's desire. Have you breakfasted? I have not. I have had neither bite nor sup since last evening. Pray order me a meal, and — wait!'

From a gold-embroidered reticule she extracted a miniature set round with diamonds. It depicted a seraphic youth with golden curls and a Cupid's bow of a mouth: an excessively flattered portrait of George Louis, executed some few years before by the Hanoverian Court painter, and which Sophia had brought with her to present to Sophia Dorothea as her birthday gift.

'Give this,' she said grandly, 'to your daughter with my blessing and the devotion of her adoring affianced, George Louis. I could fancy an escalope of veal and a bottle of Rhenish. Do me the honour, brother Celle, of sharing your breakfast with me.'

Thus was the destiny of kings and queens decided unto the third and fourth generation, and to the ultimate undoing of Sophia Dorothea.

'I cannot — I *will* not,' cried Éléonore, 'break this news to her. How am I to tell her? *You* must tell her!'

'You will know better how to tell her than I,' mumbled her husband. The sight of his wife's ashen face, and her agitation when she had learned from him the reason of this visit of her enemy, had weakened but not altered his decision. 'You must see,' he continued, looking all ways at once, 'that this marriage of our dear one to my brother's son is to the best advantage of both Hanover and Celle.'

'The best?' wrathfully echoed Éléonore. 'The worst! I cannot understand why you should contemplate such a match for our child with that young profligate George Louis. As for your cavalier treatment of Wolfenbüttel — *that* is disgraceful. He behaved with greatest dignity — to put you to shame, if shame,' she mercilessly pursued, 'were in you! I can never forgive or forget your abject submission to that woman, who has systematically insulted me and our angel girl all these years; and now, to gratify her greed and enrich Hanover's wealth purloined from *us*, she comes to you with her preposterous proposal. At least your brother had the decency not to approach you himself, but sends her to do his dirty business for him. She rules him and his Duchy with the flick of a finger. He dare not oppose her. You and he are —' She left the remainder of that unfinished, and turned disgustedly from him as he made to take her in his arms.

'My love, my life!' Tears, always his refuge in emergencies, filled his eyes and dribbled down his nose. 'Pray do not allow your dislike of Sophia to — to stand in the light of our child's future, a future that may bring her the promise of a crown, Queen Consort of a King of England as — as,' he gulped, 'the result of this union.'

'Union? And what a union! To sacrifice our darling to your nephew who is bed-ridden with his woman, the Platen's sister, following the lecherous example of his father. As for the future that may bring her the promise of a crown, I see that Sophia has stuffed you full of her *folie de grandeur*. As much likelihood of her son succeeding to the Crown of England as to a crown in heaven! I will not — will *not*,' came the repetitive crescendo, 'agree to such a match. Never — as God is my witness — *never!*'

But for all her vehement objection, Éléonore was eventually persuaded to agree. For once George William had his way with her. It is possible she was not so proof against Sophia of Hanover's *folie de grandeur* as she professed to be, nor to the *grandeur* such *folie* did imply. For should the issue of James of York, heir presumptive to his brother Charles, die childless … a far-fetched assumption since the second wife of James was young enough to bear him half a dozen children, his daughter Anne but seventeen, and her sister, Mary of Orange only four years older, so that the throne of England looked to be secure for all time to come. Yet miracles could happen. Another plague to take its toll of kings and commoners alike, then George Louis might eventually…

Supposition went no further than this remotest gleam of hope to send Éléonore, albeit with grave misgivings, to her daughter. She had anticipated mutiny and something of a scene, but not the volcanic eruption of temper that greeted the news she came to tell.

Sophia Dorothea flung herself on a day-bed; she kicked her heels upon it; she thumped the cushions with her fists. 'I won't! I won't!' Another thump directed to the shoulder of her mother, bending over her in vain attempt to soothe. '*You* to do this to me! You, Mother, to let them pass me from one to another! First Wolfenbüttel — what a name to fasten on me! Then his brother — that lump of cheese-faced suet — and now George Louis. I'd as soon be married to a pig! He *looks* like a pig, he *behaves* like a pig and he *is* a pig! Oh, Mother, how could you?' And then, aghast, she cried: 'And see what you

have made me do. I hit you! *Honour thy father and thy mother* —
but how can I honour you or Father, who have dishonoured
me? To turn Wolfenbüttel out at the door — thank God I
shan't have to be called by that hideous name — but to turn
him and his father away before they set foot in the castle. I saw
them go. I saw that wart-hog Bernstorff — yes, he *is* a wart-
hog — that's what Philip used to call him, and so do I.'

Éléonore exhaled a caught breath. Philip Königsmarck. This
was the first time she had heard his name pass her daughter's
lips since that day, four years ago, when the page had also been
turned away as result of Bernstorff's tales.

Sophia Dorothea was saying, or rather screaming, 'I saw
Bernstorff go out and speak to them, with bows and those
grimaces of his which pass for a smile of *politesse* — *toujours la
politesse* — and they rode furiously off with their cavalcade, and
if they send an army to Celle in revenge for that insult — I
hope they do! — it would be no more than you deserve. Of
course *I* was not consulted. *I* was not asked, "Will you take a
pig to be your wedded husband instead of a lump of suet?" Ah,
yes, I know who is at the root of this — our old duchess, after
whom you named me. Fancy giving me *her* name! — and now
you give me to her son. I hate you — I *hate* you, Mother and
Father. Both of you I hate, for doing this to me!'

Her lovely face was transfigured with passion; tears sprang to
her eyes and dried in their own heat; again she banged the
cushions, lifted one, poised it as if to fling at her mother's
head, thought better of it and hurled it to the floor. Éléonore
inhaled a horrified breath. Although not unaccustomed to the
captious moods and tantrums of her inflammable, highly
strung darling, this paroxysmal explosion suggested a new and
unsuspected personality, a changeling in possession of her
adored.

Éléonore's feeble protest, 'Please calm down, my angel,' brought forth another outburst.

'I will not calm down!' yelled her 'angel'. 'Am I, then, your lamb, to be led to the slaughter? Unnatural Mother, to offer me up as a sacrifice to Hanover as Abraham sacrificed Isaac to God, but God was merciful. He gave him a ram for the sacrifice instead of his son. But you aren't merciful. Why can't you offer a sow to George Louis, a far more fitting mate for a green-tusked boar than I?'

'She is beside herself,' lamented her mother when she recounted this appalling scene to her duke. 'She flew at me — in truth a virago. You must go to her and — and pacify her, for I cannot. She will — she *must* listen to you. Be tactful. Give her the miniature. It is a charming likeness,' pleaded his wife with persuasive mendacity.

Armed with the 'charming likeness', George William, in a taking, went off to his daughter's suite. This consisted of three intercommunicating apartments. There was the schoolroom, where the princess's tutors taught her the rudiments of Latin, English and High and Low Dutch, which aristocratic young German ladies were supposed to learn and to speak, although few of them did. This room overlooked the castle's moat and an avenue of lime trees. Her parlour, that commanded a view of the long entrance drive, was decorated somewhat clumsily in Gallic-Germanic baroque, not as Éléonore would have had it, but the best that Celle's workmen could attain in following their French lady's instructions. The bedroom with its alcoved bed was hung with silver brocade draperies, the marble mantelshelf carved in garlands of fruit and flowers and supported by four cupids. The ceiling, likewise, depicted cupids floating around discreetly clothed nymphs.

The duke, approaching his daughter's apartments with a sinking heart, was met by Eleonore von dem Knesebeck, curtsying and pale.

'Your Serene Highness, the princess is indisposed. She has retired to bed,' assayed the confidante with a scared look over her shoulder at Chancellor Bernstorff, apparently engaged with the princess's butler; for, of late, the chancellor had taken to himself the Comptrollership of the duke's household as well as of the State, and was often seen about the princess's apartments, where certain of her servants were rewarded with gratuities for information extracted concerning their young mistress to be reported to the Platen.

'I ought to — to see my daughter,' indeterminately muttered the duke. 'My poor little one.'

'Certainly, Serene Highness,' bleated Knesebeck, with another curtsy and her eyes up-rolled as if in prayer, for she well knew the reception the duke would be given by his 'poor little one'.

He found her lying fully dressed upon her bed. As she sighted her father, standing hesitant in the doorway with Eleonore von dem Knesebeck hovering in the background, she hoisted herself up, disgracefully to tell him: 'Go away! I won't speak to you ever again! You and Mother to have done this to me!'

'Now, now, my sweetling,' her father began, endeavouring to coax, 'you are very naughty. See what George Louis has sent you for your birthday gift, to plight his troth.'

He produced the miniature. His 'sweetling' snatched it from him. '*That* for his troth?' Still sobbing, but tearlessly, she flung against the wall the 'charming likeness' of George Louis with such violence that the diamonds framing it were scattered on the carpet, and the glass that enclosed the painted ivory splintered into fragments.

'*Mais! Ça c'est trop fort!*' ejaculated the duke in his guttural French. 'Have you taken leave of your senses?' He was habited for the hunt; his deer hounds were fretting at the castle gates, and he also in a fret to be off to his favourite, indeed, his only pastime. 'I will not have this insubordination. You are very naughty,' was the ineffectual repetition. 'That is a valuable piece of jewellery, and now it is ruined. How are we to apologise or explain to your cousin when he arrives this evening for your birthday celebration and — uh —' he cleared his throat, preparing to plunge — 'and the announcement of your betrothal to him — as to why you are not wearing his gift?'

'You can explain it,' yelled his daughter, 'by telling him that I refuse to wear his grinning face, which as much resembles him as a seraph resembles a pig, and I am not his betrothed nor he mine. And you can tell him this —' she seized her father's hand to dig her nails in its podgy palm — 'that if you make me marry him I'll *kill* myself!'

'Hey!' exploded the duke, extricating his sausage fingers from the painful embrace of hers. 'You have hurt me! Your nails are as long as a cat's claws. Now listen.' He lowered himself to the bed, and with a heightening of his mottled red colour and more clearing of his throat, 'You are a Princess of the Blood, and as such it behoves you, and all of us who are royal, to marry less for — hem — uh — uhh — inclination than for duty to the State.'

'Did you,' disconcertingly he was asked, 'marry for duty to the State or inclination? Had it been your duty to the State I would have been that old hag Aunt Sophia's daughter, and not Mother's.'

What, demanded the duke of his inner man, *have I done to deserve this? The child is more than out of herself. She's possessed of the devil!* And with what dignity and courage he could muster with those great dark eyes of hers accusingly upon him, he said, 'I married for love. A marriage of convenience was not at that time — uhh — discussed.'

'So Uncle Ernest had to have your old cast-off instead of you!'

Ignoring this outrageous remark, the duke braced himself to resume. 'It is of the utmost importance that Celle and Hanover should be reunited, and how better than by the marriage of our beloved children, you and my brother's son?' His watery stare was now directed to the glitter of spilled diamonds on the carpet. 'Do you not know that it is only your happiness and welfare that we — your mother and I — desire?'

'If that's what you desire then you had best hang a millstone round my neck and drown me in the moat, which would be far better for my happiness and welfare than to be married to a — oh, Father!' Always a chameleon of moods, she changed in an instant from a termagant to an imploring penitent. Her arms were round his neck. 'How I am wicked! How could I behave so to you and to Mother! Forgive me, do what you will with me, marry me off to a pig or a bladder of lard, or to Satan himself if you will. I am yours for the — the sacrifice. Only hurry up about it. I can understand what prisoners feel when they wait in their dungeons for their ends.' She shivered and said, 'A grey goose is walking on my grave,' and the next minute fell to laughing.

Her father, betwixt relief at this sudden transformation and feeling as if he had fallen into a bed of roses with that bundle of loveliness all about him, kissed her moistly and, in approximate English, thankfully told her: 'That is my darling

Herz. All is well that does end for the well, as our Wilhelm Shakespeare does it say, yes?'

'No, as William Shakespeare does *not* say,' she corrected between tearful giggles. 'Nor is he *our* Shakespeare. He is England's.'

At which her father, seeing her softened, or at least more tractable, countered in his native tongue, 'Which may be *your* England — one day!'

TWO

Clara, Madame Platen, emerged in unwonted good humour from her daily bath of asses' milk. She had learned that Lady Castlemaine, the King of Britain's favourite, did thus indulge, and chose to profit by example charitably to dispense among the poor, as did the king's mistress, the milk in which she had previously bathed.

'Cathie!' she called to her sister. 'I have had great news from Bernstorff! He has well earned his "von" *and* his tobacco factory. A master diplomat to feather his nest — and ours. Ilse!' to her maid, 'don't stand gawping there. Dry me, animal! Am I to catch my death of cold?'

She was wrapped in warm towels and dried, having deposited a painful pinch on the fleshy underpart of her 'animal's' arm with the admonishment: 'Careful, clumsy! Don't be so rough. I am not a mare to be groomed.' And to her sister, 'Our Gottlieb — pardon, *Baron* von Bernstorff — tells us — Ilse, fetch the letter that came by courier this morning. On my dressing table, idiot!'

The letter was fetched. Divested of her towels, her fat buttocks swaying, she walked, or rather waddled mother-naked, into the adjoining bedroom, where her sister Catherine awaited her. Seated on the bed and holding the letter close to her eyes that were somewhat near-sighted, Clara scanned the parchment and said, 'Bernstorff reports that the Frenchwoman had all to do to make herself heard. The bastard was screaming to raise the roof. She wouldn't — no, she wouldn't — aha! but this is too rich! — she wouldn't be married to a pig. She calls George Louis a pig! Ha, ha!'

Supporting her sagging bosoms the Platen rolled on the bed. Her sister joined in her laughter, saying, 'He does look rather like a pig, especially nude. So very pink and hairless; preferable to Busche, however, who is hairy as an ape.'

Reverting to the letter, Clara continued: 'Celle was sent for to cajole and coax. But it seems that for once he exerted himself sufficiently to induce her to agree to the betrothal. She, having threatened suicide, decided on the lesser of two evils, George Louis or the castle moat. The betrothal,' perused Clara, 'was announced last evening. Bernstorff's messenger lost no time, riding top speed to give account of it. *The girl*, he says, *looked about as cheerful as a morgue.* George Louis, arriving late, was in high fettle, soaked to the eyes, apparently, being fortified along the road with wine and brandy. And now —' leafing through the pages, Clara produced matter of more significance — 'there seems to be *an undertaking,* Bernstorff calls it, *that Madame Busche shall be given her* congé. This on the insistence of the Frenchwoman, and also by our old woman here, who obviously thinks it best to humour Celle's "Madame". But don't let this disturb you,' was Clara's reassurance to Catherine's gasp of, 'Me! To be thrown *out?*'

'Of course not, stupid. Gottlieb writes: *There is no necessity to terminate the relationship* — as if George Louis would allow it anyway. He is crazy about you. Have no fear — *so long,* says Bernstorff, *as discretion is observed.*'

Catherine Busche, a younger, prettier, and far less intelligent edition of her sister, received this assurance with a doubtful sniff. 'So long as discretion observed will recompense me, I wouldn't care a row of pins if he forsakes my bed and company. I've had enough of his.'

'He will never do that, my dear,' said Clara. 'The bastard of Celle is nothing to his taste. Both he and his father prefer more solid substance,' complacently she stroked her fleshy white thighs, 'than a skinny undeveloped little rat.' And wetting her thumb and forefinger to flick over the pages, 'Here,' she cried delightedly, 'is something for your recompense which will recompense us all! Gottlieb has secured for Ernest those fifty thousand thalers Celle refused him, plus one hundred thousand thalers a year —'

'A hundred *thousand*?' echoed Catherine, wide-eyed.

'— to be paid into our — into Hanover's treasury along with "the vast Wilhelmsburg estates, at the Frenchwoman's death — which,' piously added Clara, eyes to heaven, 'may the good God think fit to expedite for the benefit of more deserving recipients. So we will all rejoice to see George Louis married!'

But neither Clara nor her sister saw George Louis married. They were not invited to that fateful wedding in November 1682.

After the announcement of the betrothal, the Duchess Sophia, well pleased with her part in these unjoyful proceedings, had returned to Hanover to supervise the contracts for the marriage settlements that would substantially endow her son and Hanover's Duchy, while allowing his wife sufficient to maintain her state as Crown Princess and nothing more. She would be left entirely dependent on her husband.

It is likely the duchess derived some compensation for the effort it had cost her to make that journey to Celle and to offer her son to the 'dot of dirt's' daughter, not only because of the fabulous settlements agreed, but also for the satisfaction of knowing her hated rival thwarted in her determination to forbid the match.

We may believe Sophia Dorothea had decided that marriage with George Louis was preferable to drowning in the castle moat, even though at the first sight of her future husband it was observed she turned so pale she looked about to faint. But she managed to get through the ordeal of congratulations from the assembled company, and submitted to a moist peck on the cheek from her betrothed, who, so soon as was permissible, went off with his equerries to drown himself not in the moat but in drink, at his fate 'in having to take to wife a puny child' — as he complained to his cronies between hiccups — 'and a half-wit at that, if not deaf and dumb. N-not a word — *hic* — did she speak, and appeared not to hear when I — *hic* — spoke to her. She's about as bedworthy as a j-j-jellyfish.'

A similar disparagement of her betrothed was outpoured to the devoted Knesebeck from Sophia Dorothea.

'I was almost sick,' she affected to retch, 'when he kissed me, if you can call a wet slobber on my ear a kiss. And to think I shall have to sleep in a bed with *that*! How am I to endure it? And I'm sure he hates me as much as I hate him!'

To which Knesebeck, endeavouring to soothe, ineffectually replied, 'Highness, darling, these are early days to judge him. He was obviously nervous, as you both were, at this announcement, and all so sudden when your other betrothed was — or would have been —'

'You needn't remind me of it!' cut in Sophia Dorothea. 'I was disgusted at the way they were treated, he and his father turned out as if they had come to raid the castle. That old hag, my aunt of Hanover, is at the bottom of all this. Why, oh, why should I be victimised in order to unite the House of Hanover with Celle. I'm only being married for my money! O God, I wish I were dead!' She thrashed about the room, her hair tumbled on her shoulders, a flame of colour in her face, her words in torrents. 'Why was I born for this — why — why? Why wasn't I the daughter of a peasant, or a yokel, or the *sweep*? Then I could have married someone whom I — I — wanted to marry, and not be foisted on a sweaty-faced pig! I can't forgive Father for doing this to me — he should never have allowed that old witch, my Aunt Sophia, to persuade him to make me have her beast of a son. I tell you, Lennie, she —'

At this moment her father put his head round the door. Whether he had heard much of this outburst is doubtful. He was full of more important matters than the tantrums of Sophia Dorothea.

With conciliatory smiles he advanced into the room, holding in his hand a sheet of paper. 'Here, my heart's delight, I have prepared — or, I should say, Herr Bernstorff has prepared — a little letter for you to write to your dear Aunt Sophia.'

'A letter? Why should I write to the old — write her a letter?' demanded his heart's delight.

'Because,' was the winning rejoinder, 'it would be a pretty token of your regard for her if you assure her you will always strive to deserve her — her goodness, and that you will be a dutiful daughter to her, and —'

'I am not her daughter and don't *want* to be her daughter. Oh, Father!' She flung herself at him. '*Must* I go on with it? I can't — I can't! He's so ugly and horrible and fat. And as for writing a letter to his nasty old mother — why should I?'

Yet, despite all her frenzied appeals, she had to give in and give up. And so we find her at her writing desk laboriously copying the letter suggested by Chancellor Bernstorff; and after several attempts to insert additions of her own, to which the confidante, looking over her shoulder told her, 'Highness, dear, you can't say that. Just write what the chancellor has suggested, then everyone will be satisfied.'

'Except me!' retorted Sophia Dorothea, finally to achieve:

Madame,

I have so much respect for my lord, the Duke, your husband —
'Respect? For that blustering old ass?' — *that whatever manner they may act on my behalf I shall be content. Your Highness will do me the justice to know that no one could be more sensible than I of the many tokens of your goodness.* 'Her goodness? I like that — calling me a bastard and Mother a clot of dirt!' *I will endeavour all my life long to deserve the same and to make it evident by my respect and very humble service to Your Highness that you could not choose as a daughter one who knows better how to pay you what is due.* 'Yes, I'll pay her what is due with as much mud slung at her as she has slung at my mother and me! If I could put that in it would be the end of me and her precious son. Let him go seek another — some fat old German *frau* who would be more to his fancy than I, providing she has enough money! I say, Lennie, shall I put that in and chance it? They can't hang me for it!'

'Your Highness, no!' Lennie stayed the poised quill. 'For heaven's sake. Just imagine what you would bring upon us all if you did!'

'A revolution, maybe,' giggled Her Highness, 'if not my head on the block. Very well, then, where was I? Hmm, I've lost my place … *choose a daughter … pay you …* I've done that…'

In which duty I shall feel it my great pleasure in showing you by my submission that I am Your Serene Highness's very humble and obedient servant,

Sophia Dorothea.

'And may God forgive me for a pack of lies!'

It is possible that the duchess had reason to feel certain conscience pricks concerning her promotion of this marriage which none but herself, her husband, and his and their son's mistresses had any cause to welcome, unless it were the Duke of Celle.

He had it firmly dinned into him enough by his sister-in-law that the union of Hanover and Celle was a *coup de grâce* to end the long-drawn-out feud between him and his sole surviving brother. Nor is it unlikely that he bore in his mind the seed, planted there by the ever optimistic wishfully thinking Sophia, that, in some glorious future a grandchild of his— if not his daughter — might wear the Crown of Britain. It was this golden hope that illumined the beaming countenance of the bride's father which, by reason of its roseate glow, was seen as a red sun through fog. And, not inapposysitely, on that November morning, a blanket of fog uprisen from the river, obscured whatever brightness might have lightened the dismal day. The omens could not have been more gloomy, for with the gradual lifting of those leaden clouds came the sound of thunder, a low menacing growl that broke in unprecedented storm upon the castle and drowned the organ rolling out sonorous hymns of thanksgiving during and after the ceremony.

The Court chroniclers were lavish in their eulogies heaped upon the bride; her beauty, her exquisite deportment, her jewels, the richness of her white-and-silver gown in which she looked less like a girl than the ghost of one there at the altar.

The bridegroom, who had fortified himself for the ordeal, seemed to find some difficulty in rising from his knees, and stood swaying when assisted to his feet by his groomsmen, his young brothers Charles and Maximilian. Then his wife, joined to him before God until death should them part, walked half fainting on his arm down the aisle of the flower-decked chapel between the ranks of distinguished guests, and so to the bridal coach that would bear them to her father's hunting box at Brockenhausen for the honeymoon.

'Happy, *Happy,* HAPPY,' pealed the joy-bells, as the coach drove off drawn by six cream-coloured horses, scarlet-habited postilions and outriders followed by jostling crowds. Despite the storm they had stood in their hundreds, drenched to the skin, to cheer their Princess upon her wedding journey with God-blessings and, from many of the women, tears to see her so young and lovely yet so sadly pale, while her newly wedded husband nodded in jerky, unsmiling response to the multitude's greetings.

The rain beat against the windows of the coach with demoniac little hammer blows; the gale shrieked about the castle walls and tore from the oaks in the park and from the plane trees, the last of late autumn's withered tokens of dead summer. And to her who sat so lost and still, bewildered by the nightmare horror of these few hours, it was as if a horde of witches rode the winds to mock with eldritch laughter 'these unholy rites,' her white lips moved to whisper, 'that have fettered me to … you.'

He, rendered semi-conscious by frequent imbibition, spoke not one word throughout that dreary drive, while voicelessly she prayed, *O God, of your mercy, let me die … tonight.*

She almost did when long into the dawn she lay, torn and broken, while he, having done with her and spilled what he'd drunk in the grate, snored and grunted there beside her in his sleep.

A week dragged by which, to the wretched little bride, was a purgatorial eternity. George Louis, accustomed to and greedy for the enticements of the alcove, had no patience with, nor sympathy for deflowered innocence. That his child wife was his co-victim of a merciless State marriage, devoid of all affection or compatibility, unloving and unloved, aroused in him an unwarrantable resentment against her as the head and front of the offending which had parted him from his mistress. Her over-ripe flamboyance and experienced abandon to his possession of her body satisfied him as his ravaged young bride could not, nor never would.

Her beauty that, between the bud and blossom, had fulfilled its early promise, had no appeal for him. She was slight and delicately formed; her great dark long-lashed eyes looked to be too large for the fragile bone structure of her face under its wealth of dusky brown hair, framing the shell-like transparent skin, in direct contrast to his highly coloured, wide-hipped, blonde, full-breasted Catherine. He — also blond, heavily jowled and, despite his youth, paunchy — gravitated to women of physical similarity, doubtless due to a subconscious urge to be reproduced in his own likeness. As with many small men lacking height, he had an inordinate conceit of himself. Flattered by his woman that he was irresistible, he could not believe he was resisted. His bride's repulsion of his marital rights he took to be a deliberate disparagement of his manhood, an insult over which he unforgivingly brooded.

At table she would sit, pecking at her food served on gold plate by obsequious lackeys, and scarce a word was, passed from him to her, monosyllabically answered, if answered at all. Bereft of the comfort of her mother — even her devoted 'Lennie' had been denied her, sent in advance to Hanover to prepare for the bride's homecoming — she had. none to whom in her desolation she could turn.

So, between these two, dislike of each other mounted: to boredom on his part, on hers to increasing hate. He, to relieve the tedium of their daily, and nightly, intercourse — he was soon glutted of that — had brought to him from Hanover some of his boon companions, among them his equerry and former tutor, the cuckolded Johann Busche.

She need not now fear invasion of her undefended privacy. He no longer sought it for he went hunting by day, and spent the evenings until long into the night at faro, dice and drink, when he would be lugged from the gaming tables by a servant and put to bed, not, God be thanked, in hers, to lie in drunken torpor until the morning.

So passed the honeymoon.

'Here they come, the loving pair!' crowed Clara von Platen to her sister. Sumptuously gowned, bejewelled, bedecked for the occasion, they stood at an upper window of the Alte Palais, where the prince and princess were to take up residence. Contrary to the order of the Duchess Sophia, in accordance with the demand of the Duchess of Celle, Madame Busche had stood upon the order of her going and, unknown to the duchess, had not gone.

Loud were the rejoicings of loyal Hanoverians as the bridal couple, preceded by a military escort, entered the city in the State coach. Flags were flying, bells ringing, multitudes cheering to the sky amid shouts of 'God bless her, our Princess!'

Tears smarted in the eyes of Sophia Dorothea at this welcome to warm her frozen heart after the misery of the past few weeks. But, even as the coach with its six prancing white horses halted at the portico of her new abode, she looked up at the gaily decked facade of the palace and saw the two women leaning forward from the window. The one, her face paint-plastered, was sneeringly a-grin; the other, equally high-painted, stabbed a look of unmistakable venom at the pale young girl who had been preparing to alight, but now instinctively drew back.

Her husband had already been handed out; he now waved aside the footman and turned to give his hand to his wife. At this gesture the crowds redoubled their cheers, since he had made it evident that none save he should conduct his bride across the threshold of their palace.

'No!' Her voice was a hushed scream. 'Tell them to drive on. We have arrived too soon. There are strangers in the palace. It is not ready to receive us.'

George Louis had also seen his woman at the window, and while for appearance's sake his face was wreathed in smiles although red with rage, he hissed: 'Come out! Are you mad? Get *out!*' And loudly, for the benefit of onlookers crowding close to catch a nearer glimpse of their Crown Princess despite the guards lined up to hold them back, 'Welcome to your home, sweetheart!' Her gloved hand was seized and crushed, hurtfully, in his, while, still masked in that smile, he snarled below his breath: 'Would you disgrace yourself and me?'

She was all but dragged from the coach, his arm supporting her, since so wax-white was she and in a tremble that she seemed about to fall; and in that same smiling whisper from a corner of his mouth he bade her, 'Hold up, for God's sake!' And, loudly for the crowd to hear in case they had not heard the first time: 'Welcome home, my love!'

Home! What a misnomer for the garish brilliance and laxity of morals and manners of the Hanoverian Court that strove to ape the magnificence of Louis, the Sun King's Versailles; those interminable banquets, the singers, the dancers, the harems, the masquerades, for which the impoverished subjects of the Duchy paid in tax; and when drained of what little money they had, they paid with their lives' blood. For their masters, the royal dukes, would stake a whole regiment at the gaming tables in addition to their mistresses' jewels to be refunded from their winnings at a future night's sessions.

To the girl bride, reared in the sheltered cloisters of Celle, this overcrowded *mise en scène* of sensual eroticism and exuberant extravagance was as if she had been jettisoned into another planet as far removed from the world she had known as hell from heaven is. Yet, after those first few weeks of aching homesickness, resilient youth revived gradually to become case-hardened to conditions to be accepted as one accepts a climate. Even her nuptial obligations had become less of an abhorrent ordeal than the duty of a wife who had vowed at the altar to take this man to be her wedded husband for better or for worse.

'And nothing could be worse,' she confided to the ever-faithful Knesebeck. 'It can only be better.' *If God thinks fit to take me and the child* — she was now three months pregnant — *his child that I can never feel is mine, begot of hate.*

But this she did not say aloud. What she did say was, 'I am thankful she,' referring to her mother-in-law, 'is gone to Herrenhausen, as I will be free of her fault-finding for a while.' And folding back her upper lip she declaimed in fair mimicry of the duchess's harsh croak: '"You committed a grave breach of etiquette at yesterday's Court. Will you never learn discrimination? Dear God! How am I cursed! How often must I tell you that the Fourth Class whose presence we command as our duty to the lower orders are not allowed more than entrance to the State rooms and certainly no presentation, unless to receive some specific reward for civil or military service to His Serene Highness. Yet you deliberately approached, and engaged in conversation, a burgomaster's wife while ignoring the obeisance of the wife of the Lord Chamberlain. We cannot blame you for your neglected upbringing, poor child, since you have never been taught how to conduct yourself, bred and born as you are from the — French!" And how I kept my hands off the old bitch I don't know — only that bitch is too complimentary a word for her — isn't it, my precious?' This to a satin-coated long-eared spaniel of the breed beloved of the English King Charles. 'I am sick — sick — sick — of Court etiquette that covers excesses worse than any of Rome's emperors or Nero's.' Lifting the spaniel in her arms she showered it with kisses. 'And all because I spoke to the wife of an ugly fat old burgomaster — she is newly married and about my age, and he looked uncommonly like you-know-who. Didn't you notice? He will look very like him in twenty years' time. I am sure the poor little thing — she seemed so sad and lost and lonely — had been forced to marry him for his money. In my case it was the other way about. I am married for *my* money, of which I haven't a pfennig to call my own. Well, at any rate we can be done with these tiresome courts for at least a month.'

Every so often the duchess would go into virtual retreat at her country estate not half an hour's drive from the Old Palace where Sophia Dorothea was in residence. In the gardens of Herrenhausen with their wide grassy spaces, their stone images of fauns and dryads perpetually grinning and soundlessly piping, the Platen and others of her kind would, in the absence of the duchess, make rowdy the nights in amative pursuits to pleasure their young, and old, gentlemen. But a country house that was not owned by her did not pleasure the Platen. With the munificent gifts from his brother of Celle and the dowry of Duke Ernest's daughter-in-law poured into his coffers, his woman was building for herself a mansion named, not inappropriately, Monplaisir. Nearby, in sumptuous apartments, resided her sister Catherine.

The duchess, having heard that her order for the lady's banishment had been disregarded, flew into a rage and commanded her dismissal from Hanover on the day the newly wed Princess arrived. Madame Busche, however, if out of sight and maybe out of mind of George Louis, was, for him, not irreplaceable. He soon found other feminine attractions to engage him. His tastes were catholic and ranged from the servant girls of his household to women of easiest virtue. These diversions were most welcome to his wife.

She, having fulfilled her duty by providing him with a possible heir, was relieved of much of his proximity, both in and out of her bed. And although she found it irksome, she did endeavour to conform to the duties incumbent on her state as second lady in the land.

She had her own establishment in a wing of the Old Palace where she had been given a separate household with her chamberlain and some half-dozen sour-visaged ladies-in-waiting of the duchess's selection, chosen with a view to her son's amatory propensities. All were fiftyish, attenuated, angular, possessed of none of the florid over-emphasised proportions so much admired by the Hanoverian Princes. From these gentlewomen the duchess received daily reports on the conduct of the princess regarding any transgression of behaviour compulsory to the ethics of the Court; and it seems she frequently transgressed.

Bitterly did the duchess complain in letters to her niece of the ill-breeding and lack of etiquette on the part of her son's wife … *But what can you expect of the daughter of a nobody?* And of George Louis, for she had no illusions about him, the least loved of her sons: *He is the most pig-headed, stubborn boy who ever lived, and whose brains are embedded in so thick a crust that I defy any man or woman to discover them. He does not care for her but a hundred thousand thalers a year atone for much…*

During this first year of her marriage, the letters to her mother from Sophia Dorothea reflect a dispirited boredom; a monotony of dressing or being dressed for the ceremonious meals where again the most rigid etiquette must be observed. Assembled in the great hall of the Leine Schloss, the State Palace, the Duke, the Duchess, the Crown Prince and Princess of Hanover must take their seats at the high table. All of lesser rank must sit in order of precedence, including the younger princes. Of these, her four brothers-in-law, Christian and Ernest Augustus, were considered too young to attend being still in the nursery, but Charles — in his early teens, her favourite — must always be present with others above the salt. He had not yet run to fat, was rosy-cheeked and cherubic and, when not pinioned by the hawk eye of his mother, would convey to the silent little Princess in a conspiratorial wink his distaste for the heavy ten-course meals.

The daughter of Celle, accustomed to the civilised refinements of her French mother's Court, may have not a little wondered at the indifference to and toleration on the part of the matriarch of Osnabrück and Hanover towards the ill manners and inelegance of that Germanic company with their scandalous adulteries and undisguised concubinage. Charles, however, who had made the Grand Tour of European Courts and in particular that of the 'Grand Monarch' and, young though he was, had profited by his sojourn at Versailles to acquire something of the grace and charm of those in contact with the masters of literature and the arts comparable to none in that seventeenth-century *fin de siècle*.

Not surprisingly, therefore, did Sophia Dorothea seek the society of this young lad who, other than Knesebeck, was her only friend in a friendless world. During her pregnancy when forbidden by her doctors to ride, which she joyed to do, she must now take her outings in her gilded coach through the narrow cobbled streets of Hanover where townsfolk would watch and wait for her, loud in their greetings of the beautiful girl, still a child, some time or other to replace their dour Duchess. And to their heartening welcome she would respond with a wave of her hand or a word and a smile to lighten her sad little face at the window of her coach. Or, to relieve the dreary daily routine, she would arrange a picnic outside the city walls where rich pastures spread green aprons to the banks of the river Leine, or in the pine forest, when Charles and any young crony of his would be invited to enliven her, but always accompanied by her grim attendants. They, obeying orders from the duchess, would never for a moment relax their vigilance lest she commit some unforgivable recalcitrance. And, mischievously, to confound her ladies, she would converse with her brother-in-law in her mother's tongue since, apart from Knesebeck and one other, none of them knew a word of French.

But not her gentlewomen alone kept watch upon her.

The Platen and her well-paid *agent provocateur,* Bernstorff, had each an axe to grind in the respective duchies of Hanover and Celle. It would suit the ambitions of both to secure a permanent union between the two principalities. That the wealth of the one had been partially depleted to fulfil the terms of the marriage contract did not satisfy the Platen. Were the two combined the remaining and still vast estates of Duke William would further benefit the rapacious Clara and her partner, Gottlieb von Bernstorff.

Madame, or, to give her the full title she had obtained for her husband, now raised to the rank of Baron — Baroness von Platen — must be provided with sufficient means to maintain her state at Monplaisir as the duke's concubine. Her equipages, gowns and jewels outshone in magnificence those of the Duchess Sophia, and totally eclipsed any appertaining to the Crown Princess whose purloined wealth provided all this splendour. But the source of it, drained of her lawful due, was scorned by the Platen as 'the Interloper'. This, possibly, because Duke Ernest had evinced a more than paternal or avuncular interest in his daughter-in-law and niece. He greatly admired and was proud of her beauty and had been heard to declare her the loveliest girl in his Duchy, indeed in the whole of Germany. A fond exaggeration to rouse the jealousy of the duke's possessive mistress. Nor was he the only admirer of Sophia Dorothea. The young bloods who frequented Monplaisir to play high, drink deep and partake of the easy and gratuitous enjoyment of the Platen's insatiable indulgence, had turned their attention to the princess, despite discouragement of any attempt to win her favour.

The first to warn her of danger from the Platen's enmity was Charles. They were walking along the banks of the Leine followed at near distance by three of her elderly ladies, and Knesebeck. It was a blue and golden day, the river lay shimmering in an aquamarine glory under a sky tufted with feathery small white clouds. Bees hummed in the acacias lining their way. Bird song was clamorous among the lime trees that dropped their scented blossoms in their path.

Charles slid a glance at her whose face, under the wide-brimmed hat she wore to shield her eyes from the glare of the July sun, had a soft contented look too seldom seen, and hurtful now to see it change as in fluent French he said, 'My dear. I have this to say,' and saying it he cast another glance, not at her but over his shoulder at her women, 'there is one who shall be nameless, who is full of venom as a rattlesnake to poison the very air you or anyone whom she may spitefully suspect of —' He hesitated.

'Of?' On a caught breath she prompted him.

'Of trespass as might be —' then, seeing her face lost of its gleam, her eyes, under the shadowing hat-brim, dark with apprehension raised to his, he floundered on — 'of trespassing in what she thinks are her preserves, so overgrown with weeds and — and nettles that any who may want to pluck her — her fruits would find none worth the plucking more than an over-ripe plum.'

At which, to his relief, the momentary alarm his words had caused her, passed. In her nearest cheek appeared a dimple.

'Charles.' She laughed round at him. ''Tis you should be warned. If these —' she jerked her head to indicate those watchful three walking together, while Knesebeck walked alone — 'if they who are appointed by your mother to be the wardresses of me — and as some of them are also the minions of your nameless one — should they report to *her* that she's an over-ripe plum and as full of venom as a rattlesnake, even though your metaphors are a trifle mixed, then the Platen —' She clapped a hand to her mouth, wrinkling her nose to show her teeth, as a puppy will when about to bite in fun. '*Now* what have I said? Misery me! I am done for. Look — no, don't. She's watching us. She has eyes like a lynx. The bearded one with black prickles on her chin. I call her the Porcupine. She is as much in attendance on me as in attendance on your rattlesnake whose creature, among others, she is paid to be — including the wart-hog!'

'The who?'

His smile widened in answer to hers that was full of mischief. 'It is a name I and a — a friend of mine whom I have not seen these — almost five years — used to call him. It would seem that only zoological names apply to this delightful company … I think we had best speak English. The Porcupine understands French.'

'A friend of yours?' Charles felt a stab of something in the region of his left breast under his fine grey satin coat; for although he held the knowledge of it to himself that must be forever unconfessed, with all his boy's young heart he loved her. And as she made him no reply, he, red to the ears, asked again, 'Who is he?'

'Perhaps,' she sounded casual enough, 'you may have met him when you were in England. He left my father's Court, where he was a page, to go to school in London. His name if I remember rightly,' this was somewhat overdone and did not quite deceive, 'it is a Swedish name. Yes, I remember. It is Königsmarck.'

'What?' His crestfallen moment lifted. Excitedly he turned to her. 'Not Philip Königsmarck?'

She hushed him. 'Not so loud. His name is too well known and not well liked in Hanover and Celle. So you know him?' She managed to control the eagerness behind the query: 'Where did you know him?'

'Philip,' said Charles in his approximate English, his round pink cheeks aglow, 'my best friend in Dresden was. From his school in London he to Dresden go after a trouble I did hear he had.'

'Trouble? How — what trouble?'

'Not of his a trouble. His brother he in a trouble was.'

'His brother? Tell me. Tell all you know of him — of Philip. He was my best friend too — at Celle.'

And so he told.

When Philip Christopher, the younger Königsmarck, was sent to Monsieur Foubert's military Academy in London to complete his education, his elder brother Carl John went with him, carrying a letter of introduction from the King of Sweden to the King of England. While still in his teens he had been involved in a series of hare-brained adventures. He had fought against the Turks and almost met his death when he fell off a rock into the sea and was dragged out half drowned.

'These Königsmarcks,' Charles lowered his voice to say, 'they are like the cats. They have nine lives. More than in the sea must Carl John fall to kill him.'

As it would seem when, during a visit to Spain, he was challenged by a grandee who resented his attentions to his wife, a great beauty at the Court of Madrid with whom he had found favour, as much for his handsome looks as for his courage. Having accepted the challenge to meet her husband, the most noted duellist in Spain who had never been known to lose a fight, he winged his man in his right arm so severely that he could never cross swords in a duel again. Nor was this his only fight in Spain. His next challenge was to a bull that gored him, tossed him, and had him bleeding from a dozen wounds. Yet he fought on until he dropped and was carried fainting out of the arena.

'All this of the duel and the fight of the bull,' Charles admitted, 'was by Philip give me as by his brother him told. *Aber* — I think much of it should, as the English say, *mit* a smell of salt be take, *nicht wahr*? For *mit* — with — the so many bravura accomplishment of this Carl John, he an excellent good liar is …'

After his performance in the bull-ring, according to Charles, and with adequate allowance for embellishment from Philip, Carl John was the hero of all the women in Madrid.

'These brothers,' Charles said with envy, 'have more than their part — how do you say? — more than their share of the good looks. Their sister Aurora —'

'I didn't know there was a sister,' came interruption from Sophia Dorothea where, in the shade of a lime tree, she sat with Charles squatting beside her, and her ladies disposed in a funereal circle at discreet distance yet within earshot of the prince's cautionary monologue while they listened, in vain, to interpret. 'What a lovely name, Aurora!'

'And a lovely lady also.' Charles smoothed the mechlin at his wrists, looking down at his thick hands. *As red as hams,* he thought glumly, remembering Philip's that were white and long and thin, yet strong as steel. 'These Königsmarcks —' forgetful of her warning, he harped upon that name — 'their charm is *wunderschön.* Wherever they do go also the hearts broke of the ladies they them do follow. Not so Philip while he at school must be *mit* — with — no chance as *cavaliere servente.* Monsieur Foubert him he guard close to keep as Philip me did tell. *Aber* Carl John —'

But the adventures of Carl John had little interest for her who impatiently cut in with, 'How did Philip come to trouble through his brother, if he was so closely guarded at his school?'

'Ssh!' Charles, with a finger to his lips and a sidelong glance at the listening ladies, said, 'Please, not now. Later, I will tell. That one with the — how you call them — pricks? — has the ear too many.'

The trouble to do with the elder Königsmarck, as Sophia Dorothea later had account of it from Charles, resulted in a sensational murder trial that was the talk of London and out of it for months; a trial in which the reckless daredevil, Carl John, stood accused as accessory before the fact. And the fact of the case was this.

Carl John, Count Königsmarck, having succeeded to his father's estates in Sweden, arrived in London to receive a cordial welcome at Whitehall, not only from King Charles but from the king's ladies, who opened doors and arms to this well-favoured youth versed in all the graces to enchant them. But Carl John desired more substantial advantage than access to a lady's bedchamber. Notwithstanding his great wealth he intended to increase it by marriage to a wife endowed with as great, if not greater, wealth than his. For in those glorious rip-roaring Restoration years even the younger generation, unborn during the Protectorate, had heard from their parents or grandparents how they had sickened of godly Puritanical talk under the tyrant Cromwell to run riot with their hail-fellow-well-met beloved restored King. And in that pleasure-greedy Renaissance, money, or the want of it, was still the proverbial root of all evil. Neither men nor women lived by bread alone. Most of them lived on their wits or on the bounty of their too liberal free-handed and not always 'Merry' Monarch. And while the subjects of his Britannic Majesty were recovering from the terrors of the Popish Plot and the blood-baths of those Catholics victimised by that perjurous liar and fanatic Titus Oates, Carl John, no less than any other young spark who rejoiced in riotous living, was in need to replenish his exchequer on the premise that to them that have much shall be given.

With this end in view he sought and found the richest widow in the kingdom, daughter and heiress of the Earl of Northumberland. Her father's recent death had amplified the vast fortune bequeathed by her husband, the Earl of Ogle, to whom, at the age of eleven, she had been married. He, the son and heir of the Duke of Newcastle and scarcely older than herself, died a few months after the marriage that, since neither had reached the age of puberty, was never consummated.

The twelve-year-old widow, a pitiful little object in her mourning black, was brought by her mother to the Court of King Charles where she immediately attracted the attention of all the fortune-hunters at Whitehall, including Carl John Königsmarck.

A gawky timid child with no pretence to beauty, she was nicknamed 'Carrots' because of her red hair. The name stuck when many years later, after her third marriage, she — then Countess of Somerset — supplanted Abigail Hill, Lady Masham, as the favourite of Queen Anne.

To this unfortunate child's mother, the Countess of Northumberland, Carl John had the audacity to present himself as suitor for the hand of her daughter, Elizabeth, Lady Ogle, not yet thirteen, only to have the door shut in his face by the indignant matron. She knew something of this Königsmarck and nothing to his good. The disgruntled suitor returned to Sweden leaving his brother in the care of Monsieur Foubert. But he was not to be put down by a first attempt to gain possession of a fortune and those vast estates which would make him a lord of English lands. So, back to London he went, determined to win the prize and found that another had captured the little Ogle heiress, a widow no longer but a wife again, this time to one Thomas Thynne of Longleat in Wiltshire, known as 'Tom of Ten Thousand' for his ten thousand a year: a fabulous income in those days. It was a deplorable match in that Thynne was a dissolute roué, a drunk, and the habitué of stews from Wapping to St Giles. And once more, owing to her immaturity, the marriage was not consummated. The bridegroom, having secured for himself double ten thousand a year, parted from his bride at the church door and made off to celebrate his wedding elsewhere. He left his wife with her mother who hastened her to Holland until such time as she would be ripe for marriage.

Carl John, although furious at being tricked, as he believed, out of a goldmine had not given up hope of recovering it. Accompanied by a henchman, Captain Vratz — a scurvy rogue who had followed him on his daring escapades on sea and land — he took lodgings in London, but he did not present himself at Court. He lay low and told no one, save his schoolboy brother, of his whereabouts. Vratz, an able swordsman, acting under his master's instructions and always up and ready for a fight, scraped acquaintance with Tom Thynne in one of his haunts, a bawdy-house or gaming-house, or both and, on some pretext or other, started a row and called him out; but Tom Thynne, bemused with drink, refused the challenge. Unable to finish him off in what was known as 'an affair of honour', and urged by Carl John to get him at all costs and, if not by fair means by foul, Vratz hired a couple of ex-jailbirds to do the job with him. Accordingly, when Thynne was driving in Pall Mall in the dusk of a winter's evening, his coach was stopped by three masked and mounted men. One of them, Vratz, seized his horses, another attacked the postilions and footmen, while a third discharged a blunderbuss through the window of the coach, got away with his accomplices and left Thynne in a pool of blood to die.

It all happened in about five minutes at a time when few pedestrians were about, yet those few were enough to raise a hue and cry when the servants, stunned by their fall and the battering they had received, went to attend to their master and found the gory shambles that was Tom. The three murderers were arrested and thrown into jail. Nor did Carl John escape; he, too, was arrested and brought to trial. Tom Thynne had many friends, among them the Duke of Monmouth, the favourite bastard son of the king. All were bent on vengeance and swore to see those four, Carl John included, hanged.

'But,' said Charles, who recounted to Sophia Dorothea as much as he had heard of that *cause célèbre*, 'Carl John was not hanged. The others were. I told you these Königsmarcks have nine lives. If ever a man deserved to swing it was he who had planned the crime and made those three assassins do it for him. It was Philip's evidence that saved him. I had it all from a friend of mine who had been at school with Philip, and he wrote me a full account of it. He went to hear the trial which caused a furore and he said that when Carl John was questioned as to why one of the murderers, a Pole, had been brought from Sweden to take part in the plot to kill Thynne, Carl John declared, as cool as you please, that he had sent for this Pole — I forget his name — Grotsky or Brotsky or something — because he was a good judge of horses and he said he wanted to raise a troop of horses, a cavalry regiment, to aid King Charles in his campaigns. A blatant lie, of course,' said Charles. 'Trust a Königsmarck for that. They are the most plausible liars in Christendom.'

Sophia Dorothea pleated her fingers, looking down at them. Yes, he likely had lied to her years ago in the arbour when he … before he had left Celle. The colour burned in her face at the remembrance of the sweet surprise of his touch, child though she was when they parted and he but a boy in years.

And she, a trifle out of breath, heard Charles say, 'Then, when the judge asked Carl John to prove his statement, Philip was on his feet to tell him: "I, my lord, can prove it." He must have made a good impression on the judge and jury. My friend wrote — I still have the letter somewhere — how Philip may have rehearsed before, a mirror and dressed himself up for the part like a playactor in pink velvet and gold lace with his hair in curls on his shoulders. And he had the judge and jury eating the words out of his hand to swallow them whole, speaking in that clear voice of his — he speaks far better English than any of us here except you — and then he produced a bill of exchange for a thousand pistoles that he said his brother had given him to pay for the horses bought by this Polander to give to the king. And the judge and all the rest of them believed him. Who wouldn't?' Charles slid a smile from the corner of his mouth. 'He, with a face like an angel … angel, my fiddler's foot! He is as great a liar as his brother. Anyway, if Carl John had given him a thousand pistoles I'll wager it wasn't to buy horses for King Charles. More likely to pay for his grand pink velvet suit and the rings on his fingers and the blood mare and her foal in the stables hard by the Foubert Academy for Carl John to race at Newmarket. But whether Philip spoke truth, which is doubtful, he saved his brother from the gallows, though I'll lay Carl John primed him to produce that bill of exchange and to tell about buying those horses for the king, whose name to the majority of Englanders, and especially Londoners, is second only to God's. There never was a king so greatly loved, from all accounts. But not one of those in court was in favour of the verdict which pronounced Carl John not guilty. My friend wrote that the whole of London had hoped to see him dangling in chains on Tyburn Hill where they hang most murderers and felons. They dug up Cromwell's body after he was dead and buried to hang his bones at Tyburn. Did you know that?'

She did not know that, nor did she very much care what happened to the bones or the body of Cromwell, a name as remote to her as that of the Shah of Persia. All she cared to know was what had happened to Philip. On this Charles could enlighten her little more than that Carl John, finding London too hot for him, post-hasted to Dover and boarded the packet for France, taking with him his young brother.

Monsieur Foubert may have been relieved to see him go. The name of Königsmarck was no longer an asset but a grievous liability to his impeccable Academy.

'Where is Philip now?' asked Sophia, with a tingling in her palms. She could picture him, in his pink velvet suit, standing there in the dark crowded Court with the face of an angel, so handsome as he used to be when she was twelve and he sixteen … 'And in four years *you* will be sixteen and I'll be twenty! I will come back and we'll be married…' And now she *was* sixteen, almost seventeen, and married, not to him, and … he would never come back.

Charles was saying to wake her from a dream: 'I heard that Philip had been at Versailles as well as in Dresden. He became friendly with my kinsman, Augustus of Saxony, and travelled with him to Italy and Portugal. He still went on with his military training though from what I gather, his studies or,' grinned Charles, 'his interests were as much engrossed with Venus as with Mars. But where he is now I cannot say. I have heard nothing of him these last two years. He and Carl John, by this time, may both have lived their nine lives out.'

After which comfortless assumption no more was told of Philip to Sophia Dorothea.

THREE

Seated at her window that overlooked the tree-girt lawns of the Leine Schloss, the Duchess Sophia watched the slow death fall of autumn leaves while she waited for the news that at any hour now might announce the birth of her first grandchild. And on this windless October day, as she saw the silent flutter of those yellow leaves, she inwardly soliloquised: *Thus, in the form of atoms or monads does substance exist, as Leibnitz so admirably gives it, even in these most elementary examples of nature. Death. Rebirth. Regeneration.*

In her hand she held and, from time to time, she scanned the pages of a volume by that distinguished scholar and pedant, Gottfried Wilhelm Leibnitz, appointed by Duke Ernest at the instigation of the duchess, as custodian of the Hanoverian Library.

A woman of parts and perception, the duchess spoke five languages more or less fluently. She dabbled in philosophy, theology and mathematics. She would argue with her chaplains on the authenticity of the Gospels, and gathered to herself all the most distinguished men of letters in the principality. Chief among these, and much by her admired, was Leibnitz, and she the 'Serena' of his essays dedicated to Her Serene Highness.

As a free-thinker and disciple of Leibnitz, while denying any leanings towards agnosticism, and with all due respect to the Deity whom she allowed to be the Supreme and Perfect Monad from which all lesser monads or atoms radiate, Sophia maintained an open mind to reflect upon the riddle of the universe.

Her eyes, bright, quick, alert under lids a trifle wrinkled, since she was in her fifties and showed signs of increasing years, voyaged briskly from contemplation of tree branches to dwell upon the open page before her.

'We mortals,' she spoke aloud, as she often would, lacking other audience, 'are born to die and live again, *vide* the myth of Proserpine, emblem of spring, descended to the bowels of the earth to rise and be reborn in each springtime's fruition as did God made Man Incarnate, according to the Gospels, prove by His resurrection man's survival. By the same token this unborn atom struggling to fight its way out of the womb even as I, a Royal Stuart, daughter and granddaughter of a king, will live again when this babe who, if it be male or, if female and sole issue of my son, may carry the Crown of Britain on its head to die and live again in its monarchical descendants through me, its ancestral monad...'

Adjoining the duchess's sanctum, a holy of holies devoted to communion with herself and her high priest, Leibnitz, her women were clustered awaiting news, as did their mistress, of the pending birth. At the sound of the duchess's utterance of these, her innermost thoughts, they exchanged glances, eyebrows raised, lips quirking, and one, more daring than the rest, tapped a significant finger to her forehead. They had come to regard the duchess's obsession with monarchy as a mania.

Then, of a sudden, hurrying footsteps were heard in the outer corridor. The duchess half rose from her high-backed chair; the book of Leibnitz slid to the floor covered with Persian rugs, a fashion culled from England contrary to the prevalent custom of spreading rarities such as these on tables. Her lean body stiffened; a hand, dry and bleached as a bone, was laid for an instant to her heart, preceding a knock at the oak-panelled door and her command: 'Enter.'

Chancellor Baron von Platen, who owed his ennoblement and high ministerial office to his wife's accommodation for their sovereign's pleasure between sheets, stood bowing on the threshold. 'Serene Highness, I have the honour to inform Your Gracious Highness that the Crown Princess is delivered of a Prince.'

The duchess, gazing through the grovelling Platen as if he were a window, acknowledged his presence with a slight inclination of her head that was at the same time a dismissal. Not to this bowing, scraping automaton, her husband's cuckold, would she, by the smallest sign or gesture betray her delight and relief from mounting anxiety at what had seemed to be a long protracted labour.

The chancellor, masking offence at this icy reception of that which it was his privilege to proclaim in private to the duchess, and would be again proclaimed publicly by him with a fanfare of trumpets from the Schloss, took his dismissal, still bowing and backing, to collide with the hasty arrival of the duke. Profound apologies were swept aside and the door slammed by Ernest Augustus upon the bowing exit of his chancellor.

Red of face, heavy jowls shaking, thick shoulders heaving, gooseberry eyes tear-filling with Hanoverian sentimentality, 'Our grandson he w-weighs eight p-p-pounds,' was the sob-impeded utterance. 'A worthy successor to the bl-bl-blood. How good is God.'

'It is to be hoped,' his wife's taut lips unfolded to say, 'that God is good enough to save this worthy successor from the pox.'

'What?' The shocked Duke recoiled. 'Do you insinuate that the Frenchwoman's daughter has — is —'

'No!' Like a whiplash came the interruption. 'There is no evidence of hereditary taint in the Frenchwoman or her daughter. Would I have permitted the marriage if there were? Both have proved their price, Celle's hundred thousand thalers per annum, to be above rubies. But your son's promiscuous indulgences might have caused him to suffer a resultant penalty.'

'My God!' The flaccid mouth fell open. 'George Louis, he — has — he — he —'

'He has not,' curtly responded Sophia. 'I was at pains to have him medically examined before marriage for fear he should have incurred a distemper due to his intimacy with the woman Busche and others of her ilk. It is fortunate,' she pointedly added, 'that your promiscuous indulgences have not contaminated me. Enough of this. It serves no purpose since I am past the age of child-bearing and therefore have no further use for you,' And as the reddening Duke prepared to bluster, she rose to her feet and moved toward the door. 'I go now to see our grandson if he be visible. I have ordered all the necessary celebrations for tonight.'

The news that set joy bells ringing, trumpets blaring, the populace cheering throughout the capital was less welcome to the Baroness von Platen than to the subjects of their Sovereign Duke.

Reclining on her day-bed to rest before the evening's festivities she weighed, as a tradesman weighs his wares, the pros for and cons against the profit or loss sustained by the birth of a son to the House of Brunswick-Lüneberg.

As he stood in the immediate line of succession, it would necessitate settlements that must perforce deplete the exchequer from which she derived her welfare and wellbeing, unless — a marriage might be arranged between this future heir to the principality and her daughter. She had a daughter, presumably by Platen, kept well in the background lest its thick-jowled blonde resemblance to a certain august personage might cause remark.

Staring up at the ceiling, erotically designed with aphrodisiacal devices, she cogitated. *Five, six years' difference is immaterial in this age of child marriages. And if the Frenchwoman and her bastard could be raised to royal rank, why could not the same be achieved for the daughter of Hanover's Lord Chancellor who through my diplomacy is nominal Head of State? What of Anne Hyde, daughter of Clarendon, Lord Chancellor to Charles of England who, had she lived, would have been Queen Consort of the future James the Second?* That a principality, not a kingdom, should inflict so arbitrary a restriction on the sons of the reigning Duke, was out of all reason. She would see to it that such restriction be repealed. If Henry Tudor could marry a commoner to beget the great Elizabeth, to say nothing of a further wife, Jane Seymour, who produced the boy King Edward, surely her child and Platen's could, when the time and age of both be ripe…

Conjecture paused, while her thoughts, like bats, darted through the darkened corridors of memory. How far she had travelled since she had left Versailles, bearing on her shoulders the burden of Catherine and her father — *God rest the old devil,* she piously besought, *if he deserves to rest, which he doesn't.* Neither she nor Cathie had been welcomed by the women of *le Soleil d'Or,* and, for want of a better alternative, they had departed to explore new ground in Hanover and find richer soil therein to be — embedded.

A husky laugh escaped her at the sorry pun, and stretching her arms above her head she described a circle in the air as if she embraced an unseen presence. *After all, are not we von Meissenbergs of noble birth, of whom our father was the last of his line male, comparable with that of any French Huguenot marquis and far better bred than a Platen? ... Count von Platen. Yes!* She hugged herself; her loose-sleeved robe fell away from her arms, exposing their fleshy nakedness. *Baron is insufficient honour for him, for my devotion to the* — she grinned awry — *the State. Had I been born male I would have succeeded to the title of von Meissenberg, and now, or so soon as may be granted, I will be Countess von Platen with all due benefit accruing to support our* — *my* — *elevation.*

Her grin broadened, creasing the carmine and white lead paint with which she repaired the ravages of nightly dissipations. Rising from her couch, she went over to her dressing-glass. Seated before it she examined her reflection resulting in a frown between the thickly pencilled black eyebrows. Her full-lipped mouth curved downward, slackened, opened. Striking a silver bell on the table she called, 'Ilse! Come!'

From the closet that communicated with the bedchamber, where the cosmetics, perfumes, herbal and medicinal remedies for all vices of the skin were kept under lock and key, Ilse the maid — who had been patiently listening for that summons — emerged, advanced, and submissively bobbed. 'Gracious Baroness?'

'The water-lily lotion. Remove this,' she rubbed a cheek to leave a smear, 'and then renovate.'

She produced from a silver casket a key and handed it to the girl, who bobbed again and returned to the closet to fetch on a tray the perquisites for her lady's adornment.

While Ilse applied lotion, creams, whitening and pinkening, Clara surveyed the girl's face in the mirror to compare the natural peach bloom of her youthful complexion with her own that, strive how she might, could never disguise its coarse *peau d'orange*.

The contrast between the natural rose and cream of Ilse's face and hers seen in the looking-glass, the firm young breasts beneath the tightened bodice of her servant's dress, a stray curl or two of bright yellow hair escaped from the stiffened white coif, caused the Baroness to jerk herself from under her creature's ministrations to dig a vicious elbow in that young offending breast.

'Filth! Look what you do! Would you make a clown of me? Too much white and not enough rouge.'

Wincing with the pain of this attack in her tenderest parts, 'Pardon Gracious B-Baroness,' was the stammering reply, 'I thought you had wished me to — to lighten the —'

'Dolt! You *thought?* Can a maggot think? I did not tell you to paint me as if I were a canvas. Will you never learn? Take the hare's foot … gently, now, gently. Don't dab, just a *soupçon*. A trace, the merest touch. Gah! Why am I cursed with an animal that knows no more than an ape how to — Give it to me!' She snatched the hare's foot, flung it down and drove a fist into the girl's quivering mouth with force enough to have loosened a tooth. 'Go!' she shouted. 'I will wear the red-and-gold brocade tonight. Fetch it. Take this.' She got up, was dispossessed of her wrapper and stood revealed stark nude, scowling to note in a wall mirror the rolls of fat around her waist-line. And to Ilse, who was choking back her tears with a hand to her bruised lip, 'Go, slut! Don't stand there gaping. The red-and-gold — you heard me? Go!'

In her bed with its blue and silver draperies, Sophia Dorothea, after hours of travail, lay exhausted and at peace to gaze upon her son. Since custom did not permit a royal mother to suckle her young, the services of a wet nurse were provided to satisfy his needs. And now, his appetite appeased, he subsided and slept, enfolded in the arms of her who had forcibly ejected him into a strange new world from the comfort of the dark and cosy cavern that for nine months had been his home.

It cannot be said that Sophia Dorothea loved at first sight the curious little object ecstatically presented by the nurse; such an old, old face, wizened, red, and puckered into innumerable wrinkles; a bald head shaded with an incipient nondescript down of no colour, rather like carpet fluff, she was dismayed to think. Searching its indeterminate features for any similarity to her own she found none; yet was relieved that neither could she discern the smallest resemblance to the father who had begot him. Then, while its ugliness underwent a series of hideous contortions, a wave of rapture overswept her and joyfully she cried, 'Look, nurse, look! He knows me — he smiles at me. My blessed life!' She covered its baldness with kisses. 'He's laughing!'

She was not contradicted. Long experience in attendance on newborn royal infants had taught the midwife tact when dealing with their mothers, especially one so young as this, delivered of her first. She therefore refrained from contradiction that her nurseling, not unnaturally after a surfeit of nourishment, had been taken with the wind. Instead: 'As well he might for joy, His Precious Highness, to behold for the first time Your Serenity. There, then, there, the treasure,' was the fatuous reply. 'Your Serene Highness, pardon me if I take him just a moment — just one little *little* moment — that's my infant angel come from heaven to rejoice us!'

He was lifted from his mother's protesting arms, to be expertly patted, while he gulped, blew bubbles, made faces, wheezed, brought up milk, was returned to her who bore him and rhapsodically received while she murmured over him the foolish endearments of mothers with their babies from time immemorial.

His father was admitted. Unmoved by the transports of the pale happy girl resting on her pillows with their son nestling at her breast, he stooped awkwardly to lay a hand on her head, breathing fumes of stale wine and ale in her face. She shrank from him and drew an edge of the silken sheet to cover her sleeping babe.

'So, you're well over it now,' said George Louis with assumed heartiness. He put out a stumpy finger to his hidden son. 'Let me see him, can't you? Why cover him up? You'll smother him.' He pulled down the sheet. 'There's a look of me about him,' he decided.

'God forbid,' she whispered, low. Turning to the nurse, he asked her, 'Can't you see the likeness?'

She dipped and rose again, resorting to professional tact. 'Certainly, Your Serene Highness, the living image of Your Highness.'

'I would say his hair,' George Louis complacently stroked his curled tow-coloured wig, 'will be the same golden fairness as mine. I was flaxen as a boy, you know,' he told his wife. 'All we of Brunswick-Lüneberg are fair. Saxon. Nothing dark and Latin-French with us. My barber says mine is the best head of hair in Hanover. Don't you think,' to the nurse, 'that His Highness will be fair, if not golden-haired?'

'Without a doubt, Your Serene Highness.' More dipping and rising and dipping again. 'As fair as a cherub — which he is. I have never seen a more beautiful child, scarce six hours old.'

'And healthy too,' nodded his father, 'with a fine pair of lungs. I heard him yelling.' And, less from inclination than for appearance's sake, he bent flabbily to kiss his wife's forehead, saying, 'You must give me some more like this.'

With a cursory nod to the bobbing nurse, he left the room and his wife to her adoration.

After the birth of George Augustus life assumed a fairer aspect for Sophia Dorothea.

Noticeably her mother-in-law, the duchess, was now less critical and carping when she visited her grandson in his nursery, expressing approval of his mother's care of and attention to him and his welfare. At Celle he was as much the light of his grandparents' eyes as their daughter had been. Duke William wept and chuckled over him as he dandled him upon his knee and blessed Sophia Dorothea for the joy she brought to him in this God-sent grandchild. Duke Ernest, her father-in-law, was equally delighted. He showered gifts upon the mother and her son: a jewelled rattle for the little one; a diamond necklace for 'my darling daughter', and rings and things that, although they were bought with her money, did not decrease their donor's good intent.

All this was excellent for Sophia Dorothea; not so for Clara, now Countess, since Platen had received higher ennoblement as reward for his service to the State, or to the duke — 'for the loan of his wife', as the duchess, with more humour than rancour remarked during one of her sessions with Leibnitz. She and that learned scholar were tolerant of human frailties and extra-marital relationships, unless the rights of sovereignty were involved by an unorthodox or morganatic marriage. 'For,' pronounced the duchess, 'the lowest monad of the animal kingdom to the highest, were it king or commoner, is not immune from the call of the flesh.'

'Unless, Madame,' corrected Leibnitz, 'it were a crustacean or an hermaphrodite, as is the worm.'

Sophia cackled. Leibnitz never failed to amuse while he instructed. But Clara, Countess von Platen, was not amused. She regarded with disquiet the affection and loud-voiced admiration of the duke for his 'darling daughter', mother of this latest George. Her enmity was multiplied, accompanied by fear lest she find herself 'put down for a whey-faced smirking ninny', so did she inveigh against the Crown Princess to Platen, who cared not a jot if she were put down, with a Count's coronet on his silver and a goodly dole of the princess's portion to go with it.

It was bitter gall for Clara to see the 'whey-faced ninny' had seemed to have won all hearts by her youthful beauty, the more radiant for motherhood. It irked her exceedingly to see her drive out in her gilded coach-and-four, with her baby in her arms to resounding cheers and hand-wavings from pedestrians or women at their windows as she passed. Nor did her sister Catherine welcome the advent of the infant Prince. Talk had come to her in her near exile — not many miles from Monplaisir — that George Louis in his role of father had been more agreeably disposed towards his wife whose bed, on the few occasions when he sought it, he no longer was denied.

'With intent to fill her up with boys,' Catherine disgustedly reported to her sister.

'That's as may be,' was Clara's rejoinder. 'Don't fret yourself. If he gets her with another boy, or girl, it will be the last of them. There's heirs a-plenty with his brothers and a sister. I'll see to it that George Louis will find something tastier to warm him than his chilly little whiting of a wife. Leave all to me. You'll have him back or my name's not Clara von Platen.'

She methodically set to work. Her first approach was to the duke. To him she brought a tale to the discredit of the Crown Princess, of her indiscretions, misbehaviour, and flirtations with the various young nobles of the Court: this recounted to Ernest in the intimacy of the extra-nuptial couch. The duke, having had his fill of food and drink, was more inclined for sleep than for the attentions or complaints of the Platen.

'Foh! What of it? She's young. Let her enjoy herself while she can. She'll grow old too soon — we all do, though I'd say she'll wear better than some.' A remark that was not kindly taken by the Platen. 'And I've never seen her misbehave. She knows her place and knows — ow — ow' — a yawn interrupted him — 'knows — ow — how to keep it — a-a-ah —' A wider yawn halted him entirely. He turned his back on her and sank his nightcapped head into the pillow.

'Ernest!' Clara seized the tassel of his nightcap and tugged it off, disclosing, without his wig, his almost hairless scalp. 'Did you hear me? Are you going to allow her to go capering and giggling and sitting in corners with any young spark, to say nothing of your sons Charles and Max, to whom she allows the freedom and favours she denies her husband? Ernest! Do you hear me?'

Ernest did not hear her. He was asleep.

Finding her attack against Sophia Dorothea had fallen flat upon the duke, she tried her tactics, and with more success, upon George Louis.

A message sent to him by her page gave her instant admission to his apartment. Since the birth of his son a wing of the Leine Schloss had been allotted to the Crown Prince and Princess in preference to those of the Alte Palais.

It was morning in early spring. The trees in the garden of the Schloss were swathed in a mist of April green; daffodils swayed in the long grass edging the banks of the Leine, overlooked by the windows of Hanover's Crown Prince. Clara found him reclining on a couch with a handkerchief on his head, a glass of something on a table at his side, and on his face, that was a bilious yellow, a look of insufferable woe.

'What's this?' Wasting no time in a curtsy, Clara without ceremony asked, 'Are you sick?'

'As a dog,' groaned George Louis, 'thanks to your hospitality last night at Monplaisir. Not content with bleeding me of five hundred thalers, you gave me to drink of new wine in old bottles, enough to lay out a regiment. You had best sack your cellarer before I attend another of your orgies.'

'Is that so, indeed? If Your Serene Highness,' said Clara offendedly, 'succumbed to drink last night, it was not in my house. The finest Rhenish is kept apart for you. I am grieved to see you so poorly. Your Highness must surely be poisoned.'

'That I am.' He raised himself on an elbow to take the glass from the table, 'but this is a palliative prescribed by my wife who knows much for her age, young as she is, of medicinal remedies learned of her mother.' Yet before the glass had reached his lips, Clara had seized it and her opportunity.

'Don't touch it, Your Highness! What can a young inexperienced girl know of medicinal properties? And if learned from her mother — we may judge of the French what *their* remedies may be! I will mix you a tincture to relieve you of your sour stomach. This must be thrown down the privy. Now, a word, if I may, in your ear.' She went to the door, opened it, peered out into the corridor, saw a couple of pages playing pitch and toss, and called, 'Page! Come. Take this glass and throw away its contents.' A boy came running, took the glass, was told, 'And go. Don't either of you loiter out there. Go along.'

She watched them scuttle, and returning to the prince drew a chair close to his couch.

'It deeply irks me to tell you this,' she achieved a sigh with a sorrowful shake of her head, 'but I feel it my duty to advise Your Serene Highness that you keep a watch upon the Crown Princess, who so far forgets her dignity and duty to Your Highness, her husband, not only to flirt with all and sundry but to disparage you to them. Sir, forgive me that I am compelled to say that she makes unseemly mock of you.'

'Of me?' He hoisted himself up; the dampened bandages fell from his forehead. 'How? How *dare* she! What does she — what does she say?'

'Alas!' Another sigh, and more head-shaking. 'One must find excuse for the delinquencies of youth, which in her case are due to her upbringing that has been so sadly neglected by her French mother whom Her Serene Highness, the Duchess, rightly designates as a Nobody. Far be it from me, a mere servant of the State, in the capacity of the Chief Minister's wife, to query or to criticise the judgement of His Serene Highness, your esteemed father, in promoting this marriage, which I greatly fear will prove to be less — felicitous than we had all too fondly hoped.'

'You are right.' The loose jaw sagged; his eyes blinked to dispel the haze of the night's inebriety. 'I knew it to be a fatal mistake. We are totally unsuited. Makes mock of me, does she, with any carpet knight! God damn her! I insist you repeat what you heard her say. I have a right to know.'

'Sir,' Clara emitted a still deeper sigh to creak her honed corsage that supported the fall of the too-heavy breasts. 'At the risk of profaning my tongue with *lèse-majesté* —' Dramatically she paused.

'Get on with it,' came in a growl from him.

Clara got on with it. By the time she had finished, George Louis, whose liverish yellow face had turned a sickly lemon from shock and wounded vanity, was staggering about the room vowing damnation to and vengeance on Sophia Dorothea.

So soon as Clara, highly elated with the result of her strategy, had left him he gave an order: 'I desire the Crown Princess to attend me here — at once.'

'You believe her? You believe her monstrous lies? Then you're a greater fool than I thought — if that were possible.'

'I believe the evidence of what I long suspected,' said he in a surly tone.

'Suspected? What did you suspect? That I despise you for an ill-mannered boor who plays rough and tumble with my housemaids to make me a laughing-stock? That *chienne* — she says that I called you a *cochon*. I did and I do. You're a pig!' yelled Sophia Dorothea, well away in one of her tempers. 'But pig is too complimentary a word for you. A pig knows no better than to wallow and guzzle in a trough as you guzzle at table and fall under it drunk!'

George Louis rose up, a hand fisted to strike. She dodged and went on with a rush, 'You disgust me. Nothing I have said about you can ever — no, *never* convey how I have suffered in our marriage.' Tears were now springing; she choked them back. 'But since you have given me Georgie I thought you were kinder and that we'd be ha-happy together.'

Her hair, untidily rumpled, fell over her face. She looked even less than her seventeen years, her mouth, childishly red, in a tremble, a flag of angry colour in either cheek. 'How could you,' she sobbed, 'take heed of that wicked old woman and her lies against me? I'm your wife, worse luck, and the mother of your son. If it were not for him who is much more mine than yours — he doesn't look like you, thank God — I'd leave you. I would! I'd go back to Celle, and I will! Yes, I will, and I'll take Georgie with me.' She made for the door.

He caught her by the shoulders, twisting her round to him.

'Shame on you!' he shouted. 'Have you no decency, screaming at me like a fish hag for all the pages and my servants to hear? You're no better than a common little trull — a spoilt child. You deserve a whipping, and for two pins I'd put you across my knee and —'

But he got no further than that, for she had wrenched herself free and was at him, claws out to scratch his face had he not grabbed her hands and held them in a vice. 'Oh, no, you don't! A wildcat, forsooth.' He shook her. 'You ask me not to believe what the countess has reported of your disgraceful conduct and mockery of me, your husband. Well, I *do* believe her! You have no sense of decorum nor — nor dignity, no —'

He stopped short for he saw that she was laughing, silently at first and then with splutters. 'I can't help it. You look so funny without your wig. I've never seen you without it — you're too vain to take it off — even in bed!'

He glared at her; then he too was in the splutters, for at his age — he was little more than a boy — laughter is infectious. 'Have you seen yourself? Look at your hair, all over your face.' He dragged her to a wall mirror. 'And your gown half off your back.'

'Well, it's your fault for attacking me!'

'*I* attacking *you*! I like that! You'd have clawed my eyes out — little devil!'

'I'm sorry. Yes, I'm sorry. I know I have a hellish temper, but you shouldn't listen to that old — never mind. I forgive you. Do you forgive me?'

'Forgive? Maybe. On condition that you treat me to no more scenes like this, for I won't have it. Understand?'

She nodded, snuffling. A dewdrop trickled from her nose. She lifted her petticoat, seeking in its pocket for a handkerchief.

'Have you a handkercher?' she asked him. 'I don't seem to have one, and I'm starting a cold.'

He drew a clean piece of lace-edged linen from his cuff. 'Take this.'

She took it, blew in it, handed it back to him.

'You'd best keep it,' he told her. 'I don't want your cold.'

'Then you had better not come to my bed,' she said with an impudent upward look, 'and that will be a welcome release for both of us.' And she was off again to the door with a parting thrust. 'Why don't you send for your Busche to console you? She won't treat you to scenes though she is a common trull, but not a *little* one. She's much larger and fatter than I, or you — so you'd best buy a double-sized bed!' And out she went.

While they appeared to have patched up that quarrel, not by any means the first of its kind, Clara's stratagem bore poisonous fruit. More and more frequent were the rows between these two, and the breach that had been but a furrow widened to a chasm. Clara, watchfully alert for increasing ruptures, bethought her how to hasten a complete collapse of this marriage from which she had secured much benefit in her share of the dowry of the Crown Princess. It would suit her purpose to crush whatever chance there might have been for George Louis to tolerate if not to love his young girl wife after the birth of their son, and which might well depreciate the pecuniary advantage that she, his father's mistress, had already enjoyed.

Having heard report from one of her spies that the princess had impudently advised her husband to send for his Busche 'to console' him, Clara jumped at the idea of reinstating Catherine, and forthwith brought her again into the orbit of George Louis.

But here she was faced with a setback. The charms that formerly enticed him had waned. Catherine, as his wife so naughtily reminded him, had considerably stoutened, and while his choice lay in sirens well-covered, his fancy turned to something less cumbersome than Madame Busche.

Bitterly did she upbraid her sister Clara 'for having thrown me at his head to be cast off as if I were one of his old boots!'

'In which he may have found himself too big,' chuckled Clara. 'He is swollen head to foot with conceit. But you need not fear that he'll seek to replace you in Hanover. He'll be returning to his first love, as so I understand.'

'His first?' cried Catherine. 'Who is she? And if not here — where is she? Do you know her?'

'We all know *of* her,' teased Clara, 'though none can say exactly where she is. She travels here, there, everywhere, and George Louis travels with her.'

'Well, but who?' demanded Catherine, rising to the bait. 'Some slut he picked up at the Court of the English King when he went courting Anne of York?'

'I think not there, yet he may have glimpsed her from afar to hanker after her, and let me tell you she's no slut. Nor is she a woman.'

'What!' Catherine's mouth formed an incredulous O. The whole of her was globular; her face resembled nothing so much as a full harvest moon. Her eyes, too, were rounded in her circular red apple cheeks.

'She — you called her "she", and not a woman! Don't tell me he's one for the boys?'

'No,' Clara gurgled, 'neither he nor his father can be accused of sodomy. I merely use the feminine for what she is — in French.'

'French!' Catherine let out a gusty breath. 'O! Then she or it, or whatever, is *French*?'

'In this case,' said Clara, 'she's German.'

'Oh, be damned! You befool me.'

'No more,' said Clara sweetly, 'than you are already befooled — from birth. Come then, I'll tell you. Not you or any woman can hold George Louis for any length of time underneath her petticoats or in her bed, because his heart and soul, if he has a soul which I doubt, is held by the army. He is a man of the camp rather than the Court, and since he was fifteen and fought with his father in his campaigns on the Rhine, and at Consarbrück, the army is his one and only love.'

Which may not have been too great an overstatement.

So now the Crown Prince of Hanover was seldom to be seen in his father's Duchy, a state of affairs that caused his wife no heart-burning, and allowed her increasing pleasure in the company of her two brothers-in-law, Maximilian and Charles, but with no pleasure at all in that of their young sister, Sophia Charlotte. During the first year of the marriage, Charlotte, who, more than any of her brothers, favoured George Louis, had shown marked resentment and unfriendliness to the Platen's 'Interloper'; but since the departure of George Louis in pursuit of his 'first love', Charlotte changed sides to champion his wife for what she called her elder brother's 'nastiness' to Sophia Dorothea. Not that the sudden and embarrassing histrionics from the fifteen-year-old Charlotte received any marked response. She actively disliked her sister-in-law, a fat plain child, a born trouble-maker, ill-mannered and in awe of none save her mother, whose rod of iron implemented to bring her sons to heel when applied to Charlotte had but small effect. She, although impervious to chastisement, dared not openly defy her redoubtable mother, who would never hesitate to apply her rod of iron — or, more correctly, the birch — as punishment for insolence or any other juvenile delinquency.

'I hate my mother,' she confided to Sophia Dorothea, 'as much as I now hate George Louis. I used to love him but I don't any more. Not after the way he's treated you. Max and Charles hate him too. He's a beast.'

This conversation took place in the garden of the Leine Schloss, where Charlotte had followed her. Although Sophia Dorothea knew she was watched by her gentlewomen from the windows above she had come out to enjoy in solitude the spring sunshine and walk her dog beside the river.

Panting with her hurry, Charlotte said, 'I saw you go into the garden. You don't mind if I walk with you, do you?'

She minded very much, but, 'No, if you must,' was the ungracious rejoinder.

'Will you promise not to tell if I tell you something I heard about myself which I was not supposed to hear but couldn't help hearing?' Charlotte slid her arm in that of Sophia Dorothea, squeezing herself up against her. 'I was in the corridor outside my mother's room when she was speaking to my father.'

'Eavesdropping, were you?' Sophia Dorothea disengaged from Charlotte. She was smelling strong of onions, having just dined of and heartily devoured onion soup laden with sausages.

'I wasn't eavesdropping — as if I would!' was Charlotte's reply, with more vehemence than conviction, 'but I heard, as I was about to go into my mother's room, that I'm to be married! So what do you think of that?' Without waiting to know what her sister-in-law thought of that, Charlotte went on, linking arms again and more than ever redolent of onions. 'And my mother was saying it would be a good match for me, and then I heard — because my mother does shout, you know, so I couldn't help hearing and I heard her say that the Elector of Brandenburg wants to marry me and my father said I was too young to be married to a widower of thirty and me not yet sixteen but *you* were married at sixteen and my mother said,' again she captured Sophia Dorothea, this time with an arm about her waist, 'that if I married the Elector of Brandenburg I might one day be Queen of — I couldn't quite hear where — it sounded like Russia only it couldn't have been Russia because the King of Russia is a Czar so what do you think of *that?*' was Charlotte's triumphant conclusion to this almost unpunctuated monologue.

'I think —' determinedly Sophia Dorothea dispossessed herself of Charlotte — 'that your mother has queens on the brain. And please don't breathe onions all over me.'

'Was I breathing onions? That's the soup,' said Charlotte unnecessarily. 'But then I heard something else,' Again she captured Sophia Dorothea. 'It is something that concerns *you*. Something nice.' She sucked in her full pink lips as if she were sucking a sweet. 'I wish it was me that my father said he would take to Italy with him. Aren't you lucky?'

'He — the duke said — what?' She, who had lent but half an ear and half her face to this odoriferous recital, turned sharply. 'Did you say the duke is taking me to Italy?'

Charlotte nodded, smiling widely. 'He said you needed a holiday — were looking peaked, he said, and my mother said—'

But Sophia Dorothea did not wait to hear what Charlotte's mother had said. Shaking her off she ran to find Knesebeck and tell her this exciting news ... if it were true.

It was true, as also was the proposed marriage between Sophia Charlotte and the Elector of Brandenburg. Great were the festivities at the Court of Hanover following the wedding of the fifteen-year-old bride to her widowed bridegroom, many years her senior.

As in the case of Sophia Dorothea, the bride elect had not been told of her betrothal, more than she had gathered from a keyhole, until it was a *fait accompli;* but unlike her brother's wife, Charlotte did not rebel. She was only too delighted to be free of matriarchal autocracy, and gleefully departed with the unprepossessing, prematurely aged husband of her mother's choice, sped on her wedding journey with blessings from the duke, her father, and with tears, but not of grief from the duchess, who was as thankful to be rid of her troublesome young daughter as the daughter to be rid of her.

So soon as the wedding celebrations were over the duke, accompanied by an immense suite and the ubiquitous Platen, set off for Venice leaving his duchess to carry on affairs of State at Hanover. He would have taken Sophia Dorothea with him then, but was dissuaded by Clara from so doing on the assumption that it would not look well for the Crown Princess to leave her infant son while she went gallivanting in Italy. She had no wish to see Sophia Dorothea taking precedence above herself by right of rank where she had been received with the respect and favour due to the duke's acknowledged mistress. She was therefore not overjoyed when the Crown Princess, escorted by General von Ilten of the duke's suite, who had been sent to fetch her, arrived in Venice. With her went her Mistress of the Robes, the general's wife, Madame von Ilten, alias 'the Porcupine', and, of course, Knesebeck.

It was carnival time, and Sophia Dorothea threw herself wholeheartedly into the frolicsome gaieties, so delightful a change from the formal etiquette of Hanover. The revels and the racketings, the dancing and the prancing in the palazzi where masked nobles and their ladies romped indiscriminately with any other mask, went on day in, day out, and all night long until the bland moon waned and the stars were drowned in those lovely streets of water, greying from grape-bloom dark to rose-lit dawn.

From gondolas weaving their way through the canals and under the bridges that spanned them came shrieks of laughter, a song uprisen in a man's sweet tenor, the twang of a guitar above the murmuring voices of lovers hidden under canopies. Lamplight reflected in the water's purple sheen vied in metallic rainbow hue with the sparkle of sapphire, ruby, diamond or emerald on jewelled neck and bosom; or the glinting eyes of a tiger, a dog, a cat-faced goddess, for all wore fantastic head-dresses, some fearsomely with devils' horns and some with wings as angels.

In this ceaseless saturnalia of junketing, identities were lost; and in the Piazza of San Marco, Duke Ernest, red, perspiring, masked in the head of a donkey, stood with his niece to watch the dancers and told her, his voice booming hollowly behind the scarlet nostrils and open ass's mouth, 'I am Bottom from that English poet Shake-his-spear in his play of a dream night of summer.'

In the great shadow of the cathedral under a sky that blazed in the furnace of the sun's cremation, the drift of saffron-tinted coral clouds, deepening to crimson on that funeral pyre, were as pennons flying in rapid procession to greet the long day's death and to herald the birth of the moon.

Sophia Dorothea wore a gown of silver and a headdress crowned with a silver bow and arrow for Diana. A black satin mask hid all of her upper face save the tilted tip of her nose. 'And you,' said her uncle, hugging her close to him, 'are the most beautiful goddess of all.'

This, overheard by the Platen who, never far away from him, was voluminous in scarlet and wearing a cardinal's hat, caused her to snort into the lace of her mask worn to cover her face, since a surfeit of Italian macaroni and pasta had brought her out in pimples.

'It is all a dream,' sighed Sophia Dorothea. 'I want never to wake from it.'

But wake she did when her husband arrived upon the scene to take possession of his Crown Princess. He had not been in Venice half an hour before, craving immediate audience, he was warned by the Platen of his wife's misbehaviour. It would seem that, trusting to her thin disguise, she had allowed any masked fellow from gondolier to senator, to couple with her in the rowdy jigs of the palazzi as if she were a woman of the town.

This, were it intended further to alienate George Louis from his wife, did not achieve its purpose. Absence had made his heart, if not grown fonder, randy. A year's association with his fellow officers in camp and out of it, during his recent campaign against the Turks, and scarce a woman to be seen save in a yashmak, rendered him desirous to end his intermittent celibacy. Although her type of beauty had never appealed to him, the promise of her adolescent loveliness was now fulfilled. He must unwillingly admit her attractive to the many young Venetians who admired her, among them one, not of Venice but of Paris, le Marquis de Lassaye, who had come there for the carnival and was, avowedly, at her feet.

He had the reputation of being, or more likely believed himself to be, irresistible to women. With unflagging ardour he pursued Sophia Dorothea and, according to the Platen, was not repulsed. It may have been on her advice that George Louis persuaded his father to leave Venice for Rome when carnival week was over. So to Rome they went, the duke and his suite, the prince and princess with theirs.

And after them went Monsieur le Marquis.

The night before they left, when the jollifications had reached their height, Sophia Dorothea with Knesebeck on the Rialto, watched the last of those orgiastic revels. The rows of palazzi on either side that glorious Canal, their windows shining from a myriad lights within and from the gaily lamp-lit gondolas without, looked to be on fire. And while along the banks of the Canal frenzied youths excitedly dived into the water and came up dripping to hurl themselves upon the nearest gondola, a voice behind the princess murmured in French: 'I, too, would wish to plunge into the canal and drown myself, not for the love of this Queen of the Adriatic but for love of you, Your Exquisite Highness whom I adore!'

Or something fatuously near to this to make her turn about, startled to see a form that appeared to be encased in fish scales and masked with the head of a shark, its spiky teeth alarmingly agleam. But if its sex were indeterminate its voice was not, and recognisable as that of de Lassaye.

'Eh, well, Monsieur le Marquis,' Sophia Dorothea said, in the giggles and also in his native tongue. "I implore you do not incommode yourself in a watery grave for me, even though you would not drown, for, like a fish in water, you would be in your element, no doubt!'

'Ah, my goddess, do not make mock of me, whose heart is lacerated with your beauty.'

He fell upon his knees, and in attempt to kiss her silver shoes peeping from the hem of her gown, his shark's head slipped to reveal his face daubed with rouge, and his hair gold-powdered. Vexedly she stepped aside and all but drove her little pointed slipper into his reddened mouth, and was caught back by Knesebeck in greatest fright.

'Serene Highness! Do you not see the steps leading down to the canal? You would have been over the edge, and not in your element as is Monsieur le Marquis. Monsieur,' Knesebeck assumed her right as guardian of her Princess to rebuke him. 'Pray do not embarrass Her Highness with these unseemly advances. The hour is late, and the princess is fatigued. We now return to the palazzo, for we must be up betimes. We journey to Rome tomorrow.'

And all the way back to the Piazza Moro, the traditionally credited abode of Shakespeare's *Othello*, where Duke Ernest and his suite were lodged, the princess berated Knesebeck for being 'such a fool as to tell him that we go to Rome. Now you will see, he'll be there before us. Coincidence indeed! He had no intention of going to Rome until you told him that we will be there — tomorrow! And now I'll never shake him off!'

'But, Madame, my darling,' the confidante was near to tears, 'I am the veriest fool, I know. I can't think why I said it, only I was in such a fright with Your Highness stepping back in haste — and those steps leading down to the water — you might have slipped and fallen in — that I said the first thing I could think of to be quit of him and let him know we leave Venice.'

'So that he can follow me. And now, of course, he will.'

And so he did.

At first the princess treated his enamoured pursuit as a joke, and may have been a little flattered by his protestations of undying love. Not yet nineteen, she was still of an age to enjoy a flirtation for the fun of it, to lead de Lassaye on to let him down. But when his attentions became overwhelmingly importunate she realised she had allowed him to go too far, and refused to admit him to her presence; this the direct result of having been tamely rebuked by her uncle, and violently abused by her husband, raging up and down her salon.

'You have made a laughing-stock of me and a byword of yourself — behaving like a bawd. Where's your dignity or sense? Encouraging that painted fop. He only makes up to you because you are my wife, the Crown Princess, so that he can boast to his fellows of his conquest. He's a mountebank, a charlatan, and you let him follow at your heels and you lap up all he says. I won't have it. Understand?'

She took it hardly and there they were, the two of them, shouting at each other for all the Court to hear. She, on her part attacking him for what she called 'a case of the pot and kettle. *You* to talk to me of making a byword of myself, when you are notorious as a promiscuous adulterer! As for your false accusations — I would look higher for a lover than a painted mammet with a train of boys at his heels. Have you seen his pages? Whatever he is or may likely be he has learned at the Court of Philippe d'Orléans. We all know what *he* is!'

'A compatriot of yours,' sneered her husband. 'Perhaps you will deny that you have *not* looked higher, when here is evidence that you've looked high enough.' He flourished before her a letter, purported to have been written to the Crown Princess by de Lassaye, likely intercepted by the Platen and handed to George Louis with intent to nip in the bud his renewed relations with his wife. It was common knowledge that since his return from the wars they again cohabited.

This suited Clara not at all. She still hoped that her sister Catherine, now widowed, would be restored to her former state as favourite of the heir apparent. 'What letter? I have received no letter from him,' She snatched it and, translating from the French, read with growing dismay:

I do not desire that you should run the risk of ruining yourself by keeping up relations with me. It is better I die for you than to live unhappily without you...

'My God,' she broke off, crumpling the letter into a ball. 'This is infamous! It is utterly false, contrived by some diabolical mischief to befoul me. I have enemies enough, heaven knows, or he may have wished to revenge himself on me for having repulsed his odious advances. He, or whoever wrote this in his name says,' she smoothed the paper, reading:' Stop writing to a man who always brings misfortune in his train ... I have never written to him! And if he did write this which I doubt, for he writes very bad French for an educated Frenchman — if he did write this stuff it is a plot to ruin me, and make our marriage an even greater failure than it is at present. I think I know who is at the bottom of this. I'll name no names. Even these walls have ears. Take it!' She flung it at him, 'and gloat over it with your women, but don't bring me the garbage of the gutter, where, if you were not your father's son, you would belong.'

So that was it.

The gossips were enchanted. Here was spice enough to feed them for a month and relieve the tedium of the duke's lectures to his courtiers when, with German thoroughness, after exploring the Vatican, the Colosseum, the Appian Way and the picture galleries, he would read at wearisome length the lives of the Caesars, omitting for his bored listeners the excesses of Nero and others of the worst of them which might have enlivened those dreary sessions.

'If he would tell us of Caligula who was in love with his horse,' said the princess in an undertone of giggles to Knesebeck, 'none of us would yawn.'

And none was loth to leave Rome after a sojourn there of some six months, least of all Sophia Dorothea after her unfortunate association with de Lassaye.

Although relations between herself and her husband had been resumed despite the flare up concerning the Marquis, who had faded out, or, more or less politely, been kicked out by George Louis, these two when returned to Hanover, were once again divided. But those months in the 'passionate warm South', as the duke had hopefully foreseen and confided to his Clara, had borne fruit in the birth of a daughter named for her mother, Sophia Dorothea.

In her children she found consolation for her husband's neglect that had again increased. He wanted a boy and had been given a girl, a bitter disappointment to be vented, as usual, on his wife, who retaliated with perpetual wranglings and refusal to cohabit. They now occupied separate apartments in the Leine Schloss and met only to quarrel. The Court, always a hot-bed of scandal and intrigue, and the courtiers, most of whom were the Platen's satellites, prepared to back the duke's favourite rather than an outsider in the Hanoverian stakes. Any scrap of gossip to the detriment of the Crown Princess was retailed to Clara by those of her informants who were well rewarded for their pains, whether founded on fancy or fact. All was grist to the mills of the Platen, grinding slowly but surely to achieve her ends and sustain her power over the duke which might not be everlasting. As with all men of a certain age, he was more susceptible to younger women and, for preference, young girls.

Sophia Dorothea, well aware of the cauldron of hate simmering against her, ready at any moment to boil over and scorch her with its risen scum, had none besides Knesebeck whom she could trust, except her two brothers-in-law, Maximilian and Charles. Both had ready access to her privacy and the three formed a triumvirate in their condemnation of the Platen's arrogance and the pernicious influence she exerted over the duke.

'She is more his Lord, or — Lady Chancellor,' said Charles, a-grin, 'than her cuckold of a husband. God knows what she has in mind now to put us out and your precious George Louis in.'

'Why, what do you mean?' Sophia Dorothea, always alert for danger, looked up from her tambour frame. She was embroidering a square of satin in vari-coloured silks to decorate the front of a dress for her eighteen-month-old daughter.

'He means,' explained Max in a surly tone, 'that the duke has been persuaded by his woman to give what is called primogeniture to his eldest son.'

'Primo — what?' She poised her needle threaded with silver. 'I have never heard that word before.'

'Well, hear it now. Our revered father, who disposes when his whore proposes, has considered handing over to George Louis the whole of his territories by will or settlement instead of dividing them equally among his sons as his father and all our grandfathers did. This means that at his death George Louis will come in for the lot, Celle included, when your father dies. And the Platen will get the pickings — in hope that her fat cow of a sister will yet make her bed for your husband to lie in.'

The princess drove the point of her needle viciously into the satin. 'I wish I were as tolerant as is your mother of the duke's disregard for his obligations.'

'Our good mother,' said Max, producing a gold snuff-box and stuffing his nostrils with a pinch of its contents, has the sense to know that man is polygamous, and with the ever-present example of our cousins of England, and your King of France, she takes what you call our father's "disregard for his obligations" as criterion of his royal prerogative and his Clara's perquisites.'

Sophia Dorothea stuck out a mutinous red underlip, *like a ripe strawberry,* noted Max, *and as tempting to taste* — if he dared.

'I wish you would not call the King of France *my* king. You always do. He isn't my king.'

'Half of him is,' quizzed Charles. 'Your mother's half. And I am sure you would rather be the subject of *le Soleil d'Or* than of any of us — these sausage-eating Germans, as you so rightly name us.'

'I don't include you and Max as sausage-eaters,' she said wrinkling her nose at him with her puppyish grin that answered his. 'After all I am as much German as French and my father loves and *lives* on sausages. But what is this about primo—what d'you call it? It sounds most unfair to me.'

'It is most unfair to all of us, but it hasn't materialised yet. If it does,' Max told her brushing grains of snuff from his lilac velvet sleeve. Arbiter of elegance, he soaked himself in perfume and spent the little his father allowed him as much on clothes as on drink — 'If it *does*,' he repeated, 'will you back us up against the Platen? For I'll wager my new suit — this, which has cost me twenty thalers — that *she* has made our father cut us off.'

Sophia Dorothea vigorously nodded. 'Of course I'll back you up. I have a score to settle with the Platen. There's no end to her malice, particularly since —' She broke off, put aside her tambour frame and rose from where she sat. The two young men were also on their feet, both speaking at once.

'Since when?' from Max.

'Come on!' from Charles. 'Is this something new, or old? Particularly since you — what?'

'Yes,' Max urged her. 'When and what?'

'Since it happened at precisely nine o'clock this morning. All Hanover will hear of it, and that's another black mark on the Platen's score against me! Goodbye!' She gave them the nod of dismissal which, princes or brothers or not, they must take and bow themselves out.

All Hanover *did* hear of it, within the next twenty-four hours to set the court throbbing with the tale of a servant girl, the handmaid Ilse, attendant on the Countess von Platen!

Whispers flew between the courses of those interminable meals; fans were raised to hide the whispers, chins were stroked to hide the grins; eyes raised to be directed at the gobbling Duke, and more discreetly at his high-nosed Duchess who sat enthroned in ice. No word had passed her lips, for none must speak till spoken to, so in her immediate vicinity was silence. She ate little, but the Crown Princess ate much and with keenest appetite of 'some Frenchified concoction specially prepared for her by her own chef', as was resentfully noted by the Platen, who let all about her know that the princess spurned the food set before Their Serene Highnesses. She had reason to be vexed, as might have been the duke, were he less pachydermatous, for he too had been immediately involved in this flying rumour that had set the court a-buzz.

Diverse versions were relayed, absorbed, and swallowed with regurgitation, highly flavoured; but not until the last two days was the Crown Princess the focal point of what had better be forgotten and relegated to the bridewell where the handmaid had been sent in company with the trollops of the town for receiving the Duke, His Serene Highness's attentions, interrupted by the Platen.

All this had occasioned but a passing breeze since servant girls, and particularly pretty ones, were lawful prey for Princes as allowed to the Crown Prince whose dalliance with his wife's housemaids was known to all.

The *contretemps* and its unfortunate sequence took place at Monplaisir. Ilse had been sent to gather flowers from the garden for the countess who awaited her Duke's visit, and he, arriving betimes, had come upon the damsel with her arms full of roses, her face full of health, and as rosy as her scented burden; a tasty piece to pique a jaded palate. The duke was piqued. The curtsy, with the bouquet, dropped; the handmaid hauled up, and a sucking kiss bestowed on the ripe mouth that gasped a scared, 'Your Serene — oh, *no!*'

'Oh, yes!' was the answer to that timid recoil when, between awe of this signal honour from her Sovereign Lord, and respectful resistance, she, palpitating, overwhelmed, dared no more resist.

The duke, who may have found prolonged familiarity with his lady had bred, if not contempt, an urge for pastures new wherein to graze, made the most of opportunity to lead, or more correctly, drag the feebly protesting Ilse to a couch whereon he placed her, and himself.

It was just at this inopportune moment that the countess, finely arrayed to receive her Lord and Master, and having seen his coach arrive, came upon the pair of them in distinctly compromising attitudes. This much, and the Platen's reaction to the scene, her strident voice striking fear in the heart of the terrified maid with her petticoats up to her knees and of the no less dishevelled Duke, whose unbuttoned breeches were descending to his ankles, caused *raconteurs* side-splitting amusement. The slut had been dismissed and thrown into jail by order of the countess whose word was law; and. there in the 'spinning-house', the place of detention for women of loose morals, she stayed until tardily released with a purse of hush or conscience money from the duke, who had conveniently absented himself on a hunting expedition. But Clara had not done with her yet. Further drastic punishment had been decreed: that the miscreant be drummed out of the city for a whore.

In the few hours granted her before she be forced to undergo this lasting shame and, notwithstanding she was watched by prison warders who may not have kept too careful a guard upon her, since her unhappy plight had roused their sympathy combined with universal hatred of the Platen, Ilse bethought her of one only place of refuge. If she could evade the officers of the law she might take herself to Celle and beg mercy of the mother of the Crown Princess to grant her sanctuary.

Desperation gave her courage. A scribbled note, ill-spelt, tear-blotted, was delivered to Knesebeck by a kindly fellow servant from Monplaisir. The wretched Ilse, hiding on her ragged person the duke's peace offering, was at once brought by Knesebeck to the princess. Before her on her knees Ilse poured forth her tale, much of which was already known. But this latest bedevilment — that she must suffer the shameful drumming out of Hanover, equivalent to the whipping at the cart's tail as served in England to a common bawd — was received with greatest indignation by Sophia Dorothea.

The weeping Ilse was raised up and comforted with the promise of protection.

'No harm shall come to you, poor child. You have been most wrongfully misused.'

In thus asserting her right as second lady in the land to succour those in need of clemency, presented a chance not to be missed to 'settle a score' against the duke's powerful woman from whom she had suffered scarcely veiled insults. 'I will arrange that Her Serene Highness, my mother at Celle, will take you into her employ,' declared the compassionate Princess, exchanging a nod with Knesebeck, as near as made no matter to a wink. 'You will travel there today in one of my carriages.'

Again upon her knees to kiss the feet of her gracious lady. Ilse sobbed her gratitude, was bidden: 'Dry your tears. Take heart. My servants will escort you.'

After a whispered injunction to Knesebeck, the now joyful Ilse was conducted to the domestic quarters, fed, clothed as befitting a maid of the Duchess of Celle, and with another purse of money from Her Serene Highness pressed into her hand by Knesebeck, had been driven away.

And that, presumably, was the end of that.

But it was not.

This interference of the Platen's manifesto by the heir apparent's wife to repeal an act of cruel and unmerited injustice meted without any State authority, even though the alleged culprit were a personal servant of the countess, added fuel to her wrath, and increased the furnace of her hate against Sophia Dorothea. Yet she was too cunning to strike before the iron she heated in her blaze were hot enough to scarify. While the Sovereign of Hanover reigned with her beside him she, the power behind his Duchy, was invulnerable. *Wait,* she told herself, *until the time be ripe, when the darling will be thrown to the lions!*

Her score against the girl on whom she lavished loathing so rich it was akin to love mounted higher to be hastened by an incident indirectly connected with the 'darling'.

Maximilian, who, together with Charles, delightedly applauded Sophia Dorothea 'for having taken,' said Max, 'the wind out of the Platen's sails to throw overboard her ship's cargo of malice to injure a poor little rat of a servant whom our lecherous Father found to be more appetising than his painted old drab. But I,' he chuckled, 'have a score to settle with her, too. I know she's at the bottom of our father's intent to cut us out of his will.'

'I don't believe,' Charles told him, 'that he'll ever do it. He can't make a precedent of us. His Wolfenbüttels would raise hell if he did. And keep off the Platen. You can't get the best of her. She's got the upper hand with the duke in her pocket. You might as well try to score off a man-eater out for your blood.'

'We'll see about that,' said his brother.

He did see about it, and opportunity was offered sooner than expected. Prowling in his mother's library Max chanced upon a volume in English entitled *The Complete Herbal* by Nicholas Culpeper, M.D. He had sufficient knowledge of his grandmother's native tongue to translate a chapter on *Medical*

Aphorisms and Receipts for many diseases to which our frail natures are incident. One heading, in particular, arrested him:

OF THE FACE AND ITS INFIRMITIES

For a face full of pimples dissolve camphire in vinegar mixed with celandine water and wash the face in it. This cured a maid in twenty days that had been troubled with the infirmity for half as many years.

Aha! quoth Max to his inner man, *so what of a woman who is not a maid, with a face full of pimples for not ten, but forty years?* If celandine, whatever that may be in German … He found an English dictionary and read: *Celandine: A sort of yellow flower. Yellow? But wouldn't any other colour do as well? One indigenous to these parts, which this celandine is not.*

He took his findings to Charles and the two of them might have been seen in sniggering confabulation, to-ing and fro-ing from the still-room to the kitchens with the singular request to an astonished under-chef that a bushel of green peas, shredded, be brought to the apartment of Prince Maximilian. Also a stew-pan filled with water and a brazier of charcoal.

About this time preparations for the bi-annual banquet were astir when the reigning family received the officers of State, their wives, neighbouring Princes and lesser mortals, all in full rig; men's chests glittering with orders, women's heads and bodies sparkling with jewels. The solemn process of devouring a dozen courses diminished much attempt at conversation, each course being announced with a blare of trumpets and a procession of servants bearing aloft the laden dishes to be consumed with satisfied belchings from the duke, and equal appetite by Countess von Platen.

She, privileged as wife of the Lord Chancellor to sit with him above the salt and next in rank to the younger princes of the house, had come in all her finery of scarlet velvet laced with gold, her bosom bared to the valley of her breasts the better to display her diamonds that outshone those of the duchess and the Crown Princess.

In direct contrast to this eye-dazzling presence, Sophia Dorothea, gowned in white satin, her dark hair entwined with pearls, and about her lips a smile that came and went, toyed delicately with her food, her eyes glancing, butterfly swift, from Max to Charles and then to linger, for an instant, on the face of her arch-enemy, the Platen.

The meal neared its end. The lackeys placed dishes of fruit before the duke, the duchess and their guests. Max, turning to the Platen, said, 'Madame, may I not tempt you to a peach?' He took one, began to peel it, laid the gold-plated knife aside. 'Too blunt, I fear.' And from his pocket he produced what purported to be a sharper substitute. This he covered with his hand, while the countess replied with effusion, 'Your Serene Highness is too gracious.'

Then it happened.

As she lifted her eyes with a languishing look at the prince, her painted lips widened to a smile that exhibited two rows of exceedingly false teeth, Max raised his hand that held the article he had taken from his pocket and which now appeared to be a child's plaything, a miniature pistol. He took careful aim at the smiling countess and, full in her face, discharged the contents of the toy that were of a greenish colour like a watery pea-soup.

In the company's horrified silence, broken with titters, Max was heard to say, 'Countess, I must crave your pardon for taking the liberty of treating you, without your permission, to a medical and permanent cure of this skin eruption from which your beauty suffers and which I think you would have been unwilling to undergo. It is a prescription devised by that eminent English physician, the late —'

But he got no further. A howl as of a scalded cat interrupted him, terminating in a great guffaw. The lady's tactics advised her to condone this vulgar prank and turn the joke to herself. Now was not the time for retribution. Between her gasps of laughter, while the paint and powder streaked in rivulets down her cheeks, 'Serene Highness', she managed with the utmost good humour to convey, 'you honour me to be concerned for my unfortunate disability, which the court physicians have been unable to alleviate. I am more than grateful that you should have —' Her voice was muffled by the greenish liquid that dripped into her mouth.

The company, taking its cue from her, held its sides while applauding her gallant recovery from inexcusable insult. And all through the last of the banquet she sat dabbing at her face that showed white beneath the smear of paint, and joined in the laughter, digging a playful elbow in the prince's ribs, slyly to tell him, 'Sir, I will have my revenge for this when I take you on at ombre. It will cost you five hundred thalers!'

The duke — who had seen and heard it all, glowering down at his dish full of orange peelings — rose up, pointed a finger at his son and thundered, 'Out! Go — get out! I will deal with you later. Out, I say!'

The laughter ceased. Only a few shaking shoulders denoted that the audience had been amused. A silence fell. Max rose from his seat, bowed to his outraged father, to his mother who unconcernedly ate grapes, her high nose lifted, her nostrils slightly dilated, her lips a thin hard line. Sophia Dorothea, her eyes downcast, a dimple hovering, seized a glass of wine, sipped, choked, and was glared at by her father-in-law. Max had gone, backing from the room to turn and run, nor did he stop till he reached his own apartment, where presently Charles found him, sunk in a chair and downing a beaker of Rhenish.

'So! You're in for it now — you damned fool! What possessed you to do it there, at table? I thought you were going to have at her while she was fleecing you at cards.'

'I know, but I just couldn't resist it with her sitting next to me, nudging her great lump of a knee against mine and leering into my face. Lecherous old bitch!'

'She'll have you hanged for this,' said Charles, 'and I'll not be out of it, neither. I'll wager she's got the duke to sign a warrant for your arrest this minute. And mine, too. She'll guess we were in it together and will be only glad of the excuse to have her own back on us because we don't pander to her.'

He was mistaken.

Clara, heaping coals of fire on the graceless head of Max, persuaded the irate Duke not to take too harsh a view of a mischievous prank. 'The boy is high-spirited, and had drunk just a little too much. You must forgive him. Let it rest. I am too fond of Max and all your sons to see any one of them suffer for a boyish joke. And don't forget,' she added a careful warning, 'neither he, nor the other boys — *and* Charlotte — will be content when they learn of the will, of which I have reason to believe they already have an inkling. If you punish Max, he and Charles will the more bitterly contest your decision. Be lenient, Ernest. If I can forgive and laugh at this nonsense, so can you. After all, I love him as if he were my own, for is he not your son?'

It was a masterly stroke to regain her hold on the duke that, since the Ilse episode, had decidedly weakened. Also, by indulgence to so deliberate an insult, she offered further proof of her loyalty to, and adoration for, him whose wife in all but name she claimed to be, and which would, she judged, more readily bring the recalcitrant Max to heel in gratitude for mitigation of the punishment rightly due.

'You cannot risk,' she told his father, 'that your younger sons — and Max especially, as fourth in succession to Hanover after your grandson — should nurture grievance against you when the will is made public. You, who are in the running for the Electorate —' she played that card well aware of its worth as the wish of his heart — 'must not engender bad blood between your sons and yourself. Be advised.'

She knelt at his feet to take his podgy hand and lay it to her cheek, was lifted up, embraced and wept upon.

'You are too good, too generous, dear heart.' The ever-ready fount of Hanoverian sentimentality welled up. 'I will lock the rascal in his room for a week to bring him to his senses, although he deserves to be in jail,' said Ernest, wiping a dewdrop from the end of his proboscis. 'And I will let him and all the court — all Hanover — know that you have saved him from disgrace.'

Later, in her red-curtained bed when the satiated Duke was about to settle into sleep, 'There is one other,' murmured Clara, 'more deserving of your punishment than Max, her dupe and ally. How right the duchess was and is, to regard her as a menace to the duchies of Hanover and Celle. The sooner you have legally established the primogeniture, the better. You will find —' she tugged at the tassel of his nightcap — 'Ernest, pray attend. Do you hear me? You will find your wife strenuously opposing your decision to make your eldest son heir to all your lands and territories. She loves George Louis the least of your sons, probably because —' she grinned up at the painted ceiling where the aphrodisiacal nudities in the wavering light of bedside candles looked to be more than ever actively employed in their amorous pursuits — 'probably,' she repeated, 'because he most resembles you. Ernest!' Again the tassel was pulled, almost to bereft him of his nightcap and to rouse him from the somnolent aftermath of extra-connubial enjoyment. 'Do listen.'

'Ya-ah,' came the yawned answer. 'I-I-a-ah-am.'

'This,' persevered Clara, 'affects your future as much as that of the Crown Prince. But what you must know is that the chief opponent who will endeavour to contest your decision is — your son's wife.'

She may not have been far wrong. Sophia Dorothea, chafing against the terms of the marriage settlement that had left her dependent on the meagre allowance doled to her by George Louis, was as strongly against the duke's determination to overthrow the policy pursued by his forbears as were the younger Princes.

That Clara sought to implicate her in support of her brothers-in-law to assert and claim their rights, was evident to Sophia Dorothea; and by involving her in the rupture between the father and his sons, to widen the breach already dividing husband and wife. Having failed to restore her sister Catherine to the favour of George Louis, Clara had taken under her wing and introduced to the court the nineteen-year-old Ermengarde Melusine von Schulenberg. She was the direct opposite of Sophia Dorothea, chosen by the Platen with care for his tastes: a heavy-featured blonde Germanic type, and of unusual height. So tall was she that when the duchess first saw her she dubbed her the 'Maypole'.

George Louis — short, tubby, already run to fat — admired tall women, and Ermengarde — tallest of any, a creamy skinned, golden girl, whose empty wide blue eyes gazed adoringly at him — was his ideal of perfect womanhood. She, poor but well-born and, moderately honest, readily responded to the stupendous advantage to be offered by surrender.

She surrendered.

Jewels were showered on her; she was established in a luxurious apartment, acknowledged mistress of the Crown Prince, and successor-in-chief to the Busche. To save her face she had been provided by the Platen with a second husband, one General Weycke, who had been tempted to take to himself the widow Busche with the promise from the Platen of promotion, and that she would hold herself responsible for the wedding celebrations. These, held at the general's house, were followed by a banquet and a ball, on a lavishly extravagant scale, to which all the *élite* of Hanover were invited, including the Crown Prince and Princess. She, refusing to attend in person, sent Knesebeck to represent her. George Louis, however, in compliment to his erstwhile favourite, graced with his presence the festivities of which Knesebeck gave a full report to Sophia Dorothea. This brought a storm about the duchess when confronted by her daughter-in-law, who burst in upon her with, 'Madame! I have borne enough — too much!' In such white heat of rage was Sophia Dorothea that, dispensing with formalities and disregardful of the duchess's upreared head and refrigerating stare, 'this is the end! I leave for Celle today, never to return!' Then, belatedly remembering the formalities demanded, she bobbed, and, scarlet-cheeked, attempted an apology. 'I crave pardon, Serene Highness, for — for my —'

'Sit,' was the command. 'Compose yourself, and, if you can, explain yourself for this unwarrantable intrusion.'

The princess sat, and, endeavouring to compose herself, appeared to be struck dumb. The words boiling on her lips were muffled in a sob. Tears stung her eyes but did not fall.

She pleated the satin folds of her gown between fingers that shook, as did her voice, when she found it, to pierce that arctic silence.

'Serene High — er — ness. I implore your — your help. Your son — he — my husband has insulted me beyond endurance.'

A slight compression of those granite eyes preceded the monosyllable: 'How?'

'How, Madame? At the ball!' blurted Sophia Dorothea, not daring to look up, 'lest,' as she afterwards related to Knesebeck, 'I should be turned into a pillar of salt.'

'At the ball?' came the parrot repetition. 'What ball?'

'The wedding, Serene Highness, of his woman — she's married now — who was —'

'Who was —?'

I shall go mad, her inquisitor was silently informed. 'Yes, Madame, she was — and is — married, which you must have known being invited to it — the wedding — if you went, but you didn't, nor did I. As if I would! My lady-in-waiting, she told me —I sent her instead of me, not wishing to attend, and she told me that my husband — he led her out — not Knesebeck — his woman — he led her out to the dance as he always does before me, before anyone, and stayed beside her the whole evening.'

'Led out whom?'

'The Schulenberg, Madame — the Maypole, as you called her — and rightly, for she's as high as a church door and as wide as Shakespeare says — or something near to it — I cannot remember the exact words and — Madame, I cannot bear it — I cannot and *will* not be so publicly humiliated. I have not your phil-phil-philosophy,' sobbed Sophia Dorothea. 'If you can bear to see your uncle — I mean *my* uncle — taken in adultery with that evil mischief-maker, you know who — and I can't, and *won't!* was the finale to this incoherent speech.

'By which lucid exposition,' the fastened mouth unclosed to say, 'I understand that you attempt to criticise His Serene Highness, your uncle, and me. Or, if you object to your husband's attention to his — concubine, you can have no concept of your position as a royal wife. The peccadilloes of Princes are permissible, as from the days of Solomon. Your marriage to your cousin of Hanover, as I believe your father did forewarn you — or, if he did not, he should have done so — was a marriage of convenience, as almost every royal marriage is. Had you shown the Crown Prince the duty and affection due to him, your husband, he would not have sought elsewhere for the connubial rights you systematically deny him.'

'I — deny him?' cried Sophia Dorothea, who during this frosted homily had gained confidence to defy. 'So *that's* what he tells you as excuse for his neglect and ill-treatment of me to whom he never speaks unless to pick a quarrel. I have given him two children — one a son and heir. Ah, I see!' She drew a deep breath. 'You are in league with him against me as you have always been. I can expect no sympathy nor support from you, Madame. Ever since and before I was born you disliked and resented me as you resented my mother. And —' her temper was rising to overflow in a torrent — 'were I to take a lover you'd be the first to condemn me, while you condone your son and your husband for their —' Her voice dwindled.

That rigid figure rose up and, a finger, fleshless as a bone, pointed to the door. 'Go! Leave me before you commit yourself further.'

But having been thus far committed, there was no stopping her. The sluice gates were flung open to release the flood tides of long-held-in suppression. 'I demand,' shrieked the merciless young voice, 'that this — this Maypole, this Schulenberg, be dismissed from my presence and your court. You, who have made her a lady-in-waiting, offer a deliberate insult to me! Yet you dismissed her predecessor who had the effrontery to invite me and yourself to her wedding — or rather the Platen did. And do you forget how she and your son's woman, the Busche, stood at the window of the palace on my arrival in Hanover as Crown Princess, to shame and mock me, your son's wife? Have you no sense of loyalty or pity for me, the victim of a marriage that has been a living hell? If, at any time I chance to free myself from what you call this marriage of convenience, and live my own life away from all of you — then you've only yourself to blame!'

And having uttered the unutterable, she was out of the room like a rocket.

Long after this apocalyptic exit, the duchess, having blindly groped for the back of the chair she had vacated, sank into it, pale. The girl was demented. One must forgive, forbear with incipient insanity inherited from her French forefathers, too closely inbred.

Thus, for the sake of her *amour propre,* did she meet this unmitigated challenge. Youth in its purblind egocentricity had dealt a blow to age, but not its death blow. Never! Yet even while she gathered the remnants of her shattered pride about her, she reluctantly applauded. The girl, whether sane or insane, had spirit. That much she must allow. So, in righteous wrath, might she herself have defied injury and insult. Somewhere, far behind in the distant past of generations, the blood of this upstart Frenchwoman had stormed the royal citadel of Sophia, Duchess of Hanover. It was known that the d'Olbreuse claimed Norman descent from the barons of Conqueror William who slew the Saxon King and established his monarchy on the shores of the Britain which some day, some time, might enthrone Sophia of Hanover or her descendants. 'But, by God!' she spoke aloud, unaware that she voiced her surging thoughts, 'if I do not live to wear the Crown, my son … yes, and this wife of his may prove herself a consort worthy of my choice. As for her return to Celle…'

Sophia drummed her fingers on the arm of her chair. The girl must be locked up. A pretty yarn to spin for the Frenchwoman to unravel. And George William, poor fool, was more ready now to bow the knee to Ernest who held him and his coffers tightly bound, than to heed the ravings of a…

No! She must not return to Celle.

But return to Celle she did, and within the hour of that unprecedented scene, accompanied by none save Knesebeck. Bidding all haste to her coachman, she came to her father's castle in the same tornado of temper with which the duchess, her mother-in-law, had been besieged. To her mother she gave a garnished account of grievances galore, to be soothed and with sympathy regaled. Not so her father. He would give no quarter, lend no ear to her complaints. Bernstorff, primed by the Platen, had plied the duke with running commentaries of his daughter's indocility and high-handed misbehaviour prior to her precipitate appearance. This, when her truancy had been discovered, resulted in an emissary from Hanover sent to fetch and bring her back.

So much for her attempt at self-assertion. Subdued, defeated, she must be resigned to lifelong servitude, submissively to take whatever impost an unkindly fate might offer, with no release in bondage from 'this living hell'.

Yet, if she could have known it, release was on its way, riding with a retinue of servants, a wagon-load of luggage, cages full of songbirds, a boarhound at his stirrup and a foot-page at his horse's heels.

PART TWO (1689-1692)

FOUR

He had come to see and conquer and take Hanover by storm, not only for the beauty of his person but for his extravagant display of wealth, his retinue of twenty-nine servants, fifty horses, coaches, mules, and the magnificence of his entertainments at the house where he installed himself not far from the ducal palace.

His descent upon the court coincided with a critical time for the Duchy. The Emperor Leopold and Louis XIV were at each other's throats. On the recent death of the Elector Palatine, brother of the Duchess Sophia, Louis had invaded the Palatinate, wrecked houses, churches, and reduced the Elector's castle at Heidelberg to ruins. The wanton destruction and barbarous cruelties committed by the French on terrified villagers and townsfolk had roused universal indignation throughout Europe. The Sun King's only allies were the Sultan of Turkey and the exiled King James of England whose throne had been wrenched from him by his nephew, William of Orange.

Thus it would seem that the relatively insignificant state of Hanover could be of little importance to the chief protagonists. The Emperor Leopold, however, thought otherwise. Hanover and his brother of Celle had joined him in many of his campaigns. Their troops, hardy and well-trained, had fought courageously alongside his own; but his overtures to Hanover were not immediately accepted. Ernest Augustus dilly-dallied, disinclined to give more of his men and money in support of the emperor against the tyrant Louis. While he hesitated he was lost, urged by the Platen always ready to seize upon advantage to be gained for him and thereby for herself.

'You can make your own terms of alliance,' she told him. 'Celle will follow your lead. He always does. He is only a pawn in your game; You can checkmate Louis if you bring up your military knights to assist the emperor and win you the Electorate!'

To this suggestion the Duchess Sophia was bound to agree, notwithstanding that she guessed the source of it. One of the reasons she had tolerated the Platen's influence with, and monopoly of, the duke was that she realised the woman's canny diplomatic intuition. And so it came about that the duchies of Hanover and Celle were pledged in support of the emperor's war against France and the Turks in Morea.

It was high summer in Hanover, and despite that a state of emergency existed with troops parading the streets to the sound of drum and fife, the court had never been more gay. Balls, masquerades, carnivals and comedies prevailed. At all of these the handsome stranger from the North was the central figure. Women vied for his attention, fulsomely bestowed on each in turn; yet he had been some few weeks in Hanover before Sophia Dorothea had her first sight of him.

Since her row with the duchess and her attempt to escape from her insupportable marriage followed by the dismissal from the haven she had sought at Celle, she held herself aloof from the court and its festivities on plea of a 'malaise' for which the court physician, finding no evidence other than her word for it, prescribed various remedies and advised her to keep to her bed. She did, when he was due to visit her, and disposed of his physics down the privy. But her self-imposed indisposition soon palled, and when her parents were invited to attend a court ball in their honour, a tactical gesture in acknowledgement of the Duke of Celle's agreement to support his brother of Hanover against France, she felt bound to be present to receive them.

The Duke of Hanover opened the ball with the Duchess of Celle and then with her daughter, the Crown Princess, after which she sat sulkily apart and watched the dancers from her dais where her parents and the duke-bishop and his duchess sat in state. She saw her husband lead out the Schulenberg, splendidly attired, bedecked with jewels, her yellow hair worn high in a fontage, a fashion culled from England. The dusty haze of candles shed their light on the bright gowns of women and the multi-coloured suits of men, revolving in a glittering mosaic as the dancers bowed, retreated, and advanced to the strains of lute and viol and the aching solo of a violin.

The Crown Prince, lobster-red of face, puffing, perspiring, gazed rapturously up at his 'Maypole', while he chasséed before her and pirouetted on one toe to the admiration of his sycophants; for so fat a little man he was not ungraceful. But his wife, who watched him with a nostril curled, whispered to Knesebeck behind her chair, 'He looks like a spinning top!'

Yet it irked her to see the signal honour bestowed upon his woman, disregardful of the obligations due to herself whom he ignored for all to witness, and, for the most part, to approve. The future Duke could do no wrong, even though he wronged his wife.

Suddenly, while watching him and hating him and every moment of this garish medley of over-heated sweating bodies, the stink of them thinly disguised by sickly perfume, she stiffened. As the music wailed to its end and the couples parted she saw the bediamonded Platen, elaborately gowned in her favourite scarlet, approach one who it seemed had just arrived. He wore a suit of pink velvet, laced with silver, and, unlike the majority of those who favoured the periwig, his light brown hair hung in natural curls about his shoulders.

The Platen's curtsy was a thing to wonder at. She rose from it at his answering bow to lay a hand upon his sleeve. Her smile looked to split her face in two, exposing a row of dazzling white porcelain teeth. She led him to an alcove screened from the assembly by a coffin-shaped box filled with palms and flowering shrubs.

Something familiar in the poise of his head and the clear-cut profile had struck a chord to bring retarded recognition. *Is it … could it be?* How long, seven years since that morning when two children, wonder-charged, had found each other, then to part, and now … to meet again?

The ball was over, the guests had gone; the visiting duke and duchess in their state apartments slept. The Crown Prince having, for appearance's sake, escorted his wife to their Alte Palais, left her there and he, too, slept beside his Schulenberg. But Sophia Dorothea, lying sleep-forsaken, watched behind quivering closed eyelids, that brilliant display in which one figure vividly predominated … Who?

She saw herself panoplied in solitude, a thing apart, while courtiers bowed and billowed to the ground before her as they passed. She saw the woman who held the duke and his Duchy in her palm apprise him greedily to possess and lead him … where? Imagination was engaged to think him nothing loth to take advantage of enticement. Half Europe and all Hanover knew the power she wielded. Was it witchery, bedevilment or the craft of the experienced courtesan that had enslaved the elderly Duke, and could enslave more virile and younger men than he?

There was a moment when she saw him pause, half-turned, his eyes voyaging among that crowd of faces as if he sought one whom he recognised, or listened for a name unspoken or a word unsaid. Then that fleeting sight of him, a chance resemblance born of a child's dormant memory, was lost.

She slept at last, and strangely dreamed that she and another — faceless, formless — walked beside some water wherein a boat, shaped like a scimitar, floated among gigantic flowers, water lilies, maybe, that grew taller than a man. But as she stepped into the boat and he, beside her, made as if to follow, she saw that from his mouth gushed a stream of blood in a red vomit, and with a voiceless scream she woke to find the curtains of her window drawn letting in a flood of light, and her woman at the bedside with her breakfast tray.

'Serene Highness's chocolate,' was softly said.

'Not chocolate, no! I ate too much of sauerkraut and sausages to make me ride the night mare,' said Sophia Dorothea.

In her red-curtained bed, the Countess von Platen lifted herself on an elbow gloatingly to gaze upon the head of tousled hair and the half-hidden face of him, turned sideways on the pillow and sleeping still. She leaned over him, murmuring his name. He did not stir. His breathing, deep and regular, betokened satiation. A smile of tenderness — or as much as smeared paint would allow— came to her lips as she pulled a curl of that light brown hair and whispered, 'Dearest, you must leave me before my women come to find you here.'

He moved, flung out an arm and woke. His eyes, hazel-grey, their lashes childishly long, opened with a look of puzzlement, and passing a hand across his forehead: 'What in hell —' he muttered, 'and where — and who —?'

He spoke in a language she could not understand, and she laid her cheek to his to say again: 'My darling, you must go.'

Recollection of the night's activities came dizzily about him, accompanied by a sour taste on his tongue and a disgustful awareness of her mouth devouring his as she leaned over him. Her hands explored his body under the silken covers thrown back for coolness in that hot close-curtained room.

How had it happened? His head ached damnably. He must have been well raddled. Yes, it was coming back to him now. She had invited, or persuaded, or filled him with drink enough at the laden buffet in the palace to drive with him to this house of hers. Monplaisir. He had passed it on his rides and knew it for her house, as he had known of her. Who had not? There were a dozen or more, men and boys, at the tables. No women. He had lost — how much? A thousand thalers? Her price, in exchange for what she'd had from him and others. He had heard that nothing short of a stallion could satisfy her!

She mistook his shiver of revolt for desire in response to her voyaging touch. 'Not now, dear heart,' she murmured. 'Are you so greedy? Tonight then, again. Yes … yes, you shall have me, for I want you as much as you want me.'

'Want … you?' he muttered, and had sense enough to stay the retort, *As much as I'd want a bladder of lard!* And, sliding his legs over the side of the bed to avoid any more of her, he sought for the discarded clothes that lay in a heap on the floor. Dragging on his shirt he dressed hurriedly, for she was leaving the bed to come at him, the two white globes of her heavy breasts insinuatingly offered.

'Just this once more,' she pleaded. 'I'll lock the door against my women. I can't wait until tonight.'

And how he got away from her he did not know.

Some few days after the ball Charles came to Sophia Dorothea with the announcement, 'There is someone here who begs audience with you.'

'Who?' She turned from the window where she had been watching her children at play in the garden. Their nurse had brought them in, for the sky had clouded and rain was falling. The shrill treble of their voices diminished, elfin-like, in distance as they went.

'Can you not guess?' said Charles with a broadening grin. 'It is a ghost, if a somewhat solid one.'

Her heart was in a hurry, but she answered him cool: 'I am not good at riddles.'

'Then let him solve it for you.'

Charles darted to the door and beckoned one who stood without. He advanced, bowing, and straightened while his eyes overswept her; and as she gazed up at him, lips parted, time slid away across the space of years to find him not much changed from the boy whose image had haunted her in fleeting glimpses behind the shutters of forgetfulness.

'Philip!' His name escaped her on a breath, followed by the words, 'What a delightful surprise! Welcome to Hanover.'

Bending over her outstretched hand, he laid his lips to it in an instant's formal greeting. 'Your Serene Highness does me too much honour.'

Charles, hovering in the background, broke in with, 'I thought you would wish to see him privately rather than at a presentation. I ran into him this morning in the street. Our father has just appointed him Colonel of the Guards. So we'll be together in the same regiment, but I'm only a captain and he's my superior officer. Sir,' he saluted with a click of his heels, and then they were all laughing together, she flushed, excited, a child again and 'not a day older'. He spoke his thought aloud, adding with a courtier's grace: 'And more than ever beautiful, Madame.'

She waved aside the compliment and gestured him to sit while Charles, the irrepressible, chattered on. 'He has been here for three, four weeks and everyone is clamouring to meet him, except you.'

'I had not heard he was in Hanover,' she said, a trifle pink. 'I have been ill.'

'In the sulks, you mean, ever since that row with our mother when you rushed off to Celle and were sent back here whether you like us or not.'

'Charles!' She turned on him indignantly, red underlip caught in. Philip's mouth twitched. His eyes held a twinkle.

'And,' Charles continued undeterred, 'you were never seen in public till the ball. Didn't you see Philip there?'

'I — no. There was such a crowd. But,' hastily, 'about this appointment. Tell me,' to Philip, 'when did the duke appoint you?'

'Yesterday.' He, too, had flushed, for he guessed the duke's woman had obtained the appointment for which he had not asked nor had expected to gain him a permanency at the court. She had obviously worked to keep him in Hanover for her — convenience. To hell with that! Not again if he could help it, drunk or sober. But *could* he help it? Her influence was paramount. His refusal of a colonelcy would entail ill feeling between Sweden and the Duchy. France was angling for a Swedish alliance as also was Hanover. Besides, his sister had written to tell him she was on her way to visit him and so, 'Here I am, and here I shall stay,' he said.

'You won't stay for long,' Charles told him. 'We'll be off to the Morea within a month or two, and the sooner the better for me!'

Much could happen in a month or two. What did happen was Aurora Königsmarck.

Her descent upon Hanover caused as great a sensation as that of her brother. Her exquisite Nordic beauty, the rumours of her various intrigues at the courts of Sweden, Dresden, Saxony and France, brought young and old gallants, hopeful of her favour and her fortune, to her feet. But marriage was not for Aurora. A life of adventure coupled with the Königsmarck wealth, of which she had inherited a goodly portion, had more allure for her than wifehood. Men adored her, women loathed her, the Platen feared her for she saw that the advent of this latest Königsmarck might halt her pursuit of him she determined to capture. For the first time in her life Clara was in love. Furthermore, the Crown Princess had received this young Swedish *arriviste,* sister of Philip, with every mark of friendship. It needed not the Platen's spies to report that the two were inseparable. They were seen everywhere together, driving through the streets of Hanover or riding out with Philip in the woods beyond the capital. And in the privacy of the apartments of the Crown Princess confidences were exchanged, or perhaps extracted.

Aurora was well aware of her brother's visits to the Platen, of her efforts to entice him, and of his response to her beguilements retailed, in due course, to Sophia Dorothea. 'But,' Aurora added quickly, 'he has his reasons for — obliging the duke's woman, for your sake.'

'Mine?' She, who had paled on hearing this, now reddened. 'Why for *my* sake? What is Philip to me, or I — to him?'

'You should know. Since he was a boy and you were still a child he has held you in his heart. And — no, wait,' as the princess, alternately pale and pink, made to interrupt, 'that woman is sheer poison, to contaminate the very air you breathe. Her jealousy of you is near to madness. So Philip throws dust in her eyes to blind her that she cannot see he is entirely — yours.'

And she, a little lost of breath, enquired, 'Are you sent to me as his — his ambassador? Why cannot he speak for himself?'

'Would you listen if he did?' And receiving no reply to that, the talk returned to Aurora, a subject of which she never tired.

'I,' she said, 'am entirely possessive, as is Philip and all the Königsmarcks. What we want, we take. You may have heard of my brother Carl John, how in order to marry a widowed heiress aged twelve, he hired a couple of assassins to murder her second husband, and only escaped the gallows because Philip at the trial saved him with a pack of lies, or half-truths, shall we say?'

'On the assumption,' was suggested, 'that *del veto s'adira l'uomo*?'

'Yes, the truth may shatter the Italians, but not the Swedes, who are well versed in *le mot juste*. But let us get back to the point. Carl travelled through France with a pretty little page, and none knew him for a girl till he was brought to bed on the kitchen table of an inn where they lay the night. Carl, always in search of adventure, went careering off disguised as a journeyman dodging the police, for he left a stink behind our name in England. What happened to the baby and its mother, who can tell? Carl probably gave her a handsome pension. He was always generous to folly, as are we all. I've spent thousands on my quixotic adventures. I once had a burning passion for my father's huntsman. He was forty, I, fourteen. To keep him quiet he demanded —I forget how much — I believe I was forced to rifle my father's privy purse. We are thoroughly unscrupulous when we are in love.'

Sophia Dorothea stiffened her spine against the chair back. 'That,' she said coolly, 'I can well believe. Tell me more of your quixotic adventures.'

'They would fill volumes,' Aurora complacently replied, and which was no exaggeration, for almost two centuries later they did. 'As for Carl, he went off to the wars and died — not, as he would have wished, on the battlefield, but in his bed, of a pleurisy. Poor beautiful Carl!' Her eyes were suspiciously bright. 'I adored him. He was as handsome if not handsomer than Philip. My family is renowned for our beauty and our wickedness. Philip has been called the greatest scamp in Christendom. And my sister, who is even lovelier than I — she is married to Count Lewenhaupt — is just as daring and as wicked as the rest of us. We both ought to have been boys. My mother wanted only boys and had two of each — which, I suppose, is why I am equally attracted to women as to men. I have had lovers of all sexes, the determinate, the indeterminate, the epicene, the Sapphic. Do I shock you?'

'I have lived in Hanover these seven years since I married at sixteen, so nothing,' came the answer, with a small one-sided smile, 'ever shocks me.'

'Married at sixteen!' exclaimed Aurora. 'Me — I will never marry. I could have been the mistress of three crowned heads *before* I was sixteen, including Louis of France. But I was not enamoured of Louis. Nor would I wish to be one of a harem. Besides, if there is any seducing to be done, I'm the seducer, not the seduced.'

She threw back her head, laughing widely. She had a large mobile mouth and eyes of a startling blue under heavy almost masculine dark brows at variance with the honey-gold of her hair, fine as spun silk, and the delicate bone structure of her face. Glancing at the door: 'I think,' she said, 'there is someone at the keyhole.'

'There is always someone at the keyhole,' said Sophia Dorothea with that same small crooked smile.

'Then,' said Aurora, 'let someone who may listen carry this to Madame Platen — that Philip calls her a bandy-legged cow!'

But he or she who may have listened could not carry that, if overheard, to Madame Platen, for it was spoken in English. Yet enough had been brought to Clara and her 'investigators', as she chose to name her spies to Bernstorff, whose constant communications with Monplaisir bringing reports from Celle's council chamber, still considerably increased his yearly income. And the duke, induced by Clara, was more firmly persuaded to consider the proposed primogeniture consigning his lands and territories to George Louis, and allotting only a moderate, barely adequate, sum to his younger sons. This, Clara's revenge on Max for his sky-larking behaviour in having squirted the contents of a pea-shooter in her face amid the Homeric laughter it occasioned. He, who dared to make a fool of Clara would pay the fullest penalty in which Charles, his aider and abettor, must likewise share. That the two younger sons must also be deprived of their inheritance mattered not one whit to Clara. All four, as well she knew, detested her and would stop at nothing, short of murder, to see her fall from their father's grace.

Having disposed of the younger Princes to her satisfaction, she decided that the presence of Aurora Königsmarck in close propinquity to Philip and the princess, boded nothing to the Platen's good. Therefore the removal of Aurora was much to be desired; but Clara had no need to have manoeuvred it. Aurora had no intention of prolonging her visit, and although

Sophia Dorothea entreated her to delay her departure, she departed, having had her fill, she said, of Hanover.

Before she left and after she had paid formal farewells to the duke and duchess she was received in private by the Crown Princess. 'I cannot bear to have you leave us,' she told her. 'Why must you go so soon?'

'I can never stay long in one place. I am a bird of passage as are all we Königsmarcks, always seeking and —' Aurora looked away into a distance — 'never finding.'

'What,' was asked, 'do you seek?'

'Who knows? I am like a traveller voyaging on uncharted seas searching for a shoreless land. Who said — or do I say it? — that he who travels best knows when to return.'

Aurora's eyes dwelt on the girl, whose small slender fingers folded in her lap tightened as she said in almost a whisper: 'Do you and does he — does Philip — know when to return? Or do you — will he — for ever seek a shoreless land?'

'That depends on you.' Aurora rose and, kneeling, said, 'He will return from whatever far horizon he may seek when, or if, you call him. Princess, forgive me if I presume upon your friendship, but do not refuse what the gods offer you.'

'I do not trust the gods,' came the low-voiced answer. 'There is an old saying — I think it was from the Latin of Plautus, as my mother used to teach me — that the gods make sport of us.'

Aurora laughed lightly. 'If the gods make sport of me, I too can make sport of them!'

Meanwhile, and after Aurora had gone — journeying through France, Italy, Saxony, followed by a train of willing victims — events were moving rapidly in Hanover that were to affect the fate of these two star-crossed lovers of a love still unconfessed.

The intimacy between Königsmarck and Countess von Platen had given rise to the liveliest rumours, soon to be brought to Sophia Dorothea who might have chosen to ignore them had not Charles with every good, if blundering intent, put Philip on his guard.

'Keep away from Monplaisir or she'll suck you dry, and now that Sophie has wind of your affair —'

'I have no affair with Madame Platen,' interrupted Philip, cold.

'Whether or not in the fullest sense of flagrant delight,' grinned Charles, 'her name is coupled with yours.'

Philip's hand leaped to his sword-hilt. 'To make stink from the sewers for you to savour,' was the retort, steel-edged.

'Take it how you will,' Charles told him sulkily. 'You'd best be warned. Sophie is up and flaming that one whom she believes to be her friend should couple with, or, if you like it better, attend on her bitterest enemy.'

A muscle moved in Philip's whitened jaw. 'I am honoured that I should be favoured by the friendship of Her Serene Highness.'

'Don't be an ass! You don't have to mount your high horse with me. Go tell her what she wants to hear before we are sent off to the Morea, and who knows if we'll ever come back?'

Was it a trick-light flash of premonition, swiftly fading as a breath on glass, or the youthful bravura of one to whom the danger of war is the greatest of adventures? However that may be, Philip, struck with remorse for his too-ready response to the Platen's demands, saw the peril that would surely encompass Sophia Dorothea from his involvement with the countess. But how to be rid of his adhesion? He had found her predecessors easy enough to shake off. Not so the limpet-like Platen. Also, should the duke-bishop get wind of the association, which now was common talk, he would be dismissed from Hanover as years ago he had been dismissed from Celle. History repeated, and the last thing he desired was to leave Hanover — and one other.

He who had known the dark witchery of passion and all of passion's emptiness, searched himself to find himself hand-fasted, sealed and given, although still undeclared. He saw no way out of the impasse with which he now was faced, except by tactful withdrawal; throw in his resignation, fake a feasible excuse. Sweden demanded his return in command of the mobilisation of his King's armies. He must go. He could not go, while all his blood cried out to take from her that which no woman had denied him yet. Would she deny him? But opportunity dispensed with an excuse to go from Hanover. The treaty between the Emperor Leopold and Ernest Augustus had already been partly fulfilled by the sending of Hanoverian troops to Flanders and George Louis to the Rhine; and when Prince Charles, to his delight, was ordered to the Morea, Königsmarck begged leave of the duke to accompany the prince. The duchess hailed Philip's offer with relief.

'It is a comfort to me that you will be near to guard and watch over the prince,' she said of her favourite and much-loved son; and with a break in the harsh old voice, 'He is so young and reckless. He resembles my brother Rupert in that respect, when he was my boy's age.'

'Your Serene Highness may rest assured that I will guard the prince with my life.' He bowed over the skinny hand, ringed to the knuckles, and felt something warm and wet drop on his forehead.

Said the duchess, invoking the Deity whose existence she inclined to doubt, 'May God bless and protect you both, Count Königsmarck.'

His leave-taking of the Platen induced a scene that, even though resigned to her demanding requirements, astonished and disgusted him. A note delivered by a servant informed him she would not be in attendance on the duke that night.

When ushered to her presence he found she had taken to her bed, pleading sickness. The room stank of musk and amber. As the door closed on the woman who had admitted him, she called from behind the red curtains of her couch: 'It is a whole week, a lifetime, since you came to me. His snout-nosed Serenity is in high fettle! May the devil disparage his parts, that of late seem to have taken on a youthified new lease. He tells me he eats two dozen oysters a day, guaranteed to strengthen him where most he needs it!' She chuckled throatily and drew aside the curtains to reveal herself in the scantiest of shifts. Her arms opened to him. 'Come, dear love, I have waited too long.'

He stayed where he stood, saying formally, 'Madame, I am here in answer to your message. I have to tell you that I leave Hanover within the next few days for military service in the Morea.'

She stared aghast. 'No! You? You go to the Morea? Not possible. I will not have it. You are Colonel of the Duke's Guards. It was I who obtained your commission, which does not entail active service.'

She rose up; her bared legs were like white gigantic slugs, he shudderingly thought. Her arms entwined him. He averted his eyes from hers that clung to his with a fawning look, as that of a spaniel begging for titbits. Determinedly he disengaged. 'My duty, Madame, is at the fighting front.'

Anger and dismay showed in her face, crossed with desire. 'I know why you go — because you have had all you want of me, but I —' she broke off. An ooze of red, not paint, beaded her underlip crushed beneath a tooth. 'You can't do this to me,' she whimpered. 'You can't. No other man has had more of me than this — and this —' crudely she touched herself, 'but you have had my all. All I am now and — hereafter, if there is a hereafter which, were it hell for me, I'll share it.' Again that hoarse chuckle that was half a sob. 'I'll share my grid to burn with you, and that will be my heaven!'

She was grotesque, obscene, yet despite her coarse dramatics there was something pitiful in her unrestrained abasement. But in a moment it passed, and with an ugly animal snarl she came at him savagely to strike with knuckled fists. 'I know why you leave me. It is your whey-faced ninny who holds you. Yes, it feeds your vanity to take and break the Crown Princess as you have taken but not broken me. No, by God! It is *you* who will break! Go to her, then, *feed* on her as a guzzling boy stuffs himself with a box of sticky sweets. Go, then. Go!' She punctuated her words with vicious blows upon his rigid chest. 'Go! Enjoy your melting fondant to be sucked down and then spewed up — forgotten. But you can't forget *me*! Spew me and you'll soon return as a dog to its vomit. Aha! You'll return, if you live out there in Morea, unless you die of the fever — they all die like flies of the fever, if not from the blade of a Turk. Go — and be damned — both of you — she —'

'Enough!' He caught her thumping hands in a vice that brought from her a yelp of pain. 'Say no more, and keep your adder's tongue from one who is as far above you as a lily on a dung heap!'

Dropping her hands, and without another word or backward look, he left her standing there half-naked, nor did he see her fling herself upon the bed, pummelling the pillows, her body writhing in an agony of rage and frustration; nor did he hear her cries.

There was yet one more of whom he must take his leave, and her he had left to the last. Knesebeck admitted him to the presence of the Crown Princess.

Said the confidante, in the flutters: 'Her Serene Highness is expecting you, Count Königsmarck. Prince Charles has told you — told her — that you go with him to the Morea.'

She led him past the prick-eared women gathered at the entrance to the private apartments, and brought him to the room of the princess: a charming room furnished with an elegant simplicity more common to an English country house than to the heavy baroque and cumbersome tastelessness of Germany. Here and there *objets de vertu* from France betokened her mother's gifts; an ormolu clock that struck the hours with silvery chimes; gilt-legged high-backed chairs, their seats delicately embroidered; a chaise longue that might have had its replica at Versailles; a writing table inlaid with ivory and gold. From this, as Philip entered and Knesebeck went out closing the door conspiratorially behind her, the princess rose to tell him on a breathless rush of words, 'Charles has said — is it true? You can't have to go to the Morea. You aren't — are you — leaving us?'

He bowed, a courtier's bow, and stood erect, his voice coming coldly because his blood was hot for her whose hand made a little impulsive movement towards him. 'Madame, it is true.'

'Must you be so — formal? And must you really go?' Her voice had a break in it — to break him.

'I would give my soul to stay. You know what I would say and — dare not say.' He spoke in French, and in French was answered, on a whisper.

'Say it. I have longed to hear you say it.'

He knelt. Her hand strayed to his bent head and lingered among the blond-brown curls.

'Philip, I would give *my* soul to go … with you. Forget who I am. Remember only who I … was.'

'Could I ever forget?'

He raised himself and took her. She let herself be taken. He felt the trembling of her body and sought to find her yielding mouth.

'Love, my love. Is this, then, love between us? Is it?' wonderingly he murmured, savouring her lips.

'As it is and always has been, since I was twelve. You said you would come back. I've waited.'

'I too, have waited.' His mouth left hers. Taking her hands, feeling the soft flesh tighten to his touch, 'I have to tell you,' was the half-comical, half-penitent, almost schoolboyish admission, 'I have had a hundred women, but I have never loved, for I was given — always and utterly to you. You know that?'

'I have prayed to know it. All this time through all these waiting cruel unhappy years.' And on a strangled little cry: 'Philip! What are we to *do*? The war … suppose you…'

He stayed the words upon her lips with his. 'When I come back we'll know what to do. And I will be back again. Believe me. That's a promise.'

She leaned her head against his heart. 'How fast it beats. Is this hurry all for me?'

'All for you — and all of me. It tells you so.'

A whispered laugh escaped her. 'A hundred women! Not a man in a thousand would have dared confess it, were it true! I don't doubt it to be true, knowing what I've heard of the Königsmarcks. And the Platen — is she one of the hundred, or the hundred and one? And did this,' she touched his heart with a fingertip, and, drawn away from him, her bantering tone a trifle forced, 'go racing, jumping hurdles in this fashion for those others and — for her?'

'She is no more to me,' he answered, flushed, 'I swear it, than the sausages and sauerkraut and other loathly dishes with which I am fed at the table of the duke.'

'And at her table? Does she offer you a more palatable feast?'

'It served my purpose to accept her — offerings that were even more distasteful than those of the ducal board because she is all-powerful. And at all costs, you must believe me, I had to satisfy' — He halted, flushed still deeper at her smile, faintly mocking, as she prompted him.

'Her appetite? l am told 'tis lusty.'

He might have wished her less disinterested in his confession, with a show of jealous temper; he knew she had a temper. He recalled how, as a spoilt child, she went uncorrected in stormy scenes at Celle that passed as April showers of hail, rain and shine. Although she had acquired dignity and poise as complementary to her rank, he did not credit her with the tolerant sophistication of her mother-in-law, the duchess, when only a moment before she was melting in his arms. He had thought to have plumbed the depths of women's whimsies. He may have been dismayed to see her now capricious; he could have better dealt with tears than with sarcasm.

He made his voice firm to tell her, stating facts, cool as, seemingly, was she.

'What I had to do with the duke's woman was politic that I might remain in Hanover in an official capacity, and not as visitor, a mere bird of passage, or —'

Again came interruption, ironically gentle: 'As your sister claims you all are. Do I take it you had come here to roost at Monplaisir, and now are on the wing again?'

Very still he stood, his chin upraised, a hand upon his sword-hilt. 'Madame, I perceive that I have dared presume upon the friendship of two children. I stand rebuked for such presumption and humbly crave your royal pardon.' And like a marionette, bent double, he bowed, backed, and was out at the door before she could regain breath to recall him.

Then, to the watchful Knesebeck, palpitating at the keyhole: 'Don't let him go! He mustn't go like this — Lennie — Lennie! Run after him — he's furious — he has no sense of humour. Couldn't he see that I was only teasing? You heard? Of course you heard. You have the impress of the keyhole on your cheek. I don't care what you heard. Go after him! Go *on!*'

Knesebeck went on. Along the corridor, past the waiting women, all ears and eyes; down the wide staircase, past a group of staring pages, out into the courtyard in time to see Philip leap into the saddle and, followed by his groom, gallop hell for leather and ... away.

'Never, never, never, will I see or speak to him again!' sobbed Sophia Dorothea on the shoulder of the confidante. 'If he can't take a jest in the humour it was made —'

'But Highness, darling, it was no jest for him to confess so honestly and bravely of his — peccadilloes.'

'Honestly! Bravely! Yes, as near to bragging as could be of his hundred women! He always was a braggart. As a boy when —' Tears fell and were dried, soothingly, on Knesebeck's handkerchief. 'I hate him. He and the Platen — to *tell* me of it! "Politic"! She bleeds him white at her card tables. Everybody knows. *You* know. You told me so. You hear all that I do not.

You were born eavesdropping, as is everyone in this cursed city. Oh, I know you don't belong here. Neither do I ... Love. What does *he* know of love? As much as a tom-cat!'

So I've lost him, she moaned to her pillow that same night. *I had heaven in my hand and threw it out. And my heart out. And his heart out .... beating for me. Uh-uh! Stuff! Hearts always beat when people kiss, I suppose. No one has ever kissed me ... like that. His tongue ... does he kiss the Platen like that? Probably. I shall be sick ... But he can't want her money. They say he's the richest man in Sweden. I'd die to have him kiss me ... that way again and ... everywhere. Well, let him go back to Sweden and spend his — her money there. Not here. On the Platen's card tables or in her bed. Or in our brothels with his hundred women. Oh, God, make me hate him, for I love him. Damn and damn and damn him! And damn to hell the Platen and him too!*

Were ever lovers in such fashion wooed, nor never in such fashion to be won?

Summer passed; autumn came with boisterous gales, to tear from the swaying tree branches in palace gardens the last of their leaves that lay in heaps of dying bronze and gold on paths and lawns. The smell of woodsmoke, true herald of winter, was wafted through the Platen's windows; and while the duke's subjects groaned under the weight of heavy war taxation imposed upon them by military burdens, the Lady of Monplaisir entertained with ever more lavish extravagance the hard-up, drained-dry young ineligibles who gravitated to her gaming salons in the hope of winning back, if not their losses, some reward for their response to her demands. Any personable youth could give her temporary respite from the gnawing memory of her frustration.

Königsmarck! Even though she feasted, revelled, held banquets, attended the opera and filled her box with parasites, threw baubles, bouquets, and kissed hands to the performers on the stage, she dwelled longingly on his return. She would win him yet. She still retained what that 'whey-faced ninny' could never have, her 'magic', as she chose to call her animal attraction of the highly sexed female on which she traded, sold her wares and — waited.

One other, too, dwelled on and waited the return of Königsmarck whose name was in her secret heart, if never on her lips. At night, in her lonely bed, she saw him in some far distant land, vividly imagined on a battlefield amid gaunt rugged mountains, surrounded by hordes of yelling Turks, mowed down by red-stained scimitars. Her dream of him or someone nameless, formless, faceless, vomiting blood, recurred to haunt her; nor were her fears and anxiety assuaged by the British envoy to Hanover, Sir William Dutton Colt, who had given her some inkling, albeit guarded, of appalling conditions in the Morea.

She liked to talk to Sir William, a small lean-jawed whippet of a man who spoke French with her in not too anglicised an accent. From him she heard how report had come of fierce fighting at Prestina, where the duke's forces had been recently engaged. Then, seeing her whiten and knowing that Prince Charles, his mother's idol and — as gossip gave it — hers, since her affections as was said had been divided equally between the prince and that handsome young profligate, Königsmarck, whose brother had caused a furore some few years ago in London for his involvement in the Thynne murder — old news now — he wondered. For, mused Sir William, even dried mud sticks, and has stuck to the name of these Swedes.

'But the Turks,' he hastened diplomatically to add, having drawn his conclusion from the princess's pallor, 'are no match for Hanover's armies.' He turned the talk to opera, having witnessed a performance at the Opera House on the previous night. 'Your singers, Serene Highness, are the most magnificent, exceeding even those of Italy. Never, save in Germany,' he rose to bow, and at her gesture was re-seated, 'are such voices and such exquisite music to be found.'

For an Englishman, she reflected, *he has far less* gaucherie *than others of his kind that I have met with here. They are rough and ready as a rule, what they call the hail-fellow-well-met, from example of their late King Charles. This dog-faced gentleman has all the poise and easy flattery of a French, rather than an English ambassador.* And, although her thoughts were floating, she continued, 'The Germans are a musical race, yet I find German music too heavy for my taste. I much prefer French opera.'

'Ah, the French!' enthused Sir William with imitative Gallic gush. 'What elegance! What spirit!' His eyes under hooded lids regarded the scene of the lesser ballroom where an informal *soirée* attended by a few of the elect was assembled. The Crown Prince called for a dance and. led out his 'Maypole', glittering with jewels and gowned, remarkably, in puce. Couples decorously revolved in a coranto. 'A dance,' said Sir William, 'much in favour at our English court, but we dance it with more vigour.'

Following his discreet survey she saw her husband strutting, bowing, footing it before the Schulenberg and, with dry humour, likened him to a fat chanticleer about to tread his hen, her yellow comb uprisen as was he, tiptoe, to reach her!

She side-glanced the imperturbable Sir William. What did he see or know or think of this blatant flaunting of the heir apparent's mistress in the presence of his wife? Or was the British envoy too well accustomed to such disregard for the ethical behaviour of royalty to remark it? She had heard how

King Charles in the early days of his marriage, although perhaps not later, had paraded his mistresses for all the world and his wife to see. What, she wondered, would the British Ambassador have to tell his Monarch, Dutch William, usurper of his uncle's throne?

What the envoy saw, knew, thought or told, as recorded in his dispatches to King William, carefully avoided any allusion to the behaviour, ethical or otherwise, of royalty. He reports that the court is festive with carnival and gaieties during the New Year, but admits *dreadful apprehensions that our mirth will not end well, being concerned for the safety of Prince Charles. If he be killed, it will bring the duke and duchess in sorrow to their graves...'*

His 'dreadful apprehensions' were not unfounded. News travelled slowly, laden with contradictory reports. Prince Charles had been taken prisoner. Count Königsmarck was killed. Both were missing. Both severely wounded. The most recent information gave it that Charles had been flung into a dungeon at Constantinople ... 'Tortured to death by those barbarians, the Turks,' wailed his mother. So great was her anxiety that she broke down under the strain. The court physicians feared for her reason. Sophia Dorothea feared for hers; for apart from sharing the duchess's gloomy forebodings, the Crown Princess must contain within herself her own 'dreadful apprehensions'. She went in torment, daily expecting to hear of Philip's death.

Until now she had never dared confess that should he, who had left her suspended on a thread of love's agony, be killed she would lose all that made life bearable. So, in her solitude, uncomforted, unwatched, even by the faithful Knesebeck — who may likely have wondered to see her joyously participating in the round of pleasure, masques, balls, junketings and banquets — she could let her heart be torn; and hopelessly she prayed one constant prayer: *God, send him back to me...*

If thought could carry, Philip might have captured some ethereal winged messenger in the midst of fiercest fighting, or probably might not. To a Königsmarck war and its dangers offered more excitement in the pursuit and surrender of the enemy than in the pursuit and surrender of woman, however much desired.

It needs not much imagination to picture him charging ahead of his cavalry, leading them, cheering them on with an eye when he could spare it, for Charles, helmetless, his bright hair wind-blown, standing in his stirrups, shouting to his men, flung in the thick of the fight.

It was a bloody battle, with the odds against the Hanoverians astronomically outnumbered by the Turks. The grim grey mountains, shaped like dragons hewn from rock, surrounded the plain low-lying to the sea, where the enemy, short frocked, bare-legged, cross-gartered, all hard riders, brawny, fearless, came down like swarming locusts, brandishing their deadly curved steel weapons with triumphant howls; trampling bodies of men dead and dying amid riderless and screaming wounded horses, while the decimated duke's men struggled with their last remaining strength to hold their own.

Philip's mare was killed by the deadly thrust of a Turk's scimitar meant for him. Leaping from his fallen beast Philip took his toll of his loved mare's murderer and got him with his sword to slit his guts. It was then, amid that awful holocaust, that he saw ... and seeing, dashed on foot regardless of his life, in attempt to reach and drag Charles from the fierce attack of one, a giant with a gash across his forehead whose lance dripped red, while rags of flesh flew through the blood-stained air like monstrous scarlet butterflies.

Too late. He was too late. The Turk had driven home, straight through that brave young heart.

We have received certain news, laconically writes Sir William Colt, *that Prince Charles was killed on the spot where his body was found...*

But no 'certain news' came of Königsmarck.

FIVE

The Court of Hanover was plunged in mourning. The duchess was inconsolable, the duke consoled by the sympathetic ministrations of the Platen, and the princess in a fever of anxiety concerning the fate of Königsmarck, of whom still no 'certain' news was heard. In her solitude she wept and prayed, hoped and waited, hoping still when hope had fled.

The duchess, on receiving news of the death of her adored Charles, had fallen so dangerously ill that the court physicians despaired of her life; but in the spring of the year she rallied sufficiently to go with the duke to Carlsbad to take the waters.

George Louis returned from Flanders, where he had been in command of his regiments; no dangerous expedition this, for the allied troops were mobilising to assist William of Orange, King of England, in a final fling at his uncle James, the exiled Sovereign of Great Britain, at the Battle of the Boyne.

Absence of the Crown Prince had not made his heart grow fonder for his wife, although his ardour had increased fourfold for his 'Maypole', expressed in constant demonstration of his love and extravagant gifts for her adornment including a pair of gloves, lavishly embroidered and bejewelled. To his wife he presented another pair of gloves, of considerably less value, yet her almost schoolgirlish delight in them may have caused him a twinge — if not of conscience, for he had none concerning his relationship with Schulenberg — but perhaps a belated reminder, for appearance's sake, of his duty as a husband.

'I thought,' said he awkwardly, 'that they might be too large for you. Your hands are so small.' His tone conveyed disparagement that their smallness was a disadvantage rather than an asset. Schulenberg's hands were large, capable, outsize as she was, to enchant him.

It was springtime; the gardens of the palace were a golden glory of daffodils. From her window Sophia Dorothea looked down upon the flower borders where tall tulips stood in scarlet, yellow, parrot-hued array as of sentinels on guard. The delicate loveliness of twig tracery unfolding their shy April green of spring's welcome against a flax blue sky; a flight of birds under the pearl whiteness of a thin drifting cloud, each passing fragment of nature's perpetual design, recurrently repeated, held for her a poignant new significance, a more acute awareness of externals in which she felt herself to be but an isolated entity in this universal scheme of things, alone, unwanted, and ... unloved.

'Madame!' Knesebeck, her full-moon face radiant with smiles, her somewhat bovine eyes sparkling with excitement, burst in upon the princess and, dispensing with ceremony, announced in gasps of incoherence: 'Serene ... Your High ... he's here! Oh, my darling, he is back! He is in audience this minute ... the duchess, she sent for him. She heard he had arrived ... this morning early .... commanded him to come at once to tell her of Prince Charles ... He is there!'

'Who? Who is with the duchess?' She stayed a hand at her breast to subdue the leap of her heart, and strove to speak calmly. Not even to her faithful 'Lennie' must she betray herself, if it were true, and not a hallucination born of her longing for the return of one whom she believed was gone for ever.

'Who, Madame? Why, who but he ... Count Königsmarck! Oh my dear, my dearest!' On her knees was Knesebeck, clutching at the cold little fingers of her mistress, although her blood was warm and racing.

'I can't believe it!' The facade of calm slid from her on a whispered breath. 'I can't — I daren't believe it — it is too wonderful. Will he come to me? Shall I send him a message, or must I wait? He may not come. Why did he not tell me he had arrived? He may not,' she faltered, 'want to see me.'

'He will.' Knesebeck rose from her knees, nodding her head like a rosy mandarin. 'He will come so soon as the duchess has done with him.'

But whether or not the duchess had done with him, he did not come that day, nor the next day, nor the next; while she, who in a frenzy of impatience waited, wondered, feared. He did not want to come! He had no wish to see her and renew the promise of a passionate avowal repeated, possibly *verbatim,* to those hundred other women, and maybe now to another hundred more.

'So? Let him stew!' Thus did she unburden to the confidante, who bore the brunt of it with sympathetic clucks, unfailing optimism, and the not unlikely assumption that mischief had been made from 'that woman'. The Count was seen at Monplaisir. She gave a party to welcome his return.

'She! He went to her — *her* party! An orgy, I can well imagine!' She turned on Knesebeck, fists clenched and raised to beat the air as if it were a face. 'What perfidy! I'll not see him now should he come crawling! Never! To go to her and not to me. This is the end. He had no intention of ever seeing me again. All lies. His words and promises — all lies!'

Her hands fell to her sides, and she went to a *prie dieu* under one of the long windows overlooking the gardens. Her head was buried in her arms, her small body shaken with the tumult of her soundless sobs.

'No, Madame, dearest, you must not misjudge him.' Knesebeck, who nourished for the count a *tendresse* never told save to her innermost dreams, laid a plump hand on a heaving shoulder to administer soothing pats. 'The Platen, I am convinced of this, must have led him to believe you were not disposed to receive him. There is nothing — no wickedness that she would not do or say to injure you. And I do know — I have heard — she is so madly infatuated with Count Königsmarck that —'

'Don't!' Sophia Dorothea lifted her head. Her tousled hair falling over her face made her look, kneeling there, like an overgrown child. 'Don't speak that name to me! I will not hear it. He is as dead to me now and for ever as I thought he was — and wish he were, sooner than to have found him a liar. A hypocrite. False! O God, how I am deceived in —'

Her eyes, gazing tear-filled at the window, saw something to halt her. In the distance, limned against the feathery green of larches, she saw her children chasing in and out among the trees. The sudden swift arrowy rain of April had fallen through the sunshine, and they were holding up their hands to catch the drops with gleeful cries.

'They will be drenched!' exclaimed their mother. 'They must come in at once.' She got up to open the window and ran down the flight of marble steps, followed by Knesebeck who had snatched up a wrapper to encloak her mistress. 'Georgie! Sophie! Where is the nurse? Nurse, where are you? Come to the children!' But it was not the nurse who, in a dozen strides, had crossed the grass to seize the little Princess and lift her on his shoulder. Then, with Sophie hoisted aloft, her brother trotting at his side, he had reached the steps and stood gazing up at her, transfixed above him.

The rain had ceased as suddenly as it had come; and in the sky the ghost of a rainbow was forming.

'Mother!' From her enthronement Sophie delightedly announced. 'See who is here! And see how high am I — higher than the count.'

'Your Serene Highness.' Still bearing the daughter he bowed to the mother, while the boy darted up to her who caught him to her, hiding her face in his damp fair curls. 'So wet you are,' she breathed, and to Knesebeck, 'take him to the nursery. Count Königsmarck,' she avoided his eyes, with that in them to bring a deepening flush to her pale cheeks, and managed in tones of careful dignity to tell him, 'I had no idea you were in Hanover, Count Königsmarck. I must thank you,' she added over his head where he stood a few steps below her on the wide marble stairs, 'for so timely performing the duties of my children's errant nurse.'

Who at that moment came running, her coif half off her head, and gasping apologies between dips. 'Serene Highness,' more dips, 'they — the prince and princess — they escaped and hid from me. I and the under-nurse have been searching, but —'

'Enough.' Knife-edged, her voice cut in, glad of this diversion from his look and presence and the message in those eyes that dwelled weightily on hers. Never before had she seen them so green a grey, reflecting light drawn upward from the green rain-shotten grass. 'Take them in and change their clothes. You should keep better watch upon their play.'

The perched princess was lowered, and clasped her arms about the white-stockinged knees of the count. 'Please,' she pleaded, 'will you carry me again so high as a tree?'

'If I were permitted I would carry you so high as heaven,' was his answer, addressed not to the child who clung about his legs but to her standing on the steps above him; and with a flag of colour brightening her pallor that ebbed and flowed to the call of her blood to his:

'Sophie!' She took a step down to give a hand to the little girl and one to the boy. Both were reluctant to leave him, whom they remembered as donor of comfits; but their mother had no more to say to Königsmarck as, with a child attached to each hand, she led them up the marble stairs and through the open window, then shut and fastened it to leave him standing there.

Yet the incident had not passed unnoticed. The Platen's 'investigators', prowling in the shrubbery, were vigilant as ever, as were also certain ladies in attendance on the Crown Princess. They had seen the count lift the little girl on his shoulder and carry her to her mother, which showed a deplorable lack of etiquette on the part of the princess for permitting it, and in fact thanking the count for his care of the child and her brother. So strict was Hanoverian etiquette, out of all proportion to the comparative insignificance of a minor duchy, that none lower in rank than a Duchess or the child's nurse was allowed to touch, much less to carry, the daughter of the Crown Prince and Princess. That Her Serene Highness had appeared to encourage the count in this deliberate departure from the recognised rule of the court, and had engaged him in animated conversation — ('about as animated as an oyster') — was the comment of Sophia Dorothea when Knesebeck came to tell her how the Platen had gone hurrying off to the duke with *her* version of the scene as witnessed and heard by the ladies in attendance, gave the tatlers much to divert them.

The duke, however, home from Carlsbad after undergoing treatment at the spa, had recovered not only from his gout but from the death of his son. While his wife still grieved and was more gaunt and skeletal than ever, the duke was ready to join in the relaxations of the court, and disposed to take an indulgently avuncular view of his niece's misbehaviour as retailed, with gross exaggeration, by his mistress.

'She is lost to all sense of the decorum and dignity due to her position,' deplored the countess, 'to have allowed Count Königsmarck to carry the Princess Sophia on his shoulder and engage him without reprimand, indeed to encourage him in so grave a breach of etiquette.' To which the duke replied that etiquette could, if occasion required, allow a certain elasticity, and that he could see no misbehaviour on the part of the Crown Princess in thanking the count for his courtesy in bringing the children out of the rain. The nurse was at fault for not keeping sufficient care of her charges.

All of which was gall to the Platen. Consumed with hate and jealousy of Sophia Dorothea, she watched like a terrier at a rat-hole for the opportunity to revenge herself on the woman she chose to believe had stolen her lover.

Talk spread about the court gave it that Königsmarck and the princess were now on questionably intimate terms. The trivial incident which had aroused so much scandal, prompted by the Platen, resulted in a renewal of the count's visits to the Crown Princess, visits that were anything but intimate, as interpreted by the Platen's spies.

That Sophia Dorothea consented to receive him, even though he didn't 'come crawling', lent her free rein for resentment. We can picture the pair in the princess's privacy guarded from listeners, unless it were 'Lennie' at the door to hear.

'A whole week in Hanover, and no sight nor sound of you more than the droppings of carrion borne on the air from Monplaisir!'

'Madame, to defile you with such contamination would have been sacrilege, were I defiled.'

'Are you not — a hundred and a hundred times?'

'Your Serene Highness is pleased to harp upon one note that strikes discordantly when not played in jest.'

'Played? Jest? You call it jest to boast of conquests and —' a break here in the voice — 'to discard a — friend?'

'A friendship, Madame, on which Your Serene Highness's servant would not dare presume.' The kneeling Knesebeck, having eye in turn with ear at the keyhole, could see him bow profoundly.

'Friends once, and you betrayed my friendship and my trust. You left me in a huff and without another word when you went to the Morea, and you sent me not a word when you came back. You preferred —' sarcasm edged the voice of Lennie's lady — 'less exalted company than mine. I do not reproach you for your choice in seeking more agreeable entertainment than —'

The rest of that had been inaudible, but the reply, on reverting to the keyhole, was distinctly audible.

'It would be presumption on my part to demand audience that can only be commanded. And you did not command.'

'How could I, if I did not know you were in Hanover until I heard the duchess had received you, and that you had been received with open-armed welcome *elsewhere*?'

'The welcome, Madame, was not of my choice. But you may recollect when last we met —'

'I recollect only that before you left for the Morea, how you excused your visits to Monplaisir as — politic.'

'As they were, and must continue so to be, now I am returned to Hanover. My only hope of remaining within Your Highness's vicinity, even though I am debarred from your presence or forbidden more than formal desultory contact, is to insinuate myself in the good grace of one who is the power behind the duke, that I may continue to hold His Serene Highness's commission as Colonel of the Guards.'

'And for which appointment you are willing to debase yourself by insinuation — and to what extent one shudders to believe! — in the good grace of one whose morals, howsoever they may lead my besotted uncle, in his dotage, by the nose —' which remark, Knesebeck thought, was not a little shocking — 'and are known to be disgraceful, as you, by such association, are disgraced. Enough of this. It serves no purpose.'

Knesebeck's eye, again screwed to the keyhole, saw the princess give the nod of dismissal, which the count did not take. Instead, moving into that minute line of vision, he was seen to advance, fall upon one knee, raise the hem of the princess's gown to his lips, and there they stayed. The tiny view-point obscured what followed: a hand that alighted on Königsmarck's bent head, a touch weightless as a drift of thistledown.

The door-key which Knesebeck was holding slid from her fingers as, with pins and needles in her foot, she got up in a hurry when George Augustus came running, his sister and a page at his heels.

'Mam'zelle! Look what I've found, Mam'zelle.' For thus were the single ladies of the princess's household addressed. He held out a crumpled something, gold-tasselled and stained with the night's rain, and which his sister made as if to snatch.

'You didn't find it — I did!'

'*I* found it,' her brother contradicted, hot-faced. 'I spotted it first on the terrace by an urn.'

'You thaid it wath a dead rat,' Sophie's speech was somewhat impeded by the loss of two milk teeth, 'and I picked it up, so *I* found it. Give it to me.' She made another grab for it, but George held it high above his head — too high for her to reach.

'No!' screamed Sophie. 'I want to give it to Mama. It'th herth and I found it.'

'*I* found it — you didn't, and how could I have said it was a dead rat with gold tassels dangling from it, stupid?'

'You *did* — you did say it was a dead rat and that'th why you didn't pick it up, so I picked it up an' so I found it.'

'Who saw it first?' demanded George. 'You or me?'

Knesebeck, with a wary eye on the door, asked, 'What is it you — or both of you —' was supplemented tactfully — 'have found?'

'It'th a glove,' said Sophie, 'and I think it'th Mama's. See — it has her crown on it.'

'Not a crown,' her brother corrected, 'we don't wear crowns. We're not kings and queens.'

'Gran'mama told me,' Sophie said, 'that you may be a king one day.'

'As pigs may fly,' scoffed her brother. 'Who'd want to be a king? Bad enough to be a prince, forever *verboten* to do this or that, nor play pitch and toss with the pages, and not to say God damn what the English say, and anyway —'

'An' anyway,' Sophie interrupted, sticking to her point, '*I* found it and I'm giving it to Mama.'

'I,' said Knesebeck, interposing herself between the two of them, 'will give it to Her Highness, if it *is* her glove.' She smoothed the moist and crumpled fingers. 'I believe she did lose a pair of gloves. And where,' she asked, 'is Your Highness's nurse?'

'Not *my* nurse,' George loftily answered. 'I have a tutor, not a nurse. *Sophie's* nurse is where she always is, hunting for us, or rather for Sophie — in the grounds.'

'Your Highness should not run away from her,' Knesebeck ineffectually attempted. 'Why did you?'

'Because,' George offered his charmingly impudent grin, 'she's too fat to run after us.'

Said Knesebeck to the page, who was stifling giggles, 'Conduct the prince and princess to their apartments.' But just at that moment the door opened and Philip appeared. The children flung themselves at him.

'Count Philip!' George seized his hand. 'I didn't know you were here. Will you come with me and tell more about how you fought the Turks? You haven't told the half of it yet. Please!'

While from the room came the voice of his mother: 'What is all this?'

'*We're* all this, Mama,' cried George. 'I've found something of yours.'

'No, Mama, *I* found it.' Sophie pushed aside her brother and took possession of Philip's free hand. 'Can I come in, Mama? Count Philip will tell you I found it, won't you, Count Philip?'

He stooped to the little girl whose rosy dimpled face, upraised to his, caused a catch in his throat. Those eyes, dark-fringed, so like her mother's, but the hair, flaxen fair, which would darken with age, was her German father's heritage. Her father, that sot, who had the right to hold and claim her and her mother…

He stooped to smooth back a curl of that hair which had escaped its gold fillet. 'May I be let into the secret of what you have found?'

'Not a secret.' Sophie's widening smile showed a gap in her upper gums. 'It'th a glove.'

'Darlings,' their mother emerged to ask the inevitable question, 'where is your nurse?'

'*Sophie's* nurse,' her son told her gently, 'is looking for her in the shrubbery while my tutor devises — his word, not mine — a hundred Latin lines for me to construe for having written in my essay on Virgil *the moon is made of green cheese and so are you*. I wrote it in English because Uncle Max told me he had written that in an essay when he was having lessons with this same Herr Professor who used to be his tutor too, and he hadn't noticed it, then so I thought I'd see if he wouldn't notice it now, being much older and very absent-minded, but he *did* notice it! So I'm going to have it out with Uncle Max for letting me down.'

Said his mother, biting her lip to swallow laughter, and avoiding Philip's eyes that laughed with hers: 'It was very naughty of you and Uncle Max. You deserve not one but two hundred lines. So go and write them, and don't pester Count Königsmarck to tell you stories.'

'I'm not pestering him to tell me stories, Mama. He's going to tell me how he fought the Turks. I'm to be a soldier when I grow up, and I'll go to the wars and fight the French.'

'Not if I know it,' breathed his mother with a hand to her heart. 'And what is all this about a glove?'

All this about a glove had had its beginnings a few nights before when Sophia Dorothea, dining with the duke and duchess, had been seen by a certain lady to remove her gloves, that fell under the table. She had also been seen, since her thoughts were much engaged elsewhere, to leave the table gloveless. And after those in attendance on the duke and duchess had left the dining hall, the countess had given an order to a lackey.

'I have lost the pair of gloves I was wearing at dinner. I may have let them fall under the table. Look for them where I sat opposite the Crown Princess.'

The gloves were recovered and brought to the Countess von Platen. One of them was locked in a secret drawer of her bureau, the other flung from a window that same night to fall upon the terrace.

It was the custom of persons great and small to visit Brunswick for the annual fair, an event welcomed by the Court of Hanover and by the duke who, despite the recent death of his son, considered it as much his duty as his pleasure to attend the Brunswick revels as a sop to his cousin Anton Ulrich of Brunswick-Wolfenbüttel, who had never forgiven or forgotten the scurvy way his son had been thwarted of Celle's heiress. But the duchess, deep in mourning, refused for the first time in their married life to accompany her husband to the fair.

'Your concubine will deputise for me,' he was told; and seeing him make ready for retort to that, his dewlaps indignantly mottled, she added deftly, 'or your niece, since Count Königsmarck, your Colonel of the Guards, goes with you as your equerry-in-chief.'

He goggled an eye at her, whose thin lips stretched and parted in a smile that much resembled a grimace. 'I mislike your innuendo,' he came out with, thankful for this diversion from his 'concubine' to whom his wife seldom, if ever, alluded. 'I would not have thought that you paid heed to idle gossip which couples the name of our son's wife with Königsmarck — gossip entirely unfounded.'

'I pay no heed and lend no ear to gossip whether founded or unfounded,' was the reply from those lips, exhibiting a row of yellow teeth. *She looks her age,* inwardly remarked the duke, *which is more than mine, but I'll wager she'll outlive me, clinging to the last spark of life in hope of England's crown.* 'Yet,' his wife was saying, 'I am bound to believe the evidence of my own eyes and ears. There is a renewal of an acquaintanceship that I understand had its beginnings and was temporarily ended,' a throaty chuckle preceded the words, 'in an arbour.'

'An arbour?' echoed the duke with an eagerness that invited expansion of this further innuendo. 'How — what — in an arbour?'

'Experimentally, as children will,' obscurely croaked the duchess, and left him to think about that.

He thought about it to some purpose after his arrival in Brunswick, where loyal townsfolk had come out in full force to welcome him as, seated in his state coach, he had driven through the shouting streets that were festively be-flagged and garlanded from house to house. Banners flapped from windows, streamers floated, and Ernest Augustus, flattered at the hearty cheers that greeted him from the subjects of Anton Ulrich — with whom he had exchanged not half a dozen words in as many years — sat beaming, waving hands and bowing right and left, and was brought to the castle at eventide.

The Countess von Platen had come before, by a shorter route, to be in readiness to receive him. As the wife of the First Minister — conveniently absent, having contracted a tertian fever and, according to Clara, taken to his bed on doctor's orders — she was allotted rooms in the castle. Built on a miniature scale compared with the vast Leine Schloss, it was not large enough to house the duke's entire suite and those few attendant on the Crown Princess. The rest of the court was lodged in various inns.

George Louis, having enjoyed to repletion his Schulenberg during his leave from military duties, had rejoined his troops in Flanders, much to the relief of Sophia Dorothea. And she was not displeased to know that the colonel of the duke's bodyguard had been accommodated in a wing of the castle adjoining her own, not at all to the approval of Madame Clara. She, having supped in her chamber *à deux* with the duke and later entertained him in the extra-nuptial bed, gave him this: 'I consider it most unwise of you to have housed Count Königsmarck in close proximity to the apartments of the Crown Princess. If you are not aware of a *liaison* between them, then you are the only one who isn't.'

'*Liaison?*' The duke raised his nightcapped head from the pillow where it snuggled preparatory to sleep. The journey had been tiring and his activities with Clara had exhausted him whose spirit, however willing, was not equal to his ageing flesh. 'You can't mean to say —' he sucked his dry palate that tasted sour from the wine with which she had doused him — 'that there is any truth in this talk of — um — irregular behaviour between them?'

Clara grinned up at the ceiling which, in direct contrast to the aphrodisiacal decor of her bedroom at Monplaisir, modestly depicted figures, male and female, in diaphanous draperies: angels and seraphim reposing on clouds with lambs skipping round simpering shepherdesses. Brunswick's taste was more temperate than that of Hanover. And to her unlawful spouse she said, 'Talk enough to warn you that the relations of your son's wife with Königsmarck are too — familiar, shall we say? — to avoid remark from those who might put a misconception on a friendship dating from her childhood when your Colonel of the Guards, a page at her father's court, was dismissed for attempted rape of the princess, who was not,' a wink this time at the ceiling, 'a princess then but — let us face it — a bastard.'

'Legitimised,' muttered Ernest August, 'by imperial decree.'

'None the less a bastard, since she was born out of wedlock, with as much of French as German in her blood that might well account for her total lack of moral obligations.'

Had the duke heard the finale to this remark he might have retorted, *You're a fine one to talk of moral obligations,* but he didn't hear it; nor, if he had, is it likely he would have risked his Clara's reply to it. A gentle snore was all she got from him, rising to a nasal crescendo as he sank deep in a dream of a strangely garbed pig in a nightgown, its snout wreathed in roses and himself sucking sauerkraut from its open maw. And in his sleep he muttered, 'Wine and women don't agree...'

'Evidently not,' said Clara von Platen.

She may have derived some satisfaction from the effects of her hints upon the duke, continued with embellishment next morning.

Reminded of his Clara's revelations concerning an attempted rape — *dear God!* — on the part of his trusty Colonel of the Guards when a page at the Court of Celle, the duke-bishop was inclined to believe his mistress's word before that of his wife's innuendo. He knew Clara's intuition and diplomatic acumen to be infallible. A pity women could not take official appointments: she would have made a far better First Minister than her clod of a husband. A not improbable conclusion.

The duke regarded himself not only as sovereign head of his state, but as the father of his people. Never for one moment must the honour of his house, of his son, the heir apparent, nor of his son's wife be jeopardised by equivocal conjecture, even though there were no positive evidence of irregular intimacy between the Crown Princess and Königsmarck. The duke decided now to watch for any indication that his daughter-in-law did not behave with the dignity due to her position. Princes of the Blood were permitted certain deviations from the exigencies of marriage which, in the case of royalty, were almost always affairs of State; but their wives, like Caesar's, must be above reproach.

Meanwhile Clara, having scattered her seeds, hopeful for the fruits thereof, determined on a final bid for possession of him whom she so greedily desired and, in so far as she was capable of love, she loved. Should he deny her what she craved, then she would bring about his ruin. His days in Hanover would be numbered.

'George Louis,' she told her husband, Platen, who cared not how many lovers she had — providing none would interfere with his high office that depended, as well he knew, on his Clara's yea or nay — 'will be given ample proof of his wife's misconduct, enough to seek a divorce unless he will agree to a compromise. Our daughter to be given to his son.'

Platen drew a long lip. 'Our daughter?'

'Mine,' smiled Clara. 'A few years' difference in age is of the least importance in a royal marriage, and you might live to see a grandchild of ours on the throne of Britain.'

He had no more to say to that, had long accepted without question the parenthood of the podgy, Guelph-like girl presented to him by Clara.

'On the other hand,' she reflected, 'if all goes well and Königsmarck remains here in high favour, we may give our daughter to — him.'

'What!' Platen shot her a bolting look. Even he, who to some extent had plumbed the depths of her subtle machinations and in general approved them, since it were more than his place was worth not to, felt bound to offer a mild protest. 'Your suggestion savours somewhat of — um — of incest — yes?'

'No!' She glared at him. 'She has no relationship with Königsmarck.'

'But *you*,' he allowed himself this much to dare, 'you have.'

'*Had,*' she snarled in answer. 'Not renewed — as yet.' And left him guessing.

While the Brunswick Fair equalled, if it did not transcend, the abandoned gaieties of the Venice Carnival, the transports of the Brunswickers differed from those of the Venetians, in that a limit to the laxity of behaviour was enforced by the Duke of Brunswick-Wolfenbüttel. The fun, though fast and furious, must keep within the bounds of decency. There were no outward demonstrations of licentiousness or crapulence; no dimmed lights in corners inviting intimacy, scarcely private. Were any pastors present they could not have preached a sermon on the sins of fornication practised or witnessed in the Town Hall's assembly rooms as might have been passed with eyes indulgently averted from a gondola or in the palace of the Doge himself.

At a masquerade attended by the Duke of Hanover and all his suite, a variety of costumes, as in Venice, were worn, but none at whom a worthy burgomaster could have blinked an eyelid. There were goddesses discreetly gowned, and nymphs, scarcely sylph-like; columbines and harlequins, fat aldermen strutting in imitation armour; Knights Templar, Crusaders and clowns. The duke wore his ass's head as concession to the masque. Sophia Dorothea was diaphanous as Psyche. From a balcony above the tier of boxes reserved for less exalted persons, she, with her uncle, watched that fantasy of dancers rotating below to the squeak of fiddles, and every now and then a solo tenor voice lifted in song to hold spellbound an audience with music in its blood.

One watcher in the balcony singled out the Platen, a buxom Venus in robes of a startling transparency that revealed as much of her as was permissible to see of fleshy legs and thighs enclothed, for decorum, in tights. She was dancing a jig in a set of six with Königsmarck, unmasked and in uniform, for neither he nor any other of the duke's bodyguard could appear in costume. And now there was an interval for refreshment where, in an inner room, a buffet groaned with edibles to whet the appetite of Teutons who fancied roast geese stuffed with sausages and onions; boars' heads in aspic, salmon soaked in wine; jellied eels and hams galore baked in a dish with sugar, sack and cream, and a garnish of candied orange, and all of this washed down with various possets; rum punch, egg flip, the wines of France and Rhine wines, but in moderation. No boozing here in Brunswick, or rather none in public.

Supper was served to the royalties in the Wolfenbüttels' private suite, but Clara, much to her disgust, was not invited as guest of Duke Ulrich. This omission she attributed to Sophia Dorothea who, acting for the Duchess Sophia, could have intimated to the Duke's Comptroller of his Household those of the Hanoverian Court to be given preference: this another black, mark scored by Clara von Platen against the Crown Princess.

In the refreshment room where the crowd snatched unmannerly at food and drink, Clara chose to sit apart at a table laid for two, screened by banks of hydrangeas, and bade Königsmarck bring her a flagon of Rhenish and a slice of ham; yet when supplied with these she ate nothing, drank a lot, and leaning her elbows on the table asked, 'What time tonight are you off duty?'

'I am not on duty tonight unless commanded to wait upon the duke,' he said, and cursed himself immediately for saying so, for she seized on that to tell him, displaying a recently acquired denture of an unrealistic white, 'Then I command you to wait on me.' Her glance swept the crowd around the buffet. 'I have had all that I can stomach of these philistines. So, Philip,' he winced at that familiar use of his name, and fixed his eyes stonily above her head, dressed in a flaxen wig on which precariously perched a silver dove, 'will you ac-accompany me to my 'partment?' Her speech was slightly slurred after her fourth bumper of various wines. 'I sick-sicken of these rowdy townsfolk an' their antics —' she got up, trailing her flimsy robes behind her as she walked, a trifle dizzily, towards the entrance to the hall — 'an' I take it as an in-ins'cusable insult to me as Chief Min'ster's wife that I must mingle with the herd. This way. Through here.'

They were seen to leave by an exit into the courtyard where the lady's coach was waiting. A footman came down from his box to open the door for her. Philip bowed her in but did not follow.

'Well?' She thrust her face at him. 'Aren't you coming?'

He stood stiffly to attention. 'I cannot attend you, Madame.'

'Why — why not?' Her eyes, rimmed with black, stared from their painted lids. Somewhere a clock struck one sonorous note. 'You said you — not on duty.'

'I cannot leave, Madame, in case the duke should require my attendance.'

'The duke'll not req-require your 'tendance tonight.' Her bewigged head emphatically nodded. 'Nor'll he require,' she carefully enunciated, 'mine.' Her boozy grin revolted him. 'So in you get.'

So in he got.

command of an army, would stand abashed and shamefaced before her when she took him to task.

'She might,' the duchess smiled sourly with lips turned down; he knew that smile and what it could portend. 'I say she might, I do not say she will, seek or has sought consolation for your indifference and neglect, yet who could blame her if she did?'

'What,' he blurted, 'have you heard concerning her search for — consolation, and with whom?'

'Come, now! You take me up. I say nothing, know nothing, save to warn you what may come about should you carry too far your neglect of your husbandly duties.'

'She goes her own road,' said he in a surly tone, 'and I go mine. We don't interfere with each other's — amusements.'

'Which may not amuse the onlooker who sees nothing, not all, of the game.'

'I'll teach her,' he muttered, 'not to play the game against me!'

His mother screwed an eye at him; her long nose twitched. 'You said?'

'That I — I thank you for your warning — I'll be warned.'

'Good boy.' She offered him her cheek, withered and dry as a skeleton leaf, and dismissed him.

As the door closed on his exit, she reached for a bell on a table at her side. It was promptly answered by a lady-in-waiting. 'Serene Highness?'

'I desire the Crown Princess to attend me within the hour.'

And within the hour came Sophia Dorothea. The duchess looked her over as she rose from the bob, sulky-mouthed; her lowered lashes were dark crescent moons upon her cheeks.

'I have this to say —' the duchess cleared her throat of some catarrhal nuisance, took a lozenge from a silver box at her elbow, and spoke while she chewed — 'that now your husband is with us again after these long intermittent absences, it is to be hoped you will welcome the reunion and so give the lie to certain talk that knits your name with one unworthy of your favour.'

A streak of grey circled the iris of those eyes, myopically peering. Her doctors had advised her to wear spectacles, an advice which she ignored. Her one beauty in her youth had been her eyes, and her one vanity beyond her own appreciation of her intellect. 'I trust that these scavengers of gossip will find among the garbage where they scrabble nothing of tainted bones for them to gnaw.' A finger explored her gums to extract therefrom the remains of a jellified lozenge. This she swallowed while Sophia Dorothea, fiercely red, jerked up her head.

'Your Highness is pleased to speak in terms that I find — disagreeable.'

'No less disagreeable than I who am forced to remind you of certain indiscretions in relation to your conduct that should be more restrained.'

'Of what indiscretions am I guilty? Of what am I accused?'

The red that dyed her cheeks was fading; her breath quickened. What did she know or guess, what threat to herself and him? They had been careful, their meetings, well guarded by Knesebeck, could have aroused no suspicion, since to all outward appearance they were but the courtesy visits commanded by her to a friend of her youth: a friend, too, of Charles, so dearly loved. Did not the duchess also receive him to hear, was never tired of hearing, all he could tell her of Charles; how he died, and his last words, if any...

'Accused?' the duchess elevated her eyebrows. 'Who has accused you, unless,' her sour smile came again upon her lips, 'it were your conscience?'

That drew blood; all fear of this matriarchal tyrant was dissolved in an indignant upsurge.

'My conscience is clear, in spite of having suffered intolerable insults from your son, who parades his mistress before me and the whole court. I have not your forbearance, nor have I your philosophy that can tolerate a husband's adulterous relationships. All this —' her hand defined the nodding trees and the green stretch of lawns framed in the window — 'this land of the Duchy and all that lies beyond it — the building of your Windsor Castle in the air. No!' as the duchess, sitting rigidly against the high chair-back, made as if to speak, 'what I will say must now be said, and then I'll be forever dumb.'

And, saying it, she shed control, as once before she had defied this Medusa who could then have petrified her, but not now. No, not now!

'Do you think I care that the future of which you dream will make you a queen, or your son a King of England? I would rather be the wife of a peasant, a lackey or the village idiot than the wife of him, were he king or commoner, and to whom I'm tied, and whom I hate. Yes, I hate him, and I hate this life, and I hate — you!'

This last word flung in that old cold face had diminished to a whisper while her mouth stayed open with the shock of it. She waited in a silence as of a leaden weight about to fall upon and crush her. Only the ticking of a long-case clock disturbed that heavy stillness.

Had horns sprouted from the head of her who stood trembling at her own temerity, the duchess could not have been more horrified. That this monad, this chit, this bastard of the Frenchwoman should dare give utterance in repetition of former defiance, deprived her, for some thirty seconds, of all speech.

Then she rose from where she sat to pronounce with god-like calm, 'Poor child. You, as I have long suspected, are out of your mind. A weakness inherent from your French forbears who, I do not doubt, have bred insanity. I will have my doctors examine you for what I trust is but a temporary derangement. Go to your room. I will have a soothing posset administered as prescribed by the famous English physician, Dr Culpeper, to quicken the senses and strengthen the brain.'

It was the best she could do to preserve her dignity.

And Sophia Dorothea, considerably chastened having said her say, curtsied to the ground and backed to the door. Her petticoats raised above her ankles to hasten her speed, she ran past a huddle of pages who may have overheard the duchess's final pronouncement and were in the giggles, exchanging meaningful glances with taps to their heads, while down the corridor rushed Her Highness and was brought to a halt by Maximilian. On his way to his mother's library in search of a book he, too, may have heard enough of that scene to intrigue him. Under one arm he held a heavy volume, the other encircled her waist.

'Aha! So you've bearded the lioness.'

'The Gorgon!' panted Sophia Dorothea. 'In truth I *must* be mad.'

'You were never more sane. You've told her what I've often wished to say, but never had the guts to say it.' He cast a look behind him. 'We can't talk here. Let's go outside.'

They found a sheltered seat in the garden, screened from the palace windows. 'I too have hated George Louis,' he said, 'not only because of our father's injustice in planning to make him heir, apart from the Duchy which is his right as eldest son, but to all those territories which are not his right and should be equally divided between the rest of us as our forefathers have done. But I don't hate him now. It isn't really anything to do with him. What my father says, goes — or rather what the Platen says. You, at least,' he turned to look at her, 'will benefit when George Louis takes possession of Celle, as well as Hanover and all else besides.'

And even though his mind buzzed like an inquisitive mosquito about his perpetual grievance, he noted with approval the delicately modelled bone structure, the soft peach tone of her skin, the tendrils of dark hair clustered on her forehead. 'It is my brother who is mad,' he said, 'not to take and enjoy what is also his right.'

'Why — what?' She had not been listening. The distribution of land in the duchies, and her ultimate share in them as wife of the future duke, were of no interest to her.

'I was saying — no matter.' Max adjusted the mechlin at his wrist that had been caught up on a silver button of his velvet cuff. A shred of the lace had been torn. 'I see I shall have to dismiss my valet. As for hate,' he continued, 'I have renounced hate and the sources of it which are jealousy, envy, covetousness, greed, and all the besetting sins that obstruct the true way of life and living.'

It was her turn to look at him now. 'You talk like a pastor.'

He shook his head, a slow grin dawning. 'Not as those pastors with whom my mother delights to argue and set disputing with each other, having given them a dose of her near agnosticism. No, this man,' he opened the volume on his knee, 'who in his boyhood fell under the corruptive influence of Rome and Carthage, has revealed to me the true and only living Church as manifest in the realisation of a personal God to save us from that, abyss which is eternal severance from Him. My mother's Platonic Christianity, on which she and her Leibnitz shape their beliefs, gets us nowhere. This man —' again he referred to the book — 'who is one of the greatest intellects the world has ever known and who gives us his Confessions, I can see — on a far lower plane, of course — a certain similarity to my own perpetual gropings for the truth.'

'Well!' was all that Sophia Dorothea found breath to say. This, coming from Max, the self-indulgent dilettante who, to her knowledge, had never been concerned with any religious beliefs whatsoever, who attended church not as a duty but a penance, taxed her credulity. The thought struck her, when recovered from her first astonishment, that this reversal of his *laissez-faire* heterodoxy might be a coverage against some scheme or counterplot to thwart his father's intention to disinherit him and his younger brothers.

'At present,' Max turned over some pages, 'I am only groping in the dark where a dim light beckons. I will follow that light which may lead me to the truth through his teaching that for centuries has moulded the spirit of the Church. At the Reformation, Catholics and Protestants alike appealed to his authority, as — do I.'

In spite of her suspicion that these dialectics were expounded less from a genuine belief than from some more subtle other motive, she was impressed. 'Who,' she asked, 'is this great intellect that has so inspired you?'

'His name is Augustine.'

'Oh! You mean — not *Saint* Augustine?'

'Who else?'

'Are you — surely not — contemplating conversion to Rome? Your father would never forgive you. You will be expatriated. Cut off completely.'

'I couldn't be more cut off than I will be when the act of primogeniture comes into force. All Europe once was Catholic, and you are, or should be, Catholic, being half French.'

'My grandfather was a Huguenot.'

'But before him, right back to your Norman ancestry, you were Catholic, which is and always will be the only living Church.' He got up, tucked St Augustine under his arm and held out his hand to her. 'Let me take you back to your apartments.'

On the way through the formal gardens of the palace Max paused on the bridge that spanned the Leine, where swans, their haughty necks upraised and red bills expectantly opened, came floating to receive the titbits he carried in his pouch for them.

'They are the loveliest of all water birds,' she said. 'I am told they live for at least fifty years and sing when they are dying, maybe for joy that this life for them is ended and they will fly straight to their heaven. I wouldn't want to go to heaven if no birds or dogs are there. I wonder if we will be allowed to see our dogs again in heaven.'

He smiled down at her wide-eyed questioning face. Almost a decade of her miserable marriage had not aged her; she still retained that young look of a lost child as when he first had seen her.

'If you want your dogs in heaven you will have them. It is promised that in heaven all our wishes will be granted.'

'If I believed that,' she said with sudden passion, 'I would kill myself tomorrow.'

'Then you would never reach heaven. We can't force our way in. We must wait till we're invited. And talking of that, have you received your invitation to Königsmarck's masquerade on midsummer's night?'

She affected indifference. 'I don't know. Knesebeck has not told me if any invitation has come from Count Königsmarck. She attends to my correspondence.'

Which was almost but not quite a lie. Knesebeck's attention to her correspondence consisted of answering letters of appeal for charity, or any other impersonal matter; when addressed to Mademoiselle von dem Knesebeck, in a great sprawling hand and sealed with red wax bearing a device of two hearts entwined, they were passed to the Crown Princess unopened; and that very morning such a note had been received by Knesebeck, in cypher, to tell of the forthcoming masque.

He had already intimated that it would be 'politic' — she was beginning to detest that word and its connections — to celebrate the return of the 'Reformer', George Louis, from Flanders. 'Then,' he had said, 'we can meet with no subterfuge to bring a hornet's nest about our ears.'

None the less, the hornets, disturbed in their nest, rose up about them … to swarm.

SIX

The masquerade at Philip's house on midsummer night, attended by all the *élite,* was on a scale of extravagance that strained even his almost limitless resources. As host he received his guests dressed *à la mode,* unmasked and conspicuously recognisable among those who came disguised.

Schulenberg, easily the tallest woman there, was splendid as an Amazon, her corn-gold hair partially concealed by a jaunty silver helmet. The Platen was magnificent as a Sultana, but Sophia Dorothea wore nothing more arresting than a white domino and a mask of black velvet. The rest of the company, whether gods or goddesses, Greek slaves, Romans, peasants, Neptune — of these some half a dozen in coats of mail and curious seaweedy wigs — all wore their dazzling jewels. The Schulenberg circled her large muscular neck with emeralds, the latest gift from her prince. The Platen's heavy breast was a Milky Way of diamonds.

Card tables had been placed in one of the rooms, a long buffet in another and, leading from it, the great galleried hall where lute-players, harpists, fiddlers, provided music for those who would dance. In the gardens the lavender dusk was enlivened by lanterns strung among the trees inviting couples to take the cool evening air after a surfeit of overheated, overcrowded rooms.

Philip, giving precedence to her of highest rank, led the Crown Princess in a stately pavane, and, as prearranged, allowed himself no compromising word that might fall upon listening ears. One pair of ears had, however, chanced upon a sentence when their owner brushed against her host as the dance ended and, watching the movement of his lips to aid her hearing as the music sighed to its finale, heard fragments of a murmur: 'midnight ... the arbour on the lower lawn that overlooks the river ...'

Having performed his duties to the ladies, Philip absented himself when, during the interval, his guests surged to the buffet while the sweating musicians, grateful for that brief respite, partook of drink and eatables served to them in the gallery.

The gleaming jewels of promenading couples in those moon-silvered gardens were superimposed upon the curtain of the night lending a vivacious impermanence to tree shadows flung across the lawn that sloped to the gentle Leine, where drowned stars sank beneath the metallic light of coloured lanterns reflected in the water.

Although the darkness gave him some coverage, Philip realised that in his modern dress he must still be conspicuous among those masquers who had left the house to stroll about the lawns. Clinging to the shadows and hastening his steps, he saw her whom he sought, the white of her domino impinged upon the rustic entrance to the arbour. At the rustle of footsteps in the grass, she turned; he glimpsed her eyes through the black velvet of her mask, heard her whisper his name, but even as he gathered her into his arms and felt the weight of her body through the folds of the domino he knew he had been tricked.

'You goddamn bitch!' In hoarse English he uttered it, learned from his schoolmates in London; but she, in the feigned squeaking voice of a masquer, cried: 'Oh, oh, all is lost — we are discovered!' and in a great pretence of fright she rushed from the arbour, dropping, as she fled, a glove.

Philip stood biting his lip, more furious with himself than with her for having fallen in her trap; nor did he at first notice the two men who approached until one of them, Count Platen, in the guise of an Eastern potentate, called to him jovially, 'Aha! Mine host is pleased to entertain himself, or chooses rather to be entertained. Who is the fair incognita?'

And the other in a Roman toga, a laurel wreath binding his unwigged blond cropped hair: 'Trust our Colonel of the Guards to steal the prettiest filly from us. Come on, Königsmarck, who is she? Hallo! — what's this?'

He stooped to recover the glove the 'fair incognita' had let fall in her flight. 'So now,' the Roman George Louis, whose fat pudding face in the wavering light looked to be swollen and he, most decidedly drunk, repeated with hiccups, 'so now I — know who she — *hic* — is. And I know this glove — *hic* — it is — *hic* — one of a pair I gave my wife. Careless of her to leave prim-*hic*-facie evidence behind her.' Loudly he belched.

Philip stood stiffly at attention. 'Your Serene Highness, I am at a loss to understand you. The lady whom Count Platen calls the "fair incognita" is entirely incognita to me.'

'To you?' George Louis gave out a winey gust of breath on a sneering laugh. 'That's a good one — not to know the Crown Princess, whom you led in the dance and the — *hic* — only white dom-dom-uch-hic-uch —' He suddenly and violently retched to vomit his drink and gave Philip his chance to make off, leaving Platen in attendance.

Phew! Back on the terrace he leaned against the baluster mopping his face, while his whole being revolted at the thought that this loathly beast had the right to take and hold all he most cherished in the world.

And what, he wondered would come of this latest Machiavellian manoeuvre, in which he was certain both the

179

Platens were involved? She had instructed her husband to bring the prince there just at that critical moment, having managed to obtain or have made a copy of the glove, and had cloaked herself in a white domino. She probably had several in all colours. But how did she know they were to meet in that accursed arbour? Once again, an arbour!

Was this, as long before, to be another parting of their ways? How could he prove that it was not his Léonisse, but Platen's wife? Who would believe him against their joint denials ... and that glove?

George Louis, having overslept and received recuperation from his valet in a dose of the hair of the dog — a cup of brandy laced with raw egg — submitted his chins to be shaved, himself to be dressed and presented with a splitting, headache to Sophia Dorothea.

She, who had not overslept and had risen betimes for her morning ride accompanied by Knesebeck and Maximilian, was at her breakfast when her husband was announced.

'I wish,' said he with a baleful look at the curtsying Knesebeck, 'to speak to you — alone.' Taking the hint the confidante bobbed herself out while he produced, and dangled in the face of his wife, a glove. 'This,' he flung at her, 'is yours.'

'Oh, so it is.' Unconcernedly she took it. 'I thought it was lost. It is one of a pair you gave me. When and where did you find it?'

'I found it last night, and you,' with pointed emphasis he added, 'should know where.'

Sophia Dorothea, engaged in spooning an orange, glanced up at him, arching her eyebrows. 'What do you mean, *I* should know where? Some time ago the children brought me its fellow. They found it on the terrace. Is that where you found this?'

'No, I did not. I found it where you and our — *your* host,' he corrected, his upper lip expanding in a sneer, 'entertained you in an arbour until my arrival interrupted your — activities. Whereupon you screamed to know yourself discovered, and in your haste to get away you dropped it.' He snatched the glove, tracing with a stubby forefinger its embossed coat of arms and her initials. 'You can't deny it is yours?'

'Why should I deny it? But,' banefully she glared at him, 'I do deny that it was I who dropped that glove.'

He returned her glare with one of equal bane. 'So! You deny it — in a white domino? The only white domino in the masquerade?'

'Among four hundred guests how can you tell that mine was the only white domino?' She was beginning to see light concerning the wearer of the domino who had dropped the glove for George Louis to find.

'You admit,' he doggedly persisted, 'that the glove was yours, so who else could have dropped it?'

'There is one,' she said, still intent on her orange, 'who would go to some pains to compromise me. And I know whom *you* were with last night in the garden. I saw you leave the ballroom with him.' Which was the reason she had delayed her tryst with Philip.

'Don't,' he shouted, 'lie to me. You were always an accomplished liar.'

She sprang to her feet, her colour blazing. '*You* dare call *me* liar? If I were a man to carry a sword you'd not call me liar again. But as I can't fight you with a man's weapon — take this!' Her hand shot out to catch him a stinging blow on his flabby cheek.

'Damn you!' He caught her wrist to swing her round facing him and in rageful frenzy struck with his fist at her shoulder to receive a kick on his white-stockinged shin to make him yelp and return her a box on the ear. A ridiculous scene, and one that the listening Knesebeck at her peep-hole thought to be too dreadful; nor did she hesitate to voice her disapproval after the Crown Prince had bolted from the room with a worse than ever aching head.

'Highness, my dearest, what have you done now?' wailed the scandalised confidante.

'I hit him and he hit me back,' Sophia Dorothea rubbed her bruised shoulder, 'and so I kicked him — the beast! Calling me a liar!'

'But how could you!' gasped Knesebeck. 'Both of you behaving like —'

'Like what? A couple of street urchins? Go on, Lennie, say it.'

Lennie said it. 'Unlike any gentleman or gentlewoman should behave, least of all Serene Highnesses.'

'I have waited years,' was the complacent reply, 'to do that to him, but this is the first time I've done it and it won't be the last. It's his first time, too. There's always a beginning.'

'And, pray God,' said the confidante devoutly, 'an end.'

Sophia Dorothea helped herself to grapes and, with one in her cheek, pronounced: 'I know who wore that white domino to impersonate me. But I'll be even with her yet.'

She may have been unduly optimistic. Clara held the whip hand and knew how to wield it in her jealousy and hatred of Sophia Dorothea that had become obsessive since Königsmarck, to whom in her consuming passion she had offered herself, to be rejected.

She had devised the glove incident in order to rouse the suspicion of the Crown Prince who, his own infidelities notwithstanding, would not suffer any such diversions on the part of his wife. Hitherto he had been too engrossed with his Schulenberg, who had presented him *sub rosa* with a daughter, to pay much heed to conjecture concerning the intimacy of Königsmarck and Sophia Dorothea; but now that repercussions had been brought home to him he, as Clara had foreseen, would be on the alert. Her sole purpose was to separate the lovers, by which means the danger of propinquity might be avoided and she empowered to call him back to her. She knew that despite his vast fortune he was sinking into debt due to his reckless extravagance. She could reimburse him, however far he sank — on mutual consideration and agreement. Philip, the sybarite, would not willingly renounce his luxurious love of life and living for illicit possession of Sophia Dorothea. She still could hope. To which end she employed her strategic persuasions on the duke to make him see how necessary it was that his Colonel of the Guards should lead the Allied troops in their march upon Hamburg…

'To keep Königsmarck here in Hanover kicking his heels in attendance on you that any young aide-de-camp could do, is sheer waste of an experienced commanding officer, of which the allies on the Elbe are sorely in need. The heir apparent should not continue to risk his life in any more of your campaigns. And,' emphatically she stressed it, 'he must not be so frequently parted from his wife. I have already warned you that the intimacy between the Crown Princess and Königsmarck has caused scandal enough, and, if drastic means are not taken to end it, may become the talk not only of your Duchy but of all Europe, which might well ruin your chance of the Electorate.'

The gooseberry eyes bulged in alarm. 'How? How could any scandal in which neither I nor my son are involved affect —'

Impatiently she cut him short. 'Can't you see that the wife of the Crown Prince, who will eventually succeed to the Electorate if bestowed on you, must be protected from slanderous tongues? Your loyal subjects whose husbands, sons, and brothers have died for you and Celle in the war against France, don't relish French blood generated through your brother's "Madame". She, by her trickery and wiles, has secured royal rank for herself and her bastard and, by those same wiles may well gain the emperor's ear to confer the Electorate hat upon Celle, the elder brother, who might be considered a more likely candidate than you, the younger, as Bernstorff has reason to believe.'

'On what grounds?' He was in a great fret now. 'My brother has never so much as hinted that he looks to see himself Elector, he who cares for nothing but his hounds and the hunt.'

'And his wife.' Clara knelt beside his chair to take his hands in hers. 'My soul, my life,' she mustered a sob, 'be advised by one who lives only for your interest and your protection. You must eliminate these ugly rumours that may bring discredit to your royal name borne by the wife of your son.'

It worked. That the emperor might lend a favourable ear to the 'Frenchwoman's' wiles, which had already legitimised her marriage and her daughter, was a contingency he had never contemplated. But now that his Clara had produced so dire a possibility he realised that every step must be taken to avert it.

'Don't kneel to me, heart's delight.' She was something of an armful to raise up and plant upon his knee. 'What would I do without your unerring sense and judgment?'

'And what,' she returned his slobbering kisses, 'would I do without you? My life would be ended.'

Which she knew to be only too true. Monplaisir, her horses, coaches, her fabulous jewels and the vast wealth poured at her feet by the marriage of Sophia Dorothea, none of this would have been hers, and she and her sister still bartering their second-hand and now distinctly stale wares for small remuneration in the minor principalities.

'So, that,' she stroked his nose on the tip of which sprouted a few minute grey hairs, 'is settled. With Königsmarck gone and the *liaison* between him and the Crown Princess nipped in its bud, or its bloom, the Electorate will be safe for you and Hanover!'

Königsmarck had received his orders and passed them to those of his officers whom he had chosen to march with his two regiments in their advance to the Elbe; and now, on the eve of his departure, he sat late into the night; a chilly night for summer. The log fire his servant had lighted burned low and, stretched on a deerskin rug before it, his boarhound twitched in sleep, every so often to utter deep-throated growls and one high-pitched bay as if in chase. Philip dug a toe in the heaving ribs. 'Wake up! It's only a dream. When shall we hunt together again, I wonder, when — or — if?'

The dog rolled over, wriggling his tail. 'I can't take you with me, lad,' said Philip as the dog got upon his feet to lay his great head on his master's knee with up-gazing adoration. 'I wish I could, but you'll be waiting for me here — if I come back.'

Suddenly the dog pricked his ears, his brindle forehead puckered, nose pointing to the door that slowly opened. Königsmarck, too, was on his feet, a restraining hand on the boarhound's massive collar.

'Who?' And to that peremptory demand came the whispered answer:

'Me,' from a figure, darkly cloaked, muffled and scarcely discernible in the shadowed room lit by the flames of guttering candles and the red glow of dying embers.

'Léonisse!' He gathered her to him. 'My love, my lovely foolish love — to come here at this hour and alone. Are you alone? Where is the Sentinel?'

'In bed and fast asleep.' She stood on her toes to link her hands behind his neck. 'I told her I must see you once more before you go. We have so little time allowed us when we meet and always in fear of being followed. Spies everywhere. First the Platen's spies, and now, since she has poisoned him against me, my uncle's and … and my husband's spies. Yes —' at Philip's muttered 'God rot him!' — 'he also has his spies in the hope that he may find proof of infidelity against me.'

'And if he did?' Eagerness was in his voice and in the flicker of his eyes as his mind swooped to envisage unimaginable vistas opened out to him. 'If such were proved, would he allow your release to give him his, and — the Schulenberg?'

She shook her head. 'Even if he would divorce me — if only he would, but he wouldn't — to save his face, his pride and his mother's hope of heaven, which is England, he couldn't marry the Maypole unless she were made royal.'

'As was your mother,' he reminded her.

'Yes, but she and Father were married *before* she was made royal. My beast won't marry the Maypole, not even morganatically, although she has presented him with a great bouncing girl. Did you know that?'

He did not know that. 'And how did you know that?'

'Knesebeck told me. Won't you let me sit down?' She disengaged to seat herself in a fireside chair. The boarhound, dribbling devotion, followed to lie at her feet.

'How did you manage it?'

She laughed under her breath. 'Lennie has a cold, so I dosed her with a posset of wine, mace, and something else — to send her to sleep, and I sneaked out in her cloak with the hood pulled down over my face. We are about the same height. There are no sentries at the side gate of the palace leading to your back entrance here. Your porter let me pass, thinking I was the Sentinel who brings my notes and messages to you.'

'Yes,' his lips brushed her throat under the small rounded chin, 'that's why I chose this particular house with its easy egress from the palace!'

Her eyes searched his. 'Were you so sure that you — or I — would use it?'

'I lived in hope. I came to Hanover solely for you as our stars ordained it, and as I told you in my boyhood's first awakening when you were still a child, and will always be a child — which is one of your most adorable attractions. You have never changed, never grown up.'

Her love-warmed face was raised to his with that in it to clutch his heart; then, while sense perished at that half-promise of surrender, he felt her momentary recoil from the storm she had aroused.

'No, Philip! No.' She struggled in his arms. 'Not yet, not now.'

'Yes, now. I claim you — now. And by God,' he swore, 'I'll make you want me as much as ever in my life I've wanted you!'

The boarhound yawned, stretched himself outside the closed door of his master's room where the last of the candles had died its little death … and all sounds ceased.

From the dispatches of Sir William Dutton Colt, British Envoy to the Court at Hanover:

There is not the least appearance of danger for the city of Hamburg. The troops of Hanover march toward the Elbe and two regiments of Foot under Königsmarck ...

From which it would seem that Clara's stratagem to separate those two for any appreciable length of time had miscarried. So short an interim between Philip's departure and return after a campaign that offered little fighting, irksome to him whose breath of life was the excitement and danger of war, served only to fan the flame of his passion expressed in letters written from camp or on the march and in pidgin French or German, addressed to Knesebeck.

The first of this amazing correspondence, preserved through three centuries, suggests a doubt as to his love's reciprocation of his ardour, despite the gentle madness of her response to it in one solitary adventure...

He is not *sure of her*, is *in extremis*, he implores her to write, *if only a few lines, that he may know himself not wholly forgotten, and begs her to believe him her devoted slave.*

Her reply in a few lines to her 'devoted slave' transports him to declare himself in execrable verse of which a free translation is in something of this sort:

Alas, my love destroys me
For what is love without thee?
Such is my condition
That I sink into perdition
To nurse a fire in my heart
When we are torn apart

What then shall be my lot
Were I ... forgot?

And more and nauseating more of it, to be cherished in a casket with his letters, and taken out and wept upon and read again and yet again, and sometimes to the 'Confidante' whose romantic maiden soul was stirred in vicarious delights by these lovesick vapourings, that are not always so slavishly fond. We find him censorious to accuse her of permitting a resumption of her husband's connubial rights ... *Had you been free from blame you would not have deigned to write at all, but in spite of the way you have treated me I needs must worship you still. If you wish to comfort a poor dejected heart torn with jealousy and love let me come back...*

We may believe she advised him not to come back until all suspicion were averted. His frequent letters to Knesebeck had put the Platen's spies again upon the scent to give the duchess wind of it.

Her son received a summons: 'It is common talk that in your engrossment with your concubine you do not cohabit with your wife; which may lead her to seek, if not already sought, consolation elsewhere.'

His mouth, with its pendulous underlip, fell open. 'What's that you say?'

'What others, evil-thinkingly, do say. What all the world will say if you don't give the lie to it and put your wife where she belongs — in your bed.'

The granite eyes probed him where he sat, fists balled upon his knees, their knuckles whitening as did his dewlaps, while he digested this, breathing through his still half-open mouth adenoidally to achieve, 'I can guess with whom she is consoled — that Swedish pup of an adventurer!'

'Guesswork,' his mother told him calmly, 'is not proof. And were proof enough produced, it might redound more to your discredit than to hers. Who would blame her? Not your father's subjects warm in sympathy for your consort, who uncomplainingly and for so long has suffered your blatant infidelities.'

'No,' he gave a grunt, 'not uncomplainingly. She's a vixen in her tempers.' He glanced down at his leg which, under its white stocking, showed trace of a fading bruise. 'But if you think it diplomatic to resume cohabitation, which by — um — by mutual consent has been deferred…' He hoped by this to turn attention from his 'concubine' and the daughter she had borne him. Did the old witch, he wondered, know that, who knew too much already? 'I will,' he finished lamely, 'demand access to her apartments.'

'Which she has locked against you?'

A silence fell, broken at last by the duchess, who had taken a volume that lay on a table beside her chair. Holding the book myopically close to her large Stuart nose, she read in English:

'I was never once and do commend their resolution who never marry twice: not that I disallow of second marriages, as in cases of polygamy.' Which applies, of course, only to the male sex, not to the female,' she glanced up to inform him. *'The whole world,'* she continued, *'was made for man.'* Once more her eye pinioned her goggling son. 'With that, and in all due respect to Sir Thomas Browne, who wrote this, I disagree, but I, with him, would also be content to wish there were some way to perpetuate the species other than the most foolish, vulgar and, in view of the position of the pair, when seen in cooler senses after the event, is the most ridiculous. None the less —' she froze George Louis with a glare to halt his giggle — 'when a man occupies

so high an elevation such as yours, he owes a duty to his wife and future duchess.'

The inference of this homily, in that he might find himself cuckolded, sent him hot-foot to Sophia Dorothea, bearing in mind his mother's final injunction: 'Be tactful. Go gently. Whatever you do, you must not accuse her on suspicion, lest she retaliate to turn the tables upon you. Endeavour to persuade her that you are anxious to be reconciled. Assume, as Shakespeare gives it, a virtue if you have it not.'

Unannounced by his order to his wife's boudoir, so-named, and decorated in the French fashion he deplored — 'all this gilt baroque and what-not' — he found her at her tambour frame. At his entrance, which dispensed with its usual formality on the few occasions of his visits, she looked up sharply.

'What do you want?'

A bad beginning but, striving, as advised, to be tactful, he persevered. Standing before her, legs apart, his squat body squared: 'I've been thinking —'

'A new departure for you,' she broke in, addressing the tambour frame.

Ignoring this he stifled an unconscionable urge to box her ears — a saucy piece! — and went on doggedly, '— that it's about time we came together again. We can't live as strangers for ever. People talk, you know. After all, you are my wife.'.

At this, to gain time, she re-threaded her needle while her thoughts like scared birds soared panic-stricken; and although her heart drummed at her ribs, she said collectedly, 'You've taken long enough to remember it.'

'Here, come on.' He made a clumsy attempt to raise her chin. 'We owe a duty to each other and to the State. Let bygones be bygones.'

At the touch of his fumbling fingers, his face bent to hers preparatory to kiss, she sprang to her feet, her cheeks aflame.

'And let byblows be byblows? Is *that* your duty to ourselves and to the State? Do you think now, after all these years of your neglect and exploitation of your women — yes! She, who is brought to bed of your bastard — she whom you endow with all *my* worldly goods — is that what you would cover up by making me your scapegoat so that people cease to talk?'

All the pent-up misery of her life with him, and her fear of an abhorred relationship renewed, erupted in a torrent of recriminatory abuse until he, in the shocked surprise of her discovery, lost control to seize her by the throat that, in the heat of fury, might have caused a strangulation had she not clawed at his hands with her nails to draw blood.

'God blast you!' he shouted, releasing her, who made a bolt for the door, saying between gasps for breath:

'This is the end. I go to Celle now — at once — and will never come back! Never, *never*, never!'

At each repetition of the word her voice rose upon a scream to bring Knesebeck running, and others of her women including the Porcupine, to give full account of this marital explosion to a gleeful Platen.

The daughter of Celle could scarcely have chosen a worse time to have rushed to her father with an outrageous account of a scene with her husband that savoured of assault and attempted homicide.

George William, beset with anxiety concerning his campaign in Flanders and already impoverished by the fortune and lands bestowed upon his brother who had treacherously made overtures to France, was in no mood to heed her or her hysterics. 'He almost killed me, the brute, in his rage! Look at this.' She showed her father the bruises on her throat. 'He would have strangled me had I not dragged his hands away…' She forbore to tell the duke how in self-defence she had clawed her husband's face to draw blood. 'Oh, Father, you will never know what I have suffered in this wretched marriage which you forced upon me. For God's sake help me to end it. I have ample evidence for divorce. He has a child by the Schulenberg, who is wife to him in all but name. I have been physically and mentally maltreated and abused, and now — *now* — all but murdered! You have given him and his father the inheritance that should be mine —'

'And still is yours.' George William seized upon this side issue to stem the cataclysmic tide crashed upon him by this girl of his who surely was possessed. His skin rose in goose pimples as he essayed feebly to remind her: 'All your husband's wealth is yours.'

'Mine? I, who have not enough for my personal needs nor for those of my servants unless I go begging for it while he and his father squander your — *my* fortune on their women. Have you no love, no pity for me that you can stand by and see me so humiliated and degraded? Father, I implore you to help me to divorce him. I *must* be released from this hell which is my marriage. I must — I must!'

'You are out of your mind,' her father apoplectically exclaimed. 'What you ask is madness. Divorce? God in Heaven! Would you disgrace our name? He would defend it and bring a counter-charge against you.'

'No! How could he?' She, who had been kneeling to him, struggled to her feet. 'He has no evidence against me.'

'Has he not?'

The duke was in a stare and his daughter in a fright. Had the Platen's spies been here before her with their poison? Yes, and

Bernstorff always at her father's elbow to give him the Platen's worst construction on her meetings with Philip which, save for that once...

'Come, come,' the harassed duke broke in upon revivification of 'that once', recalled with closing eyes and parted lips. 'Let us have no more of this nonsense.' He resorted to paternal tactics to treat it as such and she as a recalcitrant child. 'All our marriages have their ups and downs. Even the happiest, as is mine with your dear mother, may have their disagreements. Go back to your husband. Take example from your excellent aunt, the duchess, who accepts with dignity proper to her high estate the, er, indulgences that are permissible in princes, as with her cousins of England. Be sensible and, er, circumspect. That's my dearest daughter.'

She jerked away from him. 'I'm sick to death of that old hag's cousins of England,' cried his 'dearest daughter', stamping her foot, narrowly to escape the duke's most painful corn encased in its velvet shoe. 'If that's all the sympathy and help you can offer, you can keep it. You —' she was tearful now — 'you're an unnatural father. I thought you loved me, but I see you never loved me. You love nothing but your horses and your hounds. You don't even love Mother or you would listen to her. She wants me to leave him. *She* knows what misery I've suffered. But you — you don't care — you don't *care*!' With which, sobbing wildly, she dashed from the room.

So that was the end of that.

Back again to Hanover along those twenty dreary miles, bone-shaken, jolted in her four-horse coach she went, to find Knesebeck anxiously waiting to hear the result of her visit to Celle. She told it in her bed, cosseted and comforted with a soothing tincture of cowslip and lavender waters and myrrh, washed down with a cup of white wine. Pulling faces between sips and the query, 'What witch's brew is this?' the confidante heard: 'So here I am, thrown out by my father who won't listen to me or my mother. She implored him to let me stay at Celle, at least while the prince and I could come to terms — whether to part, not by divorce but by mutual consent or separation. He wouldn't listen to her — roared at her — my darling dear mother. He has changed, Lennie, he is entirely different from how he used to be. You know how Mother and I could make him do anything we wanted —'

'Except to prevent your marriage.'

'Yes, that is when Bernstorff and the Platen got together to work upon him through my uncle, egged on by his old bitch —!'

'Highness, dear!' was the feeble protest, ignored.

'Who descended on us like a hurricane and drove away my other cousin and his father, already at our gates. So how am I to endure it, how to go on living with him as his wife who am no wife! I can't. Here, take this beastly stuff —' she gave the half-empty cup to Knesebeck — 'and I'll go hang myself!'

The confidante, who had heard similar threats of self-destruction during her years of devoted attendance, contributed her quota of sympathetic murmurs, and then said that which she had been burning to say: 'It is fortunate Your Highness was at Celle these last two nights, to spare you more — distress.'

'Why, what's happened?' Her first torturing thought was for Philip. 'Is he — the count —?'

'No, no,' came the hasty assurance, 'nothing of Count Königsmarck.'

'Has he written?'

'Not since his last letter, the day before you left. There cannot be another for a week at least. No, my love, it is not of him, God be praised: It is,' she paused to weigh her words in evident enjoyment, 'of some — unpleasantness that occurred between the Crown Prince and Prince Max.'

'Were they drunk?'

'No, Madame, only perhaps — sufficiently,' was the hesitant reply, 'to have loosened their tongues. Prince Max expressed his grievance against the duke's intention to enforce their primo-genitals — is that the word?'

'Almost but not quite,' Sophia Dorothea answered with a giggle. 'So Max was at it again, was he?' Forgetful of her own immediate grievance, she expectantly sat up to hug her knees. 'In what way did he express it?'

'He accused the Crown Prince of stealing his birthright, and oh, Madame,' Knesebeck announced with relish, 'they came to blows.'

'Do you mean they fought?' was hopefully asked. 'How do you know? You weren't there.'

'Major Moltke, who is in waiting on the duke in the count's absence —'

'Yes, but how does Major Moltke come into it? Was he drunk too?'

'Oh, no, Your Highness!' A blush to the eyebrows accompanied this denial. 'The major is always in command of himself — such perfect manners!'

'Which,' quizzed Her Highness, 'he seems to have exercised on you.' And watching the blush deepen to the colour of an albino beetroot, 'What happened then?'

What happened then, as recounted by Knesebeck, was the intervention of the major between the combatants, but not before the prince had been given a black eye.

'Which prince?' was asked with a quickening of interest.

'The Crown Prince, Madame. His nose, they said, was out of shape.'

'Which might possibly improve it,' said Madame with a grin. 'And then?'

'Then, Madame, Major Moltke took Prince Max away and the Crown Prince, whose nose was bleeding, swore at him and he said — they heard him say — "Don't be a fool!", they are great friends, you know —'

'Who are great friends? I don't follow you. Did the major tell the Crown Prince not to be a fool?'

'I am sorry, Highness dear,' said the still blushful confidante. 'I know I tell it badly. It was the major told Prince Max not to be a fool, and "bide your time", he said, "he's not your man", and "time will show".'

'Is that all?'

'All that I was told, Madame.'

'Oh,' said 'Madame', disappointed, 'I thought there might be more to come.'

There was a great deal more to come, as time did show.

PART THREE (1692-1694)

SEVEN

From the dispatches of Sir William Dutton Colt:

The gates have been shut for two days in Hanover accompanied by great consternation. The two Moltkes were brought to Court under guard where they are kept and their papers taken. Next day Prince Max and certain of his gentlemen were also secured and placed under guard and none of his servants suffered to come near him ... The Duke said publicly that there were designs against his person and his government. Many stories are dispersed about...

From reports relayed by those who witnessed it, the first of the many stories to cause 'great consternation' took place at Herrenhausen in the duke's gaming room. We can picture the scene.

At the hazard table sat the duke. Having dined and liberally wined, he was in jovial humour to challenge his opponent, Count Moltke, elder brother of the major. The domed ceiling decorated with painted nudities of dryads, nymphs and satyrs, appeared to be in perpetual motion from the blaze of firelight and candles reflected in the diamond buttons of the duke's red velvet coat. The dice rattled merrily, the duke raked in his winnings; Count Moltke's face grew long and the duke's pile of gold grew high as the ivory cubes bounced and slid and clicked and rolled on the green baize. Behind the duke's chair stood the major in attendance, and saw his brother's face turn pale as curds. Looks were exchanged between the pair when the count put down his last hundred, and the duke, gulping a goblet of ale, told him heartily, 'If I've played you out. I'll lend you this to play you in!' He handed a fistful of coins across the table to the count, who rose to bow his thanks.

'Serene Highness is too gracious. You have nothing but my word to square the debt.'

'I'll take your word for it.' He gestured a servant. 'Wine to the count.'

His glass was refilled, the watchers gathered close; the count won the toss and threw two sixes.

'What did I say?' His Highness was jubilant. He could afford to lose having won three thousand.

The Count rose up to bow again and tender him his winnings. 'My debt to Your Most Gracious Highness is honoured.'

'No, no!' The pile of thalers was returned. 'You may yet require a loan. The night is young. The play goes on.' His Gracious Highness leaned back in his chair, belched, and fumbled in his pocket for his snuff-box. 'Damn! I have lost it!'

The major promptly offered his. The duke got up, saying as he took the jewelled trifle, 'I need to relieve myself,' and went into an inner room, where his favourite bulldog came to meet him. 'Here, boy, have a taste of this.' His slightly inebriated Highness shoved a snuff-stained finger on the lolling tongue to see, in the flash of a second, that tongue turn blue; the dog tottered and flopped down, its head on its paws, and those eyes, just now so full of life, were glazed and dying.

'Oh, my God! My God!' Forgetful of his need that caused a leak to wet his breeches, the duke was on his knees beside the fallen body. 'My dog,' he blubbered, 'my good dog is dead. He's dead! Poisoned. Who has given him to eat? Who has killed my dog?'

Servants came running, the two Moltkes hastening, and Max, hearing the commotion, lounged from an anteroom to enquire, 'What *is* all this to-do?'

All that 'to-do' resulted in the arrest of the Moltke brothers for attempted assassination of the duke. Rumour elaborated the death of the dog as having been poisoned by snuff intended for the duke, but in point of fact the dog died, coincidentally, a natural death of heart failure according to one Jägermeister, the duke's Master of Hounds and a friend of Max. The duke stayed unconvinced. The dog was old, certainly, but not ailing. He ate well, had never been subject to heart attacks; so Max likewise was arrested on the assumption that he had persuaded Jägermeister to diagnose death from natural causes. Bulldogs, said the Master, were known to have weak hearts. He had seen similar cases of sudden deaths in bulldogs. But although no direct evidence of an attempt on the duke's life could be produced against the Moltke brothers, nor of contemplated patricide on the part of the duke's son, all three were detained in custody awaiting trial as perpetrators-in-chief of a plot to undermine the authority of the duke and his government.

Revolt was in the air. The suspected conspirators, and primarily the prince, were alleged to be implicated in a plot to oppose, by force if needs be, the act of primogeniture that had cropped up again, a hardy annual bearing bitter fruit for Max. He had adherents among the duke's subjects, in particular the Hanoverians who wished to see justice done in support of the younger brothers of George Louis. He was universally disliked, and Max the people's darling.

Locked in his room where none, not even his mother, was permitted to see him, his, food sent from the kitchens by the duke's servants, his own personal valet denied entrance, and no exit from the window which was far too high for escape with no foothold by which he might have climbed down were it possible, Max cursed his father for having brought him to this pass.

On his knees before an image of the Blessed Virgin, he prayed the Mother of God to intercede on his behalf and for those others, so wrongfully accused. His recent conversion to the Church of Rome, that had horrified the duchess and caused the duke a brainstorm, gave further rise to suspicion concerning his son's part in the plot. It was assumed he had become a Catholic in order to ingratiate himself with Louis of France, thus to secure a powerful advocate in his favour to oppose the duke's intent to deprive his younger sons of their heritage. That's as may be, but certain it is that Max and the French envoy were, as Clara put it to the duke, 'as thick as thieves'.

Ready to believe the worst of Max, the duke listened agog to her insinuations. The Platen had never forgiven or forgotten the mischievous prank Max had played upon her, squirting pea-water in her face to hold her up to ridicule in front of half the court. Were the duke disposed to deal less harshly with his erring son, Clara saw to it that to him no quarter would be granted. Nor was Max the only fly to be caught in her web spun with infinite patience to capture unwary victims. The opportunity to involve Sophia Dorothea in the plot against the duke was not likely to be missed by Clara von Platen.

'But she can't bring her into it!' fumed Max, striding up and down his empty room when this latest development had been conveyed in a basket of fruit from Sophia Dorothea where he found a hidden note. Since none of his servants was allowed in attendance, she had contrived that her French chef should concoct delicate dishes to vary the monotony of the food served him by order of the duke. In this way messages passed back and forth unknown to the ducal servants, who implicitly obeyed instructions but may have chosen to turn a blind eye to gifts from the Crown Princess.

'Madame! Madame!' A distracted Knesebeck had much to tell her mistress. 'Major Moltke — he has been questioned — under torture, it is said — to betray his associates and among them you, my darling, you!'

'Of course,' was the calm reception of this scarifying news. 'I have expected it. The Platen has only been waiting to have me locked up and my head on a charger.'

'*How* can you take it so lightly?' cried the confidante. 'He, I tell you, he's been tortured, flogged by the duke's guards to make him talk, but he wouldn't speak, not one word passed his lips, as so his brother. Count Moltke, told me.'

'You have seen Count Moltke?'

'Yes, Madame, the count has been allowed his freedom on parole. He is most anxious that you should leave Hanover. You are not safe here. He begs me to persuade you to go to Celle. They can't touch you there when you are in the care of the duke, your father. Oh, my dear one, do listen to your Lennie. Heaven knows what they will do to you if you stay here.'

'What can they do to me more than they have done to Max — lock me up? But whatever their accusations against me, I have always let it be known that I am heart and soul with Max and the younger boys in their fight to preserve their heritage. Whatever they should do to me, I will not,' declared Sophia Dorothea, 'go to Celle. Not after my father refused to hear my appeal that he should help free me from the prince. Besides, if I were at Celle how could Philip write to me there? It would take ages to send a message to tell him where I am and all his letters coming here to Hanover.'

'I could stay to receive the letters, Madame, until —'

'Don't be silly. They would want to know why you are not in waiting on me. I won't have that old Porcupine or anyone but you. Besides the Platen would soon smell a rat. I'll be bound she is sniffing at your letters already, having one or two a week — you who had only one or two a year from your sister. No, you'd have to come with me, but I'll not go. Let them throw me into prison along with the major — to hang.'

'Dear God!' cried Knesebeck paling. "The major to *hang!* No, never!'

'Is it nothing to you if *I* hang, so long as the perfect mannered major does not?' Two little front teeth became visible in the smallest of grins. 'My poor Lennie, how your heart is torn with what I hope is love not unrequited. But cheer up. They won't hang me. They will cut off my head, being royal, and I'll put in a word for the major that they cut his head off, too. Quicker and more polite than hanging.'

'Madame!' protested Lennie whose pallor had been replaced by a blush of *vieux rose* at that teasing suggestion of unrequited love, naughtily and incorrectly surmised, since the major, a bachelor of forty-five, had a predilection for boys and tame lizards which he kept in glass cages, a singular hobby. 'How can you take it so lightly? I do entreat you be advised by Count Moltke, who only suggests what the major has urged — that you be removed from danger.'

'How many more times am I to tell you — *no!* Listen to this.' She drew from its concealment in the bosom of her gown the latest letter from Königsmarck. 'He says, *I received your answer today* — that means it has taken a month to reach him, and that the suspense of waiting for a word from me has made him ill. He says he hopes to see me soon — which means that he will be coming back. He asks for two words only in reply. How could I write to him from Celle? There is none there I could trust to have my letters delivered if you stayed behind here to collect his. So, you see, I cannot go to Celle.'

Nor did she go to Celle. Her parents came to Hanover for the carnival, since plot or no plot against the duke and his government, the annual festivities must go on.

Max, still a prisoner, had been sent to the castle of Hamelin, and after interminable arguments and blustering denials that he had no hand in the plot was finally released on condition that he would submit to the paternal mandate, with, however, his own and private reservations. But since a scapegoat must be found on whom to wreak the duke's vengeance, and despite all pleas from Max, Major Moltke, as Colt laconically reports, 'was executed on Monday. The court has gone to Luisberg to be out of the way.'

And Königsmarck was back again in Hanover.

A trail of letters, as of a paper chase, preceded Philip's return at the height of the Carnival. The streets were thronged with gaping yokels, masqueraders, mummers in the skins of wild beasts or disguised as Turks, Chinamen, blackamoors, or with monstrous heads of animals perched upon their shoulders. Wagons loaded with roaring merrymakers lumbered through those narrow cobbled ways while the watchers from the bedecked doors and windows, roared and sang and shouted in unison with a noise to hit the sky. Snow fell; it was winter, and soon a snowman swathed in white cotton came riding on a gaily caparisoned mule, followed by a horde of urchins pelting him with snowballs. In the Leine Schloss the duke and duchess entertained their guests, if with less abandon with much lavishment of food and drink at banquets, balls, and levies. At all of these Sophia Dorothea was the centre of attraction.

Visiting princes from neighbouring duchies, English noblemen and foreign envoys vied each for the favour of the lovely Crown Princess, while Philip stood apart and gnawed his thumb, consumed with jealousy.

He had been warned by Knesebeck, cloaked and hooded, clogged as a peasant with a basket on her arm who called on him in secret at his house, that on no account must he pay more than courtesy attention to the Crown Princess.

'Her mother, the duchess,' said the palpitating Knesebeck, 'is suspicious, has an inkling — heaven knows how, from the Platen, doubtless, with her evil mischief-making — that there is a — a *something* between you and Her Highness. The duchess has been lecturing the princess, has told her she must not speak to you more than a passing word as she would speak to any other gentleman at court. Her Highness begs me to tell you this. And I am also to let you know that the Crown Prince has the measles.'

'The measles? What in hell,' demanded Philip, 'do I care if he has the plague!'

'Because,' bleated Knesebeck, 'Her Highness's mother, the duchess, says she must visit the Crown Prince while he is ill and show him some wifely concern.'

'Wifely concern be damned!' said Philip, boiling. 'What concern has he ever shown to her? Tell Her Highness that I forbid — no, wait, I'll write it and you can take the letter. But if you think,' he eyed her over top to toe, a twinkle dawning, 'that your hood and clogs and whatnot would deceive a cow, much less my porter, you're mistaken.'

'Your porter, Count,' said Knesebeck in considerable fret, 'seems to be quite satisfied in allowing me to pass with eggs in my basket for you.'

'He is well paid for his satisfaction, to say nothing of the eggs, new-laid, which are hard to come by at this time of the year. Now sit.' He gestured her to a chair. His boarhound, lying on the rug, got up to sniff at her who drew back in alarm.

'He is only making sure you are a friend and not an enemy. Here, Boris,' he snapped fingers to call him to heel; and the great dog came to him and sat on his rump while Philip wrote in frenzied haste.

I am extremely surprised to learn from the 'Confidante' that your mother has been preaching at you … It is cruel to think that while everybody can make love to you and you can speak to whom you will, I am the only one excluded … I believe all the fiends plot against us but they will not succeed so long as you remain faithful, yet I fear they will terrify you so that in the end they will succeed … How I hate them! And I can only implore you to hate all those who are working against me … Everyone plots against me, men, demons, even an old woman (a stab here at the Platen) *who is worse than any demon.*

Almost daily came similar outbursts that might have been written by a schoolboy in the throes of first love; but Philip, who had admitted to have had 'a hundred women', *was* in the throes of first love. His tempestuous wooing in extravagant letters addressed to the 'Confidante' while the Duchess of Celle was at Hanover were his only means of communication with Sophia Dorothea.

To the long-suffering Knesebeck she unburdened: 'They already suspect me of plotting against the duke; and the Platen, having failed-to implicate me and have my head cut off for high treason would go to any length to ruin me. Well, let them! Let them do their worst. He and I won't be here to face it. Tell him I will go with him any time, anywhere — to the ends of the earth if he wants me. He *says* he wants me but all I ever hear from him now are reproaches and complaints because of my coolness to him when we meet. How can I be anything else but cool, with Mother always preaching at me and the Platen always spying on me? Hear this, his latest.' She scrabbled among a heap of letters on the table and snatching one she read: '*With what grief have I learned you have been in other arms but mine.*' From whom has he heard *that*? And in whose arms does he think I have been? He was glaring at me last night because I spoke to the French Ambassador's attaché, a pimply boy who breathed garlic all over me. Does he think I'd go to bed with *that*?'

'Perhaps,' ventured Knesebeck, 'because of your visits to the prince while he has the measles.'

'Only because my mother insisted, and no matter if *I* catch the measles. Does he think I and the prince sleep together, he who hates the sight of me as I of him — and a sorry sight he is now that he's peeling. And why,' she swung round to ask, 'did you have to tell him I visit the prince? You might have known how he would take it. He is even jealous of my page. And listen to this,' She took up another letter. 'He says he has approached my mother in the hope that she will receive him more kindly and that I will cease to boycott him. He must be mad! Knowing she is moving heaven and earth to keep us apart. And here's something else. *I implore you arrange for me to see you tomorrow. I hovered outside your apartments last night for an hour to see if the 'Confidante' would come out. I wanted to knock at your back door, but I dared not …* Why didn't you come out? Now, tonight when all the court have retired, wait for him. You know the side entrance in the garden the way you always go? Wait there. In the dark. And bring him to me. You must get a message to him. How? I don't care how. Anyhow! Honestly, Lennie, you are the greatest fool. He will be in the ballroom for certain. Standing in corners and foaming with rage if I speak to or dance with anyone. I can't dance with him but *you* can … very well then, you must *make* him. And tell him there will be a candle in my window to let him know it is safe for him to come and he had better be disguised … how should I know what sort of disguise? A beard, horns if he likes, only for heaven's sake don't let him come in his evening clothes and glittering with jewels. Don't let him go knocking at my door, or any door. Doesn't he know there are sentries marching up and down? Well, you must manage it somehow, or *he* must. Tell him he can climb up the tree … of course, there's a tree with branches at my anteroom window … oh, God, was ever woman so cursed as I with such an idiot! All these years and you didn't know there was a tree! Tell him I'll be waiting.'

The last of the guests at that night's levée had gone; the dukes and their duchesses retired to their respective beds. The palace, wrapped in silence, slept, and no sound stirred save the muffled tramp of sentries at the main entrance gates.

Under the windows of the Crown Princess the lawns masked in velvet beneath a sky, star-studded, held spears of silver interspersed with shadows strangely shaped; formless some, or gnome-like, dwarfed or elongated others. One, more slightly solid than the rest, emerged from the brooding dark that pulsed with life unseen, untamed: the savage cry of a swift night-flying creature, the death shriek of the small captured prey, an owl's solemn hoot and a hush, fear-fallen. Tree branches traced a patterned frieze across the moon-tranced sky and at one window of the sleeping palace the single light of a candle wavered, while from the darkness came a whisper. 'Léonisse…'

In the joy of their reunion, when words and touch had been forbidden while they had hungered for each other during this past week that to them was an eternity, only the throb of hot blood in their veins spoke for them.

At last: 'Beautiful mouth! How I have longed for you. How I have been tortured to know that you can go to him who has the right to name you wife and are no wife. You are mine — *my* wife. O, God, if it could be!'

'How could it ever be, unless…'

'Unless,' he finished for her, 'you are prepared to keep your promise delivered by the 'Confidante' to come with me and be my love — for ever. Aurora would help us find a haven far from here in some other land where we would be unknown.'

'Yes … that is how I had thought to be with you, for ever, but —' his hand had wandered to her breast, its tender stalk uprisen to the love-play of his lips to drown sense — 'although, believe me, love, I would —' her words fainted on an indrawn breath — 'but I cannot. How can I leave my children?'

He drew his mouth from delicious exploration of her body that had quickened in response to his. 'You would have *my* children — mine! I see my children in your eyes.'

'My children are my life — my all.'

He flung himself away from her. 'If they are your life, your all, then what am I? If you cannot leave them begot by him whom you *hate,* am I no more than a passing adventure to console you for his negligence, a *tu quoque* retort to save your pride, one of many who will follow me when I'm discarded?'

'Don't dare to say it!' She caught at a curl of his long disordered hair that fell about his naked shoulders. Viciously she tugged. 'How can you say it? Are you my pander as you are the Platen's? Is that what you would say?'

'Great God! Only hear her! Can't you understand?' Wincing, he disentangled a curl entwined about her fingers. 'Let be. Would you have chunks of my hair out by the roots? How do you suppose I can endure the torment of knowing that you and he ... I can't! *I* would renounce all for you. My family, my whole career, everything. Why do you give me hope? Why tell Knesebeck that you would come with me, to the ends of the earth — words, words! — to bring me here by stealth and then retract. To make of me your fool!'

'I didn't. I do not retract. It is only — you must give me time.'

'There is no time.' He had left their couch and was pulling on his shirt. His chest, smooth and hairless as a child's, shone luminous in the dim light of the candle burned to its wick in the window where the curtains were now close drawn. In white-hot rage he faced her. 'I cannot and *will* not endure these secret meetings stealing to you by back doors. This continuous subterfuge is hell for me!'

'For me, too. You think only of yourself. Not of me!'

They were absurd. They suffered, they died, were resurrected. He, the first to capitulate when, her head sunk in her pillows, she was rent with soundless sobs to bring him beside her on his knees.

'My darling. My love. My life! Forgive ... I am out of myself. I can no longer think. Do with me as you will. I am yours utterly. I'll do anything you want. Anything, so long as I may see you even if I have to climb up trees like a baboon. You ask for time. Don't turn from me. Hear this. I'll give you time. There's a time for everything, a time to love, a time to hate, a time for war, a time for ... Listen. The duke, whose Electorate is within his grasp, has declared for the Allies against France. I knew he would turn again to the Allies having failed to get what he asks of Louis. The duke must keep on the right side of the emperor if he wants to wear the bonnet. He sent for me tonight — I'm telling you this, it's for you to decide — don't interrupt —' as she caught at his arm, her mouth opened to speak — 'the duke has ordered a mobilisation of troops to go forward with all speed to Flanders, and I am commanded to lead with my regiment.'

'No!' Her heart gave a startled jerk. 'You aren't going? To make me suffer as before when I went in daily dread of hearing you were killed in the Morea where we lost Charles. The torture of it! I can't go through *that* again.'

'You will not have to if you make up your mind now. We could escape together. Knesebeck will keep watch. I have a post-chaise at the ready. I am prepared to give up my all if you will give up your children.'

He felt the shudder of her body in his arms.

'Desert! You would desert?' came from her loosened lips. 'They would find and capture you — you would be shot.'

'I'll risk that to have you. But they will never take me and I'll not be shot.' His arms tightened round her. A laughing breath escaped him. 'You know we Königsmarcks have nine lives.'

A thin ghost of dawn crept through the darkened room, and in that first greying light her eyes were wide with terror.

'You — to desert!' her voice, shock-charged, lashed out at him. 'You, the soldier, a daredevil, to whom the love of war, the fight of man to man and sword to sword is ecstasy beyond all love of women! That I know. Aurora told me so. If you Königsmarcks have nine lives, those lives — as Charles once said — are dedicated to Mars, not Venus. No, Philip, no! I cannot let you sacrifice yourself, your honour — for it would be sacrifice if they allowed you to live, for even if I gave up all for you as you for me that we could be together in some distant land, the time would come when you might regret — would tire of so inactive a life. You would be,' a spark of humour gleamed, 'like some old war horse who, scenting battle at a bugle call, lifts his head and gallops off to the end of the field to return in the sulks, head down. My father had an old war horse at Celle who used to do that. Do you remember? No, whatever fate decides, you must not shirk your duty.'

A long heart-beating pause, then: 'It is not for the fates but for you to decide … if you will have it so.'

Did she detect behind that slow acceptance a note of eagerness, relief which, although she might resent it, she applauded to bring from her the answer: 'It kills me to say it — for *your* sake not mine — but you must go.'

Within a week of this meeting and with no opportunity to meet again in private, Königsmarck, in command of his regiment, and George Louis commanding the Hanoverian troops were on the march to join the Allies. During this time the correspondence between 'Tercis' and his 'Léonisse' continued unabated.

Back and forth, full gallop on their steaming horses went the couriers bearing letters from the pair of them, alternating between mutual adoration and frenzied doubts and fears. She *spends her nights without sleep and her days weeping over their separation.* She implores him *to be constant as she will be faithful.* (Neither, for all their protestations, is very sure of the other.) She *will live for him only,* he is *loved to idolatry,* etcetera.

If he, on active service, does not go without sleep nor spend his days weeping over separation from his 'goddess' whom he 'worships', she is comforted to know he is her *slave and wears her chains with joy.* Yet if, as sometimes happens, her letters are delayed, his chains are joy no longer but a torture.

Panting couriers bring evidence of unreasonable jealousy. She is accused of flirting with 'foreigners', the envoys of Austria and Italy when she attended a fête given by Sir Richard Dutton Colt. She 'drives him to madness'. He threatens suicide. He will *hasten to the front of la Grande Armée and seek a glorious death.* Then she can boast her unfaithfulness has killed him ... *Cruel one, God will punish you!*

In her reply to this she declares she can no longer bear his unjust suspicions. How could she avoid going to Monsieur Colt's fête? *I spoke very little to the Piedmontese and not a word to the Austrian'* ... she would *swear a thousand dreadful oaths* on her innocence!

Her 'dreadful oaths' may have caused him to believe she swears on her innocence too much.

A large number of letters have arrived at the camp and none from you except that you have been dancing at Monsieur Colt's fête. I will say no more. He says a great more. *I no longer doubt your inconstancy. I have neglected fortune, happiness, everything for you and you treat me like this! ... I await your letter at Antwerp.*

And from her, at Antwerp, in highest indignation: *You are just the man to pick a quarrel about nothing ... I defy you to find fault with my conduct. You must surely see that it was not for the Count's* beaux yeux *that I lingered at Hanover. I am incapable of deceiving you even in thought ... You believe I betray you Time will prove my innocence and your injustice. Good-bye!*

They did not know themselves ridiculous, they only knew themselves in love and neither, nurturing suspicion of the other, was consoled by vows of eternal fidelity. She had accompanied her parents to Brockenhausen where Max was also staying. Released from detention at Hamelin Castle and more or less vindicated by his father from any involvement in the Moltkes' attempt on the duke's life, for which the major unjustly paid full penalty, Max was still undergoing parental mistrust for his opposition to the settlement of all the duke's territories on his elder son.

That Max at Brockenhausen occupied apartments adjoining those of Sophia Dorothea, gave Philip further cause for grievance; but these doubts appear to have been, in part, allayed since she tells him she finds Max 'stupider than ever'. This in one of five of her letters delayed by floods and arriving all in one batch to satisfy him that his 'wicked suspicions' are unfounded … *What! To suspect you of inconstancy! But, dearest, remember it springs from loving you too much.*

He is delighted to hear she finds Prince Max stupider than ever, who seems to have shown her more than a brotherly warmth of affection that may have been a trifle too warmly returned: yet since 'Tercis' is reassured on that score, *the only favour I ask of the gods is to be with you always in life, or death … I would sacrifice the world to kiss your divine mouth. I am yours body and soul.* And so on *ad infinitum.*

All this to the great relief of the Confidante, who had begun to fear that the course of true love was running anything but smooth. Then, in the midst of letters full of 'joy and rapture', from the besotted Philip, in which all misunderstandings, wranglings and doubts were swept aside, comes news of the advance on Namur.

A siege! Grand dieu! she writes. *What terrors this has for me to think of you exposed to danger! All that I love, all the delight of my life is in deadly peril! I offer endless prayers for you…*

He needed them, for even before this frenzied scrawl had reached him he was in the thick of the fiercest battle of the century: Steinkirk.

The hitherto inviolate fortress of Namur had been stormed by Louis XIV before Dutch William, the British King, head of

215

the Grand Alliance, could summon his dilatory allies for its relief. Eighty thousand men stood between the English and the overwhelming forces of the French when William, in a desperate effort to gain the offensive, marched his whole army of British and Allied troops to surprise the enemy near Steinkirk. Although taken off his guard, the French general rallied the attack in the bloodiest fight within living memory, that left the French the victors by a narrow margin.

The news of the disaster came to Hanover within two days, to plunge the court in mourning for the death of many husbands, fathers, sons, killed or wounded. Sophia Dorothea, hearing of the battle, wrote frantically to Philip: *I shudder, I tremble! … I am beside myself, I hardly know what I am writing … I go in terrible fear of your life. I hate King William for he is the cause of it all.*

And then from him at camp near Wavern, his letter crossing hers: *Here I am again! I have escaped once more. Our troops did not come in for any fighting, but I did. I volunteered…* And goes on to tell her how he distinguished himself in the thick of the fight, attached to the Duke of Württemburg's regiment. He makes the most of this, for he was never behind to blow his own trumpet if none was there before to blow it for him.

I must tell you I took the precaution of sealing your letters in a packet with your portrait and gave them to an officer in my regiment with strict orders to burn them if I were killed…

More joy and hysterical raptures that did not escape the attention of the court. Whispers flew between the ladies.

'What a change is here! She went in tears, a positive Niobe, when she thought him missing, killed or wounded…'

'Yes, and writing and receiving letters to and from him by every post…'

'And what,' sniggered one, 'will Madame Platen say to that?'

What Madame Platen said to that gave Charlotte, Electress of Brandenburg, on a visit to her parents, the chance to bait Sophia Dorothea between whom and herself no love was lost. They walked together in the gardens of the Leine Schloss, attended discreetly at a distance by their women and a page. The bright harsh colours of the ladies' gowns were limned as in a living tapestry against a background of trees whose foliage, bereft of early summer freshness, had changed to the dark spinach green of late August. The heat of the day had wearied; shadows lengthened bringing cool refreshment to the parched grass of lawns. Light from a cloudless sky, that held the waning sun like a brazen shield, was reflected in the water where swans floated. One, with a trail of cygnets, came sailing, wings outspread, her beak expectantly wide for titbits.

'Hans!' The princess called to her following page. 'Bring me the croissants for the swans.'

'What,' asked Charlotte, 'are croissants?'

'Rolls shaped like horseshoes. My French chef makes them.'

'French! I wonder you employ an enemy as chef.'

'My chef is no enemy. He is my friend.' Sophia Dorothea edged away from the adhesive Charlotte, who was unsavourily breathing in her face. 'My mother brought him with her from Paris. He knew me before I was born.'

'The things you say!' giggled Charlotte. 'How could he have known you before you were born, unless,' with smiling spite, 'your mother knew him better before you were born than she knew my uncle.'

The princess flushed an angry red, but her retort to that was halted by the arrival of the page presenting a basket of bread for the swans.

'Thank you, Hans. Oh, dear!' She bent to examine a cut on his forehead. 'How did you do this?'

'I fell over a tree-stump in my hurry, Serene Highness. It is only a scratch.'

'There was no need to hurry, and it is more than a scratch. You must have it bathed and plastered. It is bleeding. Then you can come back and feed the swans! Run along now, and don't go falling over tree-stumps.'

And as obediently he ran along, 'I wonder,' Charlotte said, 'that you are so familiar with your servants — to pamper him over a scratch! But you always had a fancy for a page. I wonder —'

'What a one you are for wondering,' deftly interposed Sophia Dorothea as she broke a crust to throw to the mother swan; and setting down the basket, 'Shall we continue our walk? Hans will finish feeding them.'

'Talking of pages,' Charlotte persistently pursued, 'I was about to say that your page — or rather your father's former page — Count Königsmarck, has orders to be sent away.'

'Sent away?' was the echo, with careful indifference, while the heart of her listener froze. 'Why should the count be sent away?'

'You should know why.' Charlotte exposed two sharp canine teeth in her widening smile. 'Well, perhaps not sent away — politely told that his services should be offered to the Swedes. After all he *is* a foreigner and his first duty should be to his king and not to Hanover, although he fought for the Allies and his sister too —'

'His sister? Not his sister fighting for the Allies!' in vain attempt to stem the flow.

'No, of course not, but she has been told she won't be welcome here because of her reputation. She's notorious — the mistress of half a dozen European Princes and the latest is Prince Frederick of Saxony.'

'Indeed?' was remarked from out of a dry mouth. 'This is news to me.'

'I should have thought,' babbled Charlotte, beginning to enjoy herself as she noted the princess's pallor, 'that it would have been stale news to you considering all the letters you and her brother have been writing to each other during the whole of the campaign. It was rather ill-advised of him, I must say, to tell one of his officers to burn your letters and your portrait if he were killed at Steinkirk. You can't trust anyone in love — or war. And I regret to have to tell you,' said Charlotte in a tone of no regret, 'but I think you should be warned. Countess von Platen — how white you look. Do you feel faint? Would you like to sit down?'

'No. I — I am not faint. What of Countess von Platen?'

'Oh, she is most concerned to hear you have been in correspondence with Königsmarck and has told my father about it which points to some truth in the rumours that you and he are having an *affaire*. Not that my brother cares if you have a dozen *affaires*, knowing you are no longer bedmates and he is completely happy with his Ermengarde and his little son.'

'Daughter,' said the white lips of Sophia Dorothea.

'Is it a daughter? Or it might be a son, at least,' tittered Charlotte, 'not by George Louis. Now what was I saying? Ah, yes — the Platen has found out about your letters, and Father is furious because there must be no scandal if you are to be the Electoral Princess. Father has asked my husband to use his influence with the emperor and it is almost certain now that the duke will have the hat so you see how important it is that you and Königsmarck should not have anything more to do with each other. I only mention it for your sake, so you mustn't mind…'

For want of breath Charlotte's voice ran down. The pale princess found hers.

'I appreciate your — your interest and advice, but since it comes from Countess von Platen it has no foundation whatsoever. No letters,' blatantly she lied, 'have ever been exchanged between Count Königsmarck and myself. He would have no time nor opportunity to write letters to me or anybody else while on active service, and how could I write to him not knowing where he is? The whereabouts of the troops are, as you should know, carefully guarded.' And as Charlotte made attempt to interrupt, 'I feel I, in my turn, should warn you not to heed mischievous rumours circulated by that woman. You must realise that she has considerable influence with the duke and it is she who has persuaded him to cut you and your brothers out of their inheritance.'

This announcement was received with a startled jerk of Charlotte's head and the words, 'She wouldn't dare!'

'She would dare anything. Do you want to be done out of your territories that should be shared in equal rights between you all? Of course it is to my and my children's advantage if George Louis is given what should be yours, but I care nothing for that. I only wish to see justice done. And do you know why that woman —' Sophia Dorothea conspiratorially lowered her voice — 'has encouraged your father to deal so wrongly with you and your brothers?'

'Tell me why,' gasped Charlotte.

'Because,' desperation spurred conjecture that was nearer the mark than she guessed, 'because the Platen plans to marry her daughter to my son so that they or her grandchildren will come in for all the territories that should be yours and *your* children's inheritance.'

'No!' Charlotte seized on this. 'She can't surely aspire to — Oh, I see!' She took Sophia Dorothea by the arm. 'If her daughter — which may not be her husband's, we all know the duke — I oughtn't to say this — did have a child by her and it may well be his and not — how truly dreadful! Your son is years younger than — and such a plain lump of a girl. So that's why she influenced Father to disinherit us in favour of George Louis that her daughter may one day be the wife of the future Elector when our father dies. But I can't see why she should have made up a pack of lies about you and Count Königsmarck writing letters to each other, if she *is* telling lies —' Charlotte slid her a narrowed look — 'which can have nothing to do with the inheritance.'

'Ah, but —' circumvention was filtering out — 'if the duke refused to allow a marriage between my son and her daughter, a commoner, then she is likely to fall back on Königsmarck. He is enormously rich, as you know, and the Platen is a glutton for money. Your father has squandered much that should be yours and *all* of mine on her already.'

'Oh, no! We can't have that! I must write at once to my husband and tell him.'

'Yes, your husband should be told. I think I will sit down. I do feel a little faint. The heat...' They were passing a Gothic stone pavilion near to the water's edge.

'Yes, do. I will leave you to rest awhile. You are not pregnant, by any chance?' eagerly enquired Charlotte. For if so, and since it was known that she and George Louis had not cohabited for at least a year, or even two, then there must be certain truth in la Platen's allegations. So here was something more to tell her husband.

Sophia Dorothea closed her eyes. 'I'm not pregnant,' she said. *But,* with a fluttering heart she thought, *supposing I am?* It was possible. *His! Then nothing, nothing, not death itself could part us...*

Yet the tremble of her knees and the sickness in her stomach might have been the result of countering the shock of Charlotte's information that, if in doubtful good intent, paved hell for her ... *If not, then God send,* she prayed, *it may be so.*

The evening sun sinking to its glorious cremation dazzled her sight. Great amber clouds, rose-tinted, spread a brilliant mantle across the blue above, while the green below seemed to shine with iridescent splendour. The water sparkled as if a thousand golden coins were imprisoned in its depths. A dragonfly, a living flash of light, attracted by the brightness, settled for a moment on the leaf of a drooping willow, preened its wings and was away.

'I will leave you,' said Charlotte, hurrying off. 'I must write that letter to my husband.'

'Serene Highness.' Hans had come upon her there, so still and silent she might have been carved from the stone bench on which she sat. The boy's forehead was stuck with plaster. She roused herself to inspect him. 'Good, it has stopped bleeding. Now go back again and ask Fräulein von dem Knesebeck to attend me here. Then you can feed the swans. You will find the basket where I left it on the river bank.'

He sped to her bidding. In the distance her women were clustered in groups; some played at battledore and shuttlecock, but Madame von Ilten, 'the Porcupine', stood apart engaged in talk with a servant wearing the Platen's red-and-gold livery.

When Knesebeck arrived she said, 'We can't be overheard. Those gaggling fools are too far away; but do you see that man talking to the Porcupine? He is from Monplaisir. You remember Philip wrote that he couldn't come to see me before he left Hanover because one of the Platen's spies, a man named Mesbeck, was watching him? I expect this is he. Is there to be no end to this incessant spying on me and him?'

'Dearest,' Knesebeck seated herself and took the girl's hand in hers. 'The Countess always brings one or two of her servants with her when she visits the duchess. She is with Her Highness now.'

'Why should she visit the duchess? And why send her servant — if he is her servant — to talk with von Ilten, who is thick as thieves with the Platen?'

'The countess, holding a nominal position in attendance on the duchess, must have certain duties attached to her position. I beg you, darling, not to worry yourself needlessly.'

'I *am* worried, and not needlessly. Listen to this. The Electress has been with me and handed me a mouthful. I'll tell you…' And she told. 'You see,' when the recital was ended, 'it is certain our letters, mine and his, have been opened and read by that hell-cat. Otherwise how could they have known we have been in correspondence? You know how anxious I was when his letters were delayed, and mine too. How he raged at me for not writing, and then he received five in a batch.'

'But, Highness, all the count's letters arrived with the seals intact. And all his letters were addressed to me. I don't understand how she could have opened them and broken the seals without my having noticed it.' Knesebeck was now as greatly disturbed as her mistress.

'She could have broken the seals and had them copied — his special seal that he had made for his letters to me and mine to him, with a heart and our initials, T and L, entwined. There are no Ts nor Ls as far as I know, at court. But she with her spies could easily —'

'Madame,' broke in Knesebeck, 'I gave the letters myself to the duke's courier.'

'Yes, and how do we know he isn't one of hers, and if so is not above a bribe?'

'The duke's messenger!' exclaimed Knesebeck, aghast.

'And hers. Anything of the duke's is hers — his bed, his board, his wealth. *My* wealth. Wait! I know how we can thwart her yet — she and her spies!' The princess turned excitedly to the round-eyed Knesebeck. 'I'll have you address all my future letters to his sister, the Countess Aurora. And I'll have a different seal made. How quickly can one be made? But who would make it whom we could trust? *Grand Dieu!* She beat her hands together. 'How am I to bear it? All this subterfuge — this endless contriving. I am a coward. I should have escaped long ago. I should have gone to him that last night we had together. He wanted me to go with him — he had a post-chaise ready, servants, everything waiting. He would have given up all for me, and I failed him, but I'll not fail him again. When or if he comes back ... he *must* come back. They can't keep us apart for ever. Look!' She clutched Knesebeck's arm. 'Her man is going. I expect she has left the duchess and has sent for him to take her to her coach. Let us join the Porcupine. She's watching us. Hans is still feeding the swans. For heaven's sake, Lennie, don't look as if the devil were after us. We know Satan — or rather, she, Sathana, — is — but do learn to dissemble. Now as we pass von Ilten we must be talking. I haven't a notion what we can be talking of, for all I can think of is him!'

'Gowns!' was the confidante's suggestion. 'You remember Your Highness was dissatisfied with the embroidery on the sleeves of your new gown?'

So it was all of gowns; and Madame von Ilten, warily watching and hoping to hear something of interest, heard only, 'Yes, you will order the modiste to bring another style of embroidery for the sleeves...'

Two letters from Sophia Dorothea reporting her fears as result of what Charlotte had maliciously conveyed were received by Philip when at Charleroi, where the allied troops were awaiting an attack from the French which did not finally materialise. His reply to both these agonised epistles sent to him by Aurora from Saxony, is couched in even more than his usual exaggerated suicidal strain … *If they force me to leave you I will leave life itself…* Again he will *seek death to end my sorrows in the front of the fight … and if death does not decide my fate I will never abandon you, never … even though I were poisoned, massacred, beaten black and blue or burned alive…* After these heroics he decides that *my greatest grudge is against la Platen, on whom if I am to be robbed of my only joy, my divinity, my all, I will avenge myself … The first time I meet her off her dunghill I will insult her publicly that she will never dare to show her face again … I will give her to the bears to eat, lions shall suck her blood, tigers tear out her cowardly heart … Should their plan of sending me away come to anything you will see,* he threatens darkly, *what will happen.*

What did happen despite, these maledictions, was exactly nothing, although the catalogue of various revenges Philip intended to wreak upon la Platen must have greatly gratified Sophia Dorothea, but her hope that she might bear his child was not to be.

Meanwhile the duke, with the Electorate still in the balance, had more to engage him than the indiscretions of the Crown Princess.

'What if she has written a pack of love letters to Königsmarck?' he demands of his Clara, who had made the most of her findings. 'A couple of silly romantic young fools. He is far too good an officer for me to lose to Sweden, or to England, come to that. Marshal Podevils reports that William's Marlbrouck has his eye on Königsmarck. I have far too much to bother me,' the discomfited Clara was told, 'than to listen to a lot of balderdash about love letters! I thought you had more sense.'

'My precious heart,' soothingly she stroked his nose, 'how remiss of me to tell you what is indeed a lot of balderdash, but if King William's Marlbrouck should ask for Königsmarck I should let him go — if you take my advice.'

'Have I ever refused it?' Mollified he caught and kissed the stroking fingers. 'But Podevils will never agree to part with him. And now I must tell you that all is not so good for me with the College of Electors.'

At once she was on the alert.

He unfolded a parchment. 'The College has been in conference again. The Roman Catholic contingent are against me. They favour Bavaria to whom, at the peace of Westphalia, it was originally promised. Hear this...' And in his catarrhal throaty voice he read: '*We cannot deprive the Elector of Bavaria of what has been solemnly agreed to him.* And they go on to say: *For pretensions* — Pretensions! what insolence! — *of the Duke of Hanover there is no justification or excuse. The admission of a Lutheran would cause dissension between Protestant and Catholics.* Now you can understand why I was so bitterly against my rascally son's conversion to Rome. The Catholic Electors, although in the minority —' a dusky red of apprehension mottled his dewlaps — 'would have seized on the chance of replacing me with a Catholic and if not Bavaria, who is old and ailing, then Maximilian who, though my own flesh and blood, would be a menace to me and to my House!

'You should never have released him from imprisonment.' She did some rapid thinking. 'You must, and you will,' said she decisively, 'be given the Palatinate. This is what you must do. Agree to establish a Roman Catholic Church in all your dominions. Bavaria is three parts Catholic and Catholicism in Hanover is virtually nil. Then you must promote an Apostolic vicar here in your capital, and then — and *then* go hat-in-hand to the emperor and offer him more money and troops to assist him and so bring to an end this hellish war against France that impoverishes you and all the duchies of the Empire. Leopold has never yet refused financial aid. Go to him hat-in-hand, and you will return with the Electoral hat on your head! Serene Highness,' she knelt to him in homage of which, even from her, he could never have enough, 'be advised by one, the only one in your dominions and your life who has your interest and welfare at heart.'

Which was entirely true since his interest and welfare were her own. The more benefit to him, the more to her, even to the far distant possibility that her daughter, by a marriage to the son of that 'ninny', might become Queen Consort of England, and she, Clara von Platen, the grandmother of kings! That old hag of a duchess was not the only aspirant, she gloatingly reflected, for had not her daughter as much right to Britain's crown as any other — Guelph? And to the duke, whose podgy hand she held between her own to fondle, 'Highness, my beloved, lose no time for time is precious. Order your coach and go to the emperor — now!'

'Wonderful!' A garlic-flavoured gust was breathed into her face as his thick lips sucked at hers. 'What a diplomat is my honey-flower! If I return wearing the bonnet you will be crowned with jewels worth the emperor's ransom.'

'The only jewel I desire is this little token,' said his honey-flower, with an eye on a priceless emerald he wore on his forefinger, which would more than pay her recent card debts. She had inadvisedly taken to herself a beautiful blond young man from Denmark — she had always favoured

Scandinavians, and this one had proved to be sharper at cards than herself, 'Because you wear it always.' She touched the ring. 'It will go with me to my grave.'

'Don't talk of graves!' With some difficulty, for his hands were sweaty and the ring had stuck that he must lick his finger before he could get it off to slip it on her thumb, 'Take and wear this ring and know that my heart goes with it...'

The departure of the duke for Berlin gave the lovers opportunity, too long deferred, to meet again for one brief night. Sophia Dorothea had written to entreat him to come to her as soon as he could obtain leave. On receipt of this he wrote he would come to her at once, with or without leave, and risk the consequences. She was to expect him within the week and 'in mean disguise'.

He left the camp at Disk where the regiment was stationed, and not even his own servant knew he had gone. He went in the dress of a peasant and with this, as soon as he had passed the sentries, he covered his uniform. He wore a false beard and unkempt wig. It was a hazardous journey, not devoid of danger, for were his absence discovered he would be brought before the Field Marshal for a deserter; but danger was the spice of life for Philip. He lodged at various inns and managed to obtain a wash and shave at each halting place, although, after a shuddering inspection of bug-infested sheets, he preferred to sleep on floors.

He arrived in Hanover at nightfall. As before, the candle at her window guided him. A shadow among shadows, he crept through the enveloping dark, thankful for the moonless overcast sky. It had begun to rain, and a slight drizzle and the mist rising from the river gave him extra coverage. Knesebeck received him and brought him by devious ways to her lady's apartments.

In the joy of their reunion all petty disputes and suspicions were forgiven. 'It is only because I love you so much,' he said, 'that I am jealous of the very air you breathe. But as to those letters, I cannot understand how that she-devil, the Platen, could have intercepted them.'

'I can.' Her arms holding him in the aftermath of consummation loosened. 'She has her spies here in the palace among my women and my men — and yours, too. You spoke of a man, Mesbeck —'

'Yes, he is, or was, a servant to an officer of my regiment.'

'The same officer whom you asked to burn my letters to you and my portrait if, God forbid, you were killed?'

'It might have been. Let us forget it.' His lips played with hers. 'We have so little time together.'

'How can I forget? We must never forget that every precious moment, every word we write to each other may be watched and read. Oh, my love, my love,' her arms tightened round him again, 'I have thought and thought of ways and means to allay suspicion and quiet that woman's insatiable desire for you and her hate of me. There is only one way,' she told him in a choked little voice, "though it kills me to say it —'

'What, my darling, what?' He took her chin between his hands, gazing down into her eyes that clung to his with a feverish intensity. 'I would do anything for your protection and our love, even to go to her and make believe that I am willing to — to — to give her what she wants of me —'

She shuddered, drawing away from him. 'You read my very thoughts as in a book!'

'The print,' he kissed her mouth, 'is clear. Your eyes inscribe it. So, for our love's sake, I must degrade myself to pleasure her?'

'No degradation if to safeguard us and yourself.'

He said in wonder: "You are marvellous! Will I ever understand your sex, or you? How can you agree to a renewal of a relationship which from the beginning was nothing of my choice! She got me — that first time on my arrival here at the duke's ball when I was — was, er —'

Her small even teeth became visible in a fleeting smile. 'Somewhat tipsy?'

'Yes,' he shamefacedly admitted, looking like an overgrown schoolboy, 'and more than somewhat, but that was before I knew you were my life and my whole world. And now you throw me back at her whom I loathe and who revolts me to touch.'

'Not to — touch,' she said with whitened lips, 'only to flatter her, invite yourself to her salon, make her think I am just another of your —' she glanced up at him with mischief in her eyes that brought back the colour to her cheeks — 'your hundred women. The hundred and first.'

'Always the first! There has never been another. Never!' He clutched her to him. 'You don't know what you ask of me. My gorge rises at the very thought of her. Besides, when do you suppose I shall have the chance to visit her? I'll be suspended after this, no further leave granted, if nothing worse.'

'You can make your peace with Marshal Podevils. You are far too valuable an officer to suspend or punish. Tell him you have had a message from your sister, say she is dangerously ill and no time to be lost if you were to see her alive. That you were so concerned you could not even wait to ask permission.'

He started away from her. The worm of doubt, suspicion, crawled again. 'With what dark devilment are you possessed that you can offer me so glib a subterfuge to contrive that I present myself to Podevils with lies to shame my honour! You, so full of love-vows and now to drive me to her whom I abhor. In what other ways am I deceived?' He seized her wrist fiercely to twist it. 'Do you wish by artful conniving to be rid of me? Am I supplanted by one of those foreigners you received at Colt's fête,' his eyebrows shot up in furious mockery, 'with such royal *politesse* to one of whom you spoke no word, and with the other — as reported — you danced wonderfully!'

She heard him stunned, stabbed by a spiral of pain from her wrist. 'Let be, let be! You hurt —' He let fall her hand, while she, a flag of angry colour in each cheek, flared out at him. 'So you too have your spies! God's Grace,' eyes to heaven, she entreated, 'must he always mistrust me? I danced with no man at Colt's fête, and if I had, is that a sin? Can you not see that what I advise is more abhorrent to me than to you? But if we are to safeguard ourselves and our love — should any love be left to us, for where there is mistrust there can be no love — Ah, forgive me,' childishly she pleaded, her mouth in a tremble, 'you make me say what I wouldn't dream of saying only you torment me with your doubts and accusations. Your letters are full of them.'

He gathered her into his arms. 'Only because I fear that every man who sees you, unless he be a eunuch, must want you as I do.'

A dimple hovered near her mouth. 'That's all very comforting, but it doesn't help the present issue. Darling heart, you must see that what I hate to have advised is our only hope of misleading her who would go to any wicked lengths to have

231

you at her feet. The more you avoid her the worse for me — and you. She is old and vain, her youth has gone. In you she hopes to revive it. Maybe,' she drew in a sharp breath, 'maybe she loves you, if her kind can love, and she loathes me because you and I —' she linked her hands behind his neck, drawing his face to hers — 'Oh, my soul, let us not lacerate each other when we are together for so short a time. Let her not destroy us.'

'We destroy ourselves with too much loving.' He unclasped her hands, his lips wandered over hers teasing, taking and, withdrawing, said, low-voiced, 'Do you forget there was once a Man who destroyed Himself for love of the world and — us?'

She clung to him. 'I must not forget Him and His love, in my love for His creature, but — I do. I live only for you and for our future.'

He seized on that. 'You have decided on our future? You will come with me and share my life in some remote Arcadia? You will?'

'I will.' She breathed it as a prayer.

They clung together in an agony of rapture until a grey ghostly finger crept through the curtained window.

'Go now, my love,' she whispered, 'before dawn breaks.'
He took her hands again in fierce gladness. 'When I come back it will be for ever — evermore!' It was an almost farcical anti-climax when he put on his false beard, covered his uniform with stinking rags, and backed from her saying, 'I cannot come near you now for I have visitors and — goddamn,' vigorously he began to scratch, 'they welcome me home!'

Between laughter and tears she, from her window, watched him sneak out like a thief in the dark.

EIGHT

From the dispatches of Sir Richard Dutton Colt:

A courier is come hither with the welcome news that the Electoral bonnet was given on the 9th of December, 1692, and just now we have had advice that the new Elector will be here this day…

At long last the laboured endeavours to secure for himself the dearest wish of his life had been granted to the Duke-Bishop of Hanover. His return was heralded with clamorous rejoicing, a triumphal procession through the streets of his capital, and the beaming, bowing Elector seated in his gilded coach acknowledging the cheers with hand-wavings right and left and an occasional kiss from his gloved fingertips to any pretty little curtsying maiden in the front of the crowd, to occasion more cheers for such godly condescension.

The Duchess Sophia was no less gratified than her spouse at their elevation, but in her case for more personal reason. As Electress of Hanover she thought to be one step nearer to the coveted throne of Great Britain and Ireland. A drifting straw on the winds of chance to snatch, yet — she snatched it. Since there was no likelihood of issue from William and Mary, joint reigning monarchs, and the Princess Anne, heiress apparent, who, after several miscarriages, had only one surviving child, a sickly boy with a head too large for his body but, as reported, a prodigious amount of brain inside it; yet should he outlive his mother all hope would be gone, if not …

Then again, wishful thoughts were swamped in the fear that Anne, as was known, favoured her half-brother, James,

Catholic son of her exiled father. But Sophia was comforted to believe, however much Anne might wish to see her brother righted, Protestant Britain would have a Papist's head on the block rather than see the Crown upon it.

And watching the elation of her spouse in his new found dignity, it would seem, Sophia indulgently reflected, that the glory was mounting to *his* head under the Electoral hat. Never had been such fêtes and banquets, balls and masques and lavish entertainments held by the new Elector and attended by hordes of foreign princes, envoys, and dukes from other duchies who could not have been more outwardly delighted and inwardly consumed with envy that Ernest Augustus had brought off a *coup* bestowed on one far less deserving than many of his numerous kin.

Sophia Dorothea, henceforth to rank as Electoral Princess, was compelled to attend all these functions; no ordeal for her since Königsmarck, recalled to Hanover, must also be present in his official capacity, even though they must not by word or look afford any occasion for gossip. Contrary to expectation, and much to Philip's relief, Marshal Podevils instead of enforcing disciplinary punishment for his absence without leave, had taken a lenient view of it, possibly because he guessed what would be the result of the duke's visit to Berlin, and that Königsmarck's attendance would be commanded by the new Elector.

But when the duke, his suite and George Louis, had set out on their mission to Berlin, Sophia Dorothea, who should also have accompanied them, had been seized the day before departure with a sickness. Together she and Knesebeck devised an emetic to cause vomiting. A warming-pan filled with hot coals at her feet, and piles of blankets heaped upon her body induced a formidable sweat; a hare's foot applied to each cheek simulated a fever sufficient to convince Dr La Rose, the Court physician, called to her bedside by Knesebeck in a fair pretence of fright fearing Her Serene Highness at death's door, who assured her that Her Serene Highness was, God be thanked, in no danger of her life, but suffering from an inflammation of the stomach. He pronounced her quite unfit to travel. Should no more vomiting occur he would prescribe a course of 'rubbing' (a seventeenth-century form of massage). She must be kept absolutely quiet and he would send his apothecary with a soothing physic to alleviate the pains of the stomach. 'I wish Your Serene Highness a speedy recovery, pray God.' Bowing and backing, he talked himself out.

'And that,' said Sophia Dorothea, throwing off the blankets, 'will let Philip in. If the apothecary is to bring me physic today there is no reason why he should not bring another dose — tomorrow!'

Tomorrow, and tomorrow … And despite the risk they ran in furtive meetings, Philip, disguised as an apothecary, was sneaked in by the 'Confidante'. He had written on hearing of her 'illness':

Poor child! What are you not suffering? To be rubbed without being ill is too much! La Rose said he thought it would be very inadvisable for you to travel for your illness might come from you being enceinte *… Mind you do not undeceive them! They certainly spy upon us but tell me if you think it possible for us to meet tomorrow.* Pour l'amour de Dieu, *let me see you. I love you a thousand times more every day … I have the sweetest dreams about you … Arrange for someone to wait for me in the gallery at eleven o'clock.*

With half the court in the train of the duke, those left behind were free to indulge in their various recreations. The younger male members were invited to Monplaisir where Platen, in anticipation of her status as 'Vice-Electress' entertained right royally. Although confident that the result of the duke's visit would be successful there might be a hitch or some disastrous obstruction from other claimants to the Electorate. Should such be the case, she must be covered against any depreciation of her perquisites. The duke's promise of financial and military support to the emperor must hold good whatever might be imperial decree. Her card tables offered certain compensation to young unwary victims fallen to her lure. She could still dispense favours to whet youthful appetites to her — and their, more doubtful — satisfaction.

Among those invited to la Platen's *soirées*, Philip was reluctantly beguiled to accept. And this, we have his written word for it,

...grieves me that, while you think it a mean action on my part, you advise me to it ... I am willing to aid your plan to be civil to her, even friendly, but never could I make her believe I like her, hating her as I do ... It was a gross insult to our love. I will tell you all about my visit to her when I see you. She looked hideous in a yellow gown ... You cannot love me as I love you for, at your bidding, I have sinned against our love...

Sinned! *O, God,* she prayed, *let me not doubt him.* If he had sinned with her, for all that he had written she looked hideous in a yellow gown, then she would be done with him, finished, never see or speak to him again ...

'If he has betrayed our love,' she let 'Lennie' bear the brunt of it, 'I'll kill him or myself or both of us!' Dreadful lascivious images floated before her mind's eye. 'Yes, I'll kill him if I should know him coupled with that cockatrice!'

'But, darling Highness,' Knesebeck strove with reminder to soothe, 'it was at your wish he should visit her. Are you not inconsistent?'

'Inconsistent? How? Who would have believed he would do as I in lunacy suggested?' was the more-than-inconsistent hot reply to this.

Knesebeck gave up.

Yet, at their next stolen meeting, all fears, doubts and memory of lunatic suggestions were dissolved in the transports of mutual rapture. Nor did he tell her 'all about' his visit, for what actually occurred, if told, might have ended less in rapture than in rupture.

Clara, having dined and wined to her advantage the party of young men, 'my pretty fellows' as she severally named these chosen as much for their face value as for their inefficiency at cards, she let them go with pledges of reimbursement at their next session in return for the delights of her alcove. Only Königsmarck, who had learned a trick or two from her, found himself lost of some few score thalers instead of the few hundreds and in some cases thousands that had left Clara's 'pretty fellows' with nothing but their shirts unless they could call upon their fathers or the Jews. And as the last of them went, a hand in his empty pouch, he muttered, 'She's bitched me properly, the old sow!'

Then, as Philip rose from the gold-piled baize to go with them, Clara turned to catch the mechlin at his wrist, tearing it. 'Oh, no, my handsome, no, you don't!'

She was still seated at the table leaning her bejewelled breast against it; bared to the bosoms it revealed all of its twin hillocks save the nipples, from which unlovely sight Philip averted his eyes. She had aged, he observed, in these six months of his absence, and the 'hideous yellow gown' she wore fadged ill with the paint on her face that bore marks of late nights and gallantries; but her hair, thick and black as ever, dressed high in plaits and curls with one ringlet drooping to her shoulder, showed not a thread of grey. He could not deny her obvious physical attraction that, allied to remarkably acute perceptibility, would account for her hold upon the duke through all these years. Had she been his duchess he might not, decided Philip, have sought for a mistress. She would have amply sufficed.

She was saying, as with a long-handled silver scoop she raked in the scattered gold pieces carefully to gather them into heaps before her, 'I'll let you off your winnings if you,' she gave him a languishing look from under lazy-lidded eyes, 'will take me — on.' She rose up, her breast heaving with desire; her arms entwined him. 'How I've longed for this,' she murmured, 'have waited. I had hoped — had meant — never to engage with you again. There were times when I hated the very thought of you for your — withdrawal the last time we were together, you remember? But you have me, Philip, damn you! Yes, I'm yours and all that I am, which no man but you has ever had...' Her arms slackened. She went from him and moved towards the door that communicated with her bedchamber; her voice came to him thickly. 'Come to me now — this once, only this once. I need you, God knows I need you. Come.'

Against his will, his strength, his erring faithlessness, bemused with too much drink and with the nagging thought that should he now refuse what she demanded she would bring ruin to himself and her without whom, as he had written and from his heart had spoken truth to believe, he *could not live*, he followed where she led...

'No man,' she kept repeating to nauseate him, her greed in part assuaged, 'has ever had from me what I give and take from you with only half yourself. I know — I know I'm old for you in your full youth. I'm forty-odd but I am still of child-bearing age. Philip, if what I've had of you tonight should bear you fruit, I'd ask no more than that and to be near you, to see you, to hear you say you love me — the mother of your child.'

He suppressed a shudder.

She continued, stroking his cheek that in the shaded light sprouted a fine fair stubble. 'You haven't shaved today. You are still a boy. Your chest,' her hand caressed it, 'is as smooth as a ten-year-old's. All I ask of you, my dear, my little one, is that you *like* and — want me. I do not ask for love from you, for I know you can never love other than yourself. I know you, Philip, through and through. I know that what you feel for that —' she halted, biting her underlip until a drop of blood oozed from it — 'I'll not name her, but what you think is love for her is but the reflection of you, seen as Narcissus saw and loved his mirrored self in water. She is so trivial a creature, ungrown and undeveloped, immature, although she has borne her sot of a husband two children. But any child, as I am told she was — having just reached puberty when he raped her on her marriage night — could have conceived. She is still a child. She can offer you no more of love than you, when a page at her father's Court, played at fumbling together. I know how she rants and raves about you to her woman, the 'Sentinel'. Ah, you start at that! Yes, her letters are not all so confidential to her "Tercis".'

'You —' he caught her straying hand — 'you have intercepted them?'

'Why not? When I see you courting disaster, not only for yourself but for her. Listen to me, my foolish one. She has a possible future so stupendous — not that she could ever support it with the dignity and state that is required — none the less she may yet wear the crown of the greatest kingdom, parallel with France, in the whole world. Greater than Germany, a kingdom that vanquished Spain and will yet vanquish France, for when Louis dies — as he must some time — France will fall. If you love her, as I believe you think you do, you will cease this clandestine intrigue. No good can come of it. Should the duke, the Elector as he is now — we only wait for his return with the bonnet on his great swollen head — have proof enough of her adultery, then the fat will be in the fire to burn the pair of you!'

He had left her with the assurance that her advice would be considered.

'Not to be *considered*. For your sake,' she clung to him, 'your word on it. Your promise!'

She raised herself clutching at his arm, her face on a level with his; her eyes, smudged with the mascara on her short stubby lashes, were wet with unfallen tears. 'Give me your promise. I need you, Philip, I want you. I won't share you. It must be all or nothing between us. If you refuse me,' her loosened lips were squared against the break in her voice, 'I am not one to take refusal — I, who hold in my hand Hanover and Celle and the Palatine, as it is bound to be. I do not share my spoils, but I would give up all for you. Don't — don't deny me.' And she whimpered like a child bereft of its toy, which struck him as both obscene and pitiful. 'Don't deny me what I must — *must* have of you. All of you. He, Ernest Augustus, has now his heart's desire. He can do without me, but I — I can't do without you — *all* of you. Platen would divorce me, were he —' her harsh laugh scraped her throat — 'were he paid enough, for I will have my full compensation when the duke's old bald head — you should see how bald he is without his wig! — is covered with the bonnet!'

Was she deranged? he asked himself as he rode the few miles back to Hanover. He could well believe it. Women of her age did sometimes run amok. He had heard that childless women of fifty had been known to conceive — even Sarah of old, aged sixty was it, or seventy? And staring between his horse's ears he spoke aloud as he often did, airing his thoughts in his native tongue to this favourite of all his stables, successor to his loved mare killed by a Turk's scimitar in the Morea.

'If she should carry my seed in her foul womb, although I took as much care as she'd allow me between her bouts … How could any man, unless he were impotent, fail to rise when she … What a woman! How she gives and takes, a storm-tossed Aphrodite, but if by some god-blasted chance she should conceive by me, then I will kill her, and — it. I swear before Almighty God I will! She threatened me. Behind her lust I sensed her threats to my lovely one and to myself. I'm sure she knows we plan to escape. She has read our letters. How many? Not these latest sent by Aurora, but others. I don't care what she may do to me — if she should secure my dismissal all the better. I'd be free, our way made more easy.

'But what of my love? What of her? Guarded and watched like a felon. And what of you, my Rufus? Yes, prick your ears. You hear me. We've been together in the forefront of the fight. You itch, as do I to smell the blood and sweat of war again, the spice of danger, the hell-for-leather charge leading our troopers to scatter the enemy and come through unscathed as we did at Steinkirk, trampling the dead and dying, you with scarce a scratch and I with no more than my kneecap grazed by the bullet from a Frenchman's musket. You know as I know that we can neither enjoy life as gentlemen of leisure, you browsing in Arcadian pastures and I sunning myself on a Mediterranean shore with her beside me, enjoying domestic bliss in some white-walled villa with our children playing round us. Would you want that, my Rufus, and would I? For there is more in life for you and me than this haphazard thing that men call love … yes, for men it *is* haphazard, but not for you. Your love for me, your god, as is my dog's, is soul-possessing. Only the love of man for woman is ephemeral, frail, unlasting, swayed by every cast of an eye, every inviting tip of a tongue …

'If I fail her now, what is the alternative? This continuous creeping up back stairs for the delight of her body, her exquisite response. She was unawakened till I took her; she had known rape from that beer-barrel of a husband. Her husband, my God! She was *demi-vierge*. That was her most adorable attraction. To hear her little sighs and screams of love when I bring her to her climax … Is not that worth more than all the danger and excitement of war? But would it last? You, my stallion, three-year-old, you have not yet known the joys of mating, but you will — you will when I serve you to that fine young Arab mare of mine to match your own hot Arab blood, but it would be for you only one first glorious mating, no time for you to tire. Will I tire? Only *our* time can tell.'

He dug his heel lightly to the sweating side of his horse, who leaped forward for the last lap of the short homeward ride to his stable, where a bran mash and a bedding-down awaited him.

When the celebrations following the Elector's return from Berlin were over, the court settled again to its normal routine while Philip still remained in Hanover awaiting his orders to march against the Danes in what looked to be war between

Denmark and the Brunswick Princes. The King of Sweden, in alliance with Denmark, had threatened to confiscate Königsmarck's estates should he continue to serve under a belligerent Elector, which put Philip in an invidious position; yet he preferred to risk the loss of his property in Sweden, or even imprisonment for desertion from his king and country, than to be separated from her whom he repeatedly had said he 'worshipped'. As for Sophia Dorothea, she had been sent on a visit to her parents at Brockenhausen to get her out of harm's way. The Platen's warning to Ernest Augustus of a *liaison* between those two had caused him to consult his wife. She, taking a malicious pleasure in passing this information to her bugbear, 'the Frenchwoman', succeeded in giving Éléonore much unease imparted to her husband, with the result that more than ever was their daughter under constant vigilance from the Electress at Hanover and the Duchess at Celle.

George Louis, when told of these precautions, entirely approved them. He, gone with his regiment to Flanders, had a score to settle against Königsmarck concerning an unfortunate incident which, apparently forgotten by the Electoral Prince, was not to be forgiven. Sophia Dorothea would hear more of this from Philip.

Meanwhile these two, in direct defiance of authority, were in constant communication, meeting with every possible and dangerous contrivance. In a letter from Brockenhausen Philip is told: *You can come in by a back door and stay twenty-four hours without the least risk. You know the usual signal … I think only of the joy of seeing you. If joy can kill it will kill me…*

This particular meeting, however, was not entirely joyful. When after their transports had subsided, he told her of a circumstance in which he had been involved while at dinner with her husband and other officers of the prince's regiment and some of Philip's guards, prior to the departure of George Louis for Flanders.

'I may have had a drop too much,' he said, 'but the sight of him sitting there in state at the head of the table and looking like a performing pig at a circus, decked out in gold-laced uniform and covered in orders and ribbands and medals, and the thought that he has the right to have and to hold you — O God! I suffer hell to think of it!' He buried his head in her breast. 'I'm haunted with vile imaginings —'

'As I am when I think of you with her!'

So now they were at it again.

'There has been nothing between me and that randy old bitch,' he protested loudly, 'as I have told you a hundred times.'

'You are too easy with your hundreds — your hundred women. You admit you went to Monplaisir.'

'Only because you advised me to go. I had to simulate desire.'

'To — simulate! Then you *have* been with her. You have been intimate! You can't deny it. You come from her to me. I hate you — *hate* you for doing this. How could you so deceive me? Love? What love have you for me more than for any whore? You have made of me your whore!' She turned to dig her teeth viciously in his neck.

'Damnation! You have the incisors of a vixen!' He lifted her face, contorted with the storm of her temper and the hideous images invoked by his words. 'Listen. Why torture yourself? It was at your insistence I went to her — played cards with her. You made me go to her, I would never have seen her again but that you advised it to throw dust in her eyes and avert suspicions from us.'

'I did not insist. I only meant that you had better make her think that by visiting her, you and I are not — what we are, and that your professed love for me in your letters — and what damning evidence is in them, if she has read them, are facsimiles of those you write to your hundred other —'

'Stop! You are behaving like a foolish child. You contradict yourself at every turn.'

'Don't be so cruel. Is this how we must meet, to wrangle with each other as we do in our letters, that in yours shout love in every line and in the next accuse me of flirting with any foreign envoy and my brother, Max?'

'Yes, Max. He is here at Brockenhausen, is he not?'

'And why not? He is visiting my parents. Have you any objection to that? Oh, Philip,' and she was in his arms again, her lips fondling his. 'Our time together is so short. Why waste it in all this silliness? Go on to tell me about the regimental dinner and him looking like a performing pig — which he is! Oh!' she slapped a hand to her mouth. 'I oughtn't to have said that of him whom I vowed to honour and obey for better or for worse, only that when I repeated the words after the pastor I added "not" to myself so that I wouldn't be telling a lie at God's altar.'

'Darling! Darling!' Rapturously he kissed. 'You are still such a young thing. You have that same wondering look you always had when you were twelve. I adore you!'

'And I adore you, but do tell what happened.'

'Well, it was all because of my jealousy of him who has the right to have and hold you, which made me lash out at him as I did. I should have held my tongue and let my loathing of him and all that you have endured with and through him, boil inside me instead of —'

'Yes, yes!' impatiently she interrupted. 'Keep to the point.'

'This is the point. You remember I was at Dresden before I came here — that's when I first met Charles — and during dinner the other night, the talk turned to Saxony where I had seen the drilling of the Elector's troops and compared the military discipline of Saxony as better than that of Hanover.'

'Did you tell George Louis that?'

'I, er, I said something of the sort. I'll allow that I and all of us were rather raddled and George Louis more than half seas over. It may have been, in the state I was, that I had at the back of my mind some idea of provoking him to cross swords with me. I'm a far better duellist than he could ever be, and if he — his rank be damned — could have been man enough to meet me I'd have run him through to rid you of him though it brought me to the scaffold.'

'Don't!' She hushed a scream. 'For heaven's sake! Did you — you didn't fight him?'

'No, although my hand was on my sword-hilt and — no, dear love, there's nothing to fear. He asked me sarcastically why I had left Saxony to come here since it was evident I found the Saxon army vastly superior to his or, as he said, his father's, whom I serve. Whereupon, my blood being up and I itching to have at him and slice that porcine face of his in half, I replied that I would not serve under a prince, duke, Elector or whatever, who destroyed, as did Saxony's Elector, the life and happiness of a beautiful virtuous wife by flaunting before his court a worthless Messalina, which classical allusion is as near as dammit to the Maypole's second name of Melusine. That rocked the company until they saw his face purple as an over-ripe plum. He got up and made as if to come for me and then flopped down again. He was too full to stand.'

'Oh, my dearest,' she gave a gasp of laughter, 'you must have been full to have said what you did.'

'Nothing half so full as he who, were he one quarter sober, would have flung his glass of wine in my face, but he didn't. I almost did, and Electoral heir or nothing he'd have had to call me out. But he sat there lurching forward in his seat, and my neighbour next to me — that same officer to whom I entrusted your letters before Steinkirk — seeing my hand worrying my sword-hilt and myself on my feet, he pulled me down and hissed in my ear, "Stay! You go too far!" and then, through a silence you could have cut with a knife, he called for a song and we all yelled out in chorus in which George Louis joined:

'One man's speech
Is no man's speech,
We must hear all.'

'And which I took to be apt enough apology from me, as so it seemed did the prince, for he applauded, banging his fists on the table to make the glasses jump, and then he slid from his chair and was lugged out by a lackey, but not before he'd spilled what he couldn't hold.'

She shuddered. 'He was like that on our wedding night after he'd done with me.'

'Don't talk of it!' He fastened his mouth to hers, and presently said, 'Do you wonder I want to kill him? These damned Germans — they are always soaked. We Swedes can hold our drink. They can't.'

'My father is German and he is never soaked, and don't forget that I —' she tweaked his nose — 'I am half German, so you mustn't despise me because I am what — I partly am.'

'You are not half German, you,' he said and fell again to kissing, 'are half goddess and half angel and entirely divine.'

All of this was heaven for Sophia Dorothea.

Dawn's finger pierced the lifting night when, in his drab apothecary's guise, he sneaked out through the back door with his head in the sky and his words idiotically floating on the air. 'Madonna! Angel! Goddess! I adore you. I have drunk you to your lovely dregs and am greedy now to drink of you again…'

Nor did he know that one, hidden behind a yew hedge patiently waiting and watching to mark his man, yawned in his hand and said *sotto voce:* 'You make me laugh, Count Königsmarck.' And, having followed him to see him mount his tethered horse and ride away, he made another person laugh, not mirthfully, when he repeated these inanities to her.

It was to be the last meeting between 'Tercis' and his 'Léonisse' before Philip had his marching orders to join the Electoral Prince's armies on the Elbe. The Danes were up in arms; negotiations pending for a settlement, not yet finalised, boded more than ever gloomily for war hastened by the unpredictable bombardment at Ratziborg led by the Danish Commander-in-Chief, who had taken too much upon his own initiative.

Meanwhile she, who should have gone with the Electoral Court to Herrenhausen, found an excuse to visit her parents at Celle in the hope that she and Philip might have a chance of meeting once again, but it was not to be. He could not even write, he says, before he left Hanover, for he was hustled off with everything packed and all of them ready to start. *Since twelve o'clock the night before last I have been perpetually on horseback … No engagement has yet taken place though we are within speaking distance of the Danes; there is only the river between us…'* And later, 'We are hard pressed here. The truce is broken. We shall bang away at one another tomorrow…*

Which eased her not at all.

And to her at Celle a day or two after Philip had left Hanover came Max, travel-stained with hard riding and in a towering rage. 'Look here! I'm in bad enough odour with my father as it is without this latest crime that's fastened on me — thanks to you!'

She stared in stunned amaze. 'What on earth — ' Her one fear was for Philip, her sole thought that he might be endangered through her fault. 'What have you done, and how am I involved?'

'Not you. Me! It's what I've done, or am supposed to have done.' Striding up and down the room he stopped to wheel round on her. 'You told my mother, and she passed it to my father — curse him! — that you resented having my apartments adjoining yours at Herrenhausen, which is why you have refused to go there and have stayed on here. You insinuated that I had made unwelcome advances to you while our rooms were in close proximity at Brockenhausen, which is a monstrous lie and you know it! You couldn't feign another illness like you did to get out of going to Berlin when Philip was in Hanover, so you trumped up *this* against me. Attempted incest with my brother's wife! That's what is going about. A mean artful feminine trick. Can you wonder I prefer the company of men to women?'

She had whitened. 'It is you, or they, who lie! All I told the Electress was that it would be more circumspect for you to occupy other apartments than those allotted to you at Herrenhausen which are my husband's. He complained of you being next to me at Brockenhausen. I'll wager the Platen is at the back of this. She is out to make any mischief to damage me — and you, because she knows I am on your side about the settlement that takes from you and the younger sons *and*

249

Charlotte, the lands that should be yours and are now handed over to George Louis, and which, if she achieves her ends, will eventually be her dough-faced daughter's, your half-sister, by your father, if, God forbid, she is married to my son.'

He shrugged impatiently. 'We are all aware of her motives in urging my father to disinherit us, but you can rest assured that her bastard will never be mated with one of our stud. George Louis has too much pride in his blood-stock for that. So you did,' he reverted to his argument, 'make my proximity to your apartments at Herrenhausen the excuse for staying with, or near, to Königsmarck, which is as good — or bad — as saying I'm not to be trusted where you are. Well, I'm not!' He caught her roughly to him and forced his mouth on hers, fast closed.

She fought to free herself; her small clenched fist shot out to catch him under his chin. 'You're mad!' she panted. 'As if one of your lot is not enough!'

He rubbed his under-jaw, sheepishly grinning. 'Right. One is. But I'll tell you this, I'm not proof against the tricks you've learned to bring a man who *is* a man to want to wring your neck or tumble you. Yet I'm but *half* a man, or I'd have had you when I had the chance with only a communicating door next to your bedchamber, that I could hear ecstatic groans and sighs and sounds between you and your — visitor. Hah! That's hit you, hasn't it? So you use me to cover up for him!'

'How dare you say it!' Frantically she sought to counter this attack. 'You, a Catholic, who, if you follow the teaching of your Church, have committed a mortal sin in lusting after your brother's wife to commit adultery in your heart.'

'A thousand times and every night when I am lodged beside you, as so have *you* a thousand times, and not only in your heart but in your act.'

'No, no!'

'Yes, yes,' he teased, 'but I'll not tell on you, since there's no need to tell what the whole court knows, or *thinks* it knows, with la Platen ever on the watch. She has roped in another of her henchmen to do her dirty work. He is, or was, a servant of one of Philip's officers. Name of Mesbeck.'

'Oh, yes,' she breathed, 'I've heard of him. So he *is* one of hers.' She groped behind her for the back of a chair and sank into it, still pale. 'That accounts for his letters having gone astray, mine too, maybe … Here's a fool I am!' She dug her nails in her palm; her breath came fast. 'I should have bitten out my tongue before I spoke of letters.'

'Which is nothing new to me. But listen, silly one,' he now spoke earnestly, 'every move of yours is watched. There was never so reckless, rash, foolhardy a pair of lovers as you and he. You deserve to have what's coming to you.'

'And what is that?' She laid the back of her hand to her lips, choking back a stifled cry. 'I cannot bear much more.'

'That,' said he, producing from his pocket a jewelled snuff-box, and pausing to inhale a pinch of spicy bergamot, 'that,' he repeated, 'is banishment for Philip, if not worse.'

'Banishment!' Joyfully she echoed it. 'If it were, I'd be banished with him, and we'd be in paradise together.'

'Or in hell,' he told her dryly, 'hell for him if not for you. I never cease to wonder at you women. We, of the stronger sex, as so we mistakenly claim, have as much chance against you, once you have determined on your prey, as a rabbit has against a boa constrictor. So you would follow him in his exile, and what will you live on? Love? That won't feed you, nor your children, for you will give him his children. Wonder is that you have given him none already.'

She covered her ears. 'I'll not listen to your insults. Leave me. I'll hear no more.'

'Very well.' He turned to go, and she was after him, tugging at his sleeve.

'No! Say what you have to say — and then — out of my sight!'

'But not, I hope, out of your mind.' He disengaged her hand to lift and kiss it. 'This is what I have to say. La Platen — and was there ever a more persevering disciple of Satan than she? — has another of her spies nursed beneath her petticoats, or in her red-curtained bed shared with my senile father, though what use her latest acquisition is to her more than his tongue, which for talk is as long as a lizard's — but I digress. Do you know or have heard of one de la Cittardie?'

'Do you mean that mincing little Frenchman who was often at our *soirées* — a friend of France's envoy?'

'The same: a king, or, more appropriately, queen of gossip who flits from court to court picking up every scrap of garbage he can gather to amuse his lady — or gentlemen — friends. I am one of them who has been all ears for what he puked at the Platen and, incidentally, at me. I submit to his attentions for your sake, little sister, and this is what I've learned. That Königsmarck is in a tight spot, financially. He's in debt up to his neck. And you,' he pointed an accusing finger, 'have been pestering your father for a separate establishment and an adequate allowance to support it, *and* Königsmarck, under the rose!'

Apprehension seized her. 'Not true ... all lies!' And inconsequently: 'How do you know?'

He, brushing invisible snuff from the lapel of his riding coat, answered airily, 'How does a bird know where to find its worm or a bee its honey, or a scavenger its pickings from the gutters? Just as Bernstorff picks from Celle's council table the crumbs that your father lets fall to be carried to the Platen — at a price. She holds Bernstorff in her pocket. From whom do you suppose he got his vineyard and his von? This sudden urge for some return of your dower of which you have been cheated, comes most timely if your father will oblige, which he won't, that you may ease Philip of his debts or part of them.'

'Why,' she asked, her eyes fear-haunted, 'do you come to me now with all of this? Are you also one of her spies? Who prompts you to it? And — and at *your* price? You, too, are in debt. Your father keeps you short. Oh, I didn't mean that. I don't know what I *do* mean, or whom I can trust. Are you to be trusted? Have you come here to —' she faltered in worried uncertainty — 'to lay me on the rack?'

'No, to save you from the rack.' His eyelids flickered. He came close to her, not touching. 'As I can't have you and my brother doesn't want you, all *I* want is to see you free from all of this.' He waved his hand, a long-fingered sensitive hand inherited from his Stuart forbears. 'You are wasted on us. You may be wasted on Königsmarck, but at least with him you can make your bid for freedom, even if you have to live in a four-roomed villa and in flagrant delight five hundred miles from Hanover — and us. As for me, I join an army on the Elbe tomorrow and I'll not be at Herrenhausen, so that excuse won't hold. I'll be seeing Philip. Is there a message for him?'

'Tell him … no. I'll write it for you to give him.' She moved to her bureau and, taking pen and paper, wrote:

I tremble at all I hear of your embarrassments … I do not give up hope of getting my wish from my father but there are difficulties although my mother assures me that all she possesses in the world is for me. She urges Bernstorff to allow me thirty thousand crowns from the Duchy estates, but this terrible war will delay the business…

She nibbled the end of her quill, glancing round at Max who stood restively tapping his riding crop against his booted toe. 'I'm almost done,' she told him, and her head again bent to her pen.

You tell me you will be obliged to seek some corner of the earth and beg bread that you may not starve. Do you think, I will ever give you up whatever happens? Nothing would keep me from following you. I would starve with you, but we may yet be happier than we think. Let us love and comfort each other whatever may befall … I kiss you in spirit. I would give my blood to be kissing you in reality.

She sealed the letter and handed it to Max, who slid it into his pocket. Taking her chin to raise her face to his, he dropped a kiss upon her forehead, saying, 'I'll let him know that he has no cause to be jealous of me,' and laughed, a very little, turned and left her.

NINE

The brief war with the Danes had come to its indeterminate end with a postponement of the peace treaty, disaster to the Allies, and for the French a triumph with the capture of Charleroi and Ghent.

The Electoral Prince, George Louis, returned from the campaign in Flanders, was on his way back again to Hanover. And now, more than ever did his wife redouble her efforts to persuade her parents to grant her a separate establishment and sufficient means to support it; this, of course, a blind. Her sole thought and every action was bent on escape, urged by Philip's letters constantly inciting her to revolt and to fly with him to some far distant corner of the earth …

Oh, my divine Léonisse, I know you have more to lose than I but if you will not waver I will show you a constancy that will last till death.

Yet waver she did. To escape this purgatorial life … yes, she would go to any lengths for that, but was torn between her all-absorbing passion for Philip and love for her children. How could she desert them for a nebulous paradisiacal future offered by him which he vowed would be hers, or would it be paradise — lost? True, she had more to lose than he without the loss of her children; yet rank, position, the pomp and glitter of the court and of her high estate held no allure for her. She would renounce all to live in dishonour and comparative poverty with Philip in 'some far distant corner of the earth', if she could, but … could she? His letters, as ever, alternate between exaggerated avowals of eternal love, reproaches for her reluctance in acceding to his demands that she give up everything for him as he would give up all for her, and the usual undercurrent of egotism.

For mercy's sake, think of all the risks I run for you! ... Ignominious dismissal, ruin, confiscation of his estates, and an end to his military career ... *Delay is dangerous. If you have a spark of love for me you would not hesitate...*

He drove her crazy.

She dared not let him know that with the return of the Electoral Prince the apartments in the Leine Schloss had been prepared for them by the Electress Sophia, hoping to allay the spate of talk which had risen once again to link the name of Königsmarck with that of the Electoral Princess.

La Platen had been busy, and Sophia Dorothea was commanded to the Presence.

'Serene Highness has sent for me?'

The old cold eyes were fixed on her, taking her measure, noting the bloom of youth in its blossom that seemed to shine as if from some inner radiance; the natural result, as was cynically surmised, of sexual intercourse defined by the poets as 'Love'.

'My son, your husband,' she said, 'is on his way home to you. It is time you and he readjusted your lives together and that you pay him the connubial duty and respect which is his right. There is evil talk concerning you and one who shall be nameless.'

'Madame!' She had lost her fear of tyranny; she was fighting for her love and for her life. 'What respect or connubial duty has your son ever shown to me? As for evil talk that settles like blow-flies on an open drain, you know, as do I, the source of it who also shall be nameless.'

The slightest inclination of that head, its almost-white hair crowned with a diadem of pearls, acknowledged the source of it while her reply retained unruffled calm.

'It is to quell the source of it that I, who make no accusations but only as your well-wisher and the mother of your husband, ask that you, my —' after an infinitesimal pause, she conceded the word — 'daughter, give the lie to defamatory suspicion. My son, and his and your son, are, God willing, the progenitors of Hanover's future and of possibly a greater future yet. Reconciliation with your husband is the only means to such an end. An unblemished end. You understand me?'

'Yes, Madame, I understand you, but do you,' was the unquavering demand, 'understand me? I have suffered intolerably insults, injury and neglect from him to whom as a child I was married, who has robbed me of my fortune to squander on his women. I have suffered enough. I will suffer no more. Let the world — your world — in which I have no part, this petty Electoral State that clings to improbable grandeur, know that I, a wife in name only, scorn to degrade myself by sharing marital relations with the mistress of your sop or any loose woman, or my own serving maids. I retain my separate apartments or go my separate ways.'

For an instant those faded eyes were closed as if to avert a blow, while remembrance hovered of just such another defiance from this girl, the Frenchwoman's bastard, before and after the Swede had come to court to soil the name of Hanover …

'Bad blood, bad blood.' The thin lips mouthed the words. 'What's in the bone is out — in the flesh. I was to blame. It was I,' the thought prompted painful reminder, 'who brought about this marriage, and must take to myself the wrong of it.'

She rose from her throne-like chair. The harsh voice rang strongly.

'I, too, have suffered. It is the penalty of royal birth that their women should dedicate their lives to the service of that State to which they have been called, and to accept without question the extra-marital indulgences of Princes. Few royal marriages are of mutual love. Yes, my uncle Charles, the murdered King of England, although his marriage was politically arranged, married for love but she was a royal Princess. He did not betray his kingship by taking to wife the daughter of the King of France as your father did betray his dukedom to beget you out of wedlock by a daughter of France who was a — commoner.'

'From which, Madame, you greatly benefited, as unfortunately I do not; for, had I remained the "bastard" that, despite my legitimacy and the royal rank granted me by the emperor's grace you persist in regarding me, I would not have been called in service to your son as a brood mare is called to be served by a stallion — at a price!' And without waiting for the gesture of dismissal after that staggering retort, she bent with her petticoats wide to the ground, was up and at the door.

'Girl!' she was peremptorily recalled. 'I should chastise you forcibly for this impertinence, and were you still sixteen as when you came to us, I would take you across my knee,' those thread-like lips were drawn back against two yellow teeth in the ghost of a smile, 'as I took my sons and my daughter in their nonage *and* their teens to spank them!'

And now, surprisingly, a wetness rolled from under a parched lid, slowly to trickle down the high pinched nose. 'Do not think I cannot understand you. I am not without heart, shrivelled though it be. But I am and always have been one to set self aside for duty to my calling. Had I been born of peasant stock I might have dared to speak as you have spoken. Go, and think on what I ask. No! What I command. The State apartments in the palace are prepared for the homecoming of the Electoral Prince and you. Go to them and await your husband there.'

'M-Madame,' the princess stammered. The sight of that tear, as if a face carved from granite had wept; the knowledge of what it must have cost this dominant old woman to reveal for a second's glimpse her 'shrivelled heart', caused Sophia Dorothea a pang of something near to pity, and, for a moment, near to love.

She knelt, took that dry blue-veined hand in hers and laid her cheek against it. 'Serene Highness, forgive me. I am half distracted — torn between my duty and my —'

'Instinct,' decisively cut in the duchess. Withdrawing her hand she went back to her seat, and having dispensed with what might have been catarrhal irritation or the result of involuntary emotion that impeded clearer speech, 'Women,' she stated, 'are the higher mammals and man's superior, though he will not admit it. We contain within us the generative organs. We are the reproductive agents. We select our mates as does the female spider that devours her mate after copulation; but our methods are more subtle if equally destructive. Was it not the mother of us all who brought about the fall of man? "The woman tempted me"? He hid behind her — I almost said her petticoats —' again that ghostly smile — 'yet I think the fig leaf was not then in vogue. Alia! I see you shrink. You mislike plain speaking. You prefer the facts of life romantically rendered as "Love", which is how humankind, *vide* the ancient Greeks, present carnal attraction between the sexes as their mythical Eros. I,' she continued, addressing not Sophia Dorothea but some invisible presence, 'am a realist. I delve beneath the surface, as did Plato, seeking to find the human soul as it exists corporeally between the rational, the physical and the spiritual. But you, a romantic, follow your emotions that lead you into danger as surely as did Eve lead the human race to its destruction until the Higher Power, Love, in its immortal Essence, saved us. Go, then. Think on what I say, and, if you have heard a word of it, remember this: The only happy end to a romance is to leave it — unfinished.'

She gave the nod of dismissal, and taking a book — *Religio Medici* by Sir Thomas Browne — from the table at her side, was at once immersed.

'So what are we to do?' The princess flung herself about the room in one of her frenzies. 'How can we meet if the prince and I are, to all intent, cohabiting? Of course we shall do nothing of the sort. He is no more desirous than I of what the Electress calls "copulation". Female spiders, that's what she says women are who devour their mates, or as near as makes no matter. I couldn't follow half she said, and I wouldn't want to devour the prince. A broiled ham, as he so clearly resembles, would be more tasty. But Max said something of the sort too, only he likened us to boa constrictors … oh, Lennie, help me.' She rounded on the confidante who, during this outburst, had stood fingering a letter and managed at last to interrupt.

'Highness, I have just received this!' She held out the letter, which was snatched.

'From him! Why didn't you give it me before? How dare you keep it from me?'

'Madame, you did not give me the — the chance to —' faltered Knesebeck. 'You have been so upset about the —'

'Quiet! Let me read it.'

The letter read and re-read, Knesebeck was told: 'He says that everyone knows of our *affaire*. That's nothing new. And now he tells me he is mad with grief and rage at being parted from me and then goes on to say, to make *me* mad, that he is off to Hamburg on the morrow. Not our morrow, but last week when he wrote this. So he is in Hamburg. He wants to raise money from his estates if my parents won't give me what I should have. I didn't know he has estates in Hamburg. He cares more for money than he does for me. Money is a curse. I was married for my money, and now I'm loved for my money!'

'Highness, dear,' was the unconvincing protest, 'you know that is not so. He only wants sufficient money that you and he may be together.'

'How? *How* can we be together? Do you mean that I should run away with him when we can't even meet?' She wrung her hands. 'Not even able to *meet* now that I'm to be imprisoned in the State apartments. If he finds out that the prince and I are, apparently, united, Philip will kill him or himself, and then we'll *never* be together.' She sank on to a couch, beating the cushions with her fists. 'I've borne enough today to put me in my grave. What with the Electress and her awful prophecies of destruction to me if Philip and I … and now to have this from him saying he is off to Hamburg without making the least effort to see me, but —' she jerked up her head — 'how *can* he see me when, or if, he does come back except at court when we mustn't so much as speak to each other? Don't stand there staring like an idiot. Can't you say something? Have you no ideas?'

Striving to say something, Knesebeck came out with, 'Dearest, pray calm yourself. Let us not look on the worst side. You and the count have met often before under cover of your Lennie.'

Which occasioned more hysteria from Sophia Dorothea. 'Do you mean that I,' she spluttered, 'go to meet him hidden in your skirts? Do have some sense.' Her laughter turned to rageful tears.

'I meant, Highness —' it was Knesebeck's turn to be hysterical — 'that I who have always only your — your interest at heart — have covered up for you — ha-ha-have,' sobbed the confidante, 'given my life, my maidenhood to you —'

'You talk,' giggled Her Highness, 'as if I'd raped you! Oh, my Lennie,' a swift chameleon change here from termagant to penitent, with kisses, caresses, apologies and: 'What a beast I am! You are my only hope, my only friend. I rely entirely on you for help, but you *are* rather — no, never mind. Can't you think of some way of covering up for me again?'

'There are always the back stairs, Madame, as exit from the State apartments.'

'The back — oh, you mean the back stairs of the pages. How do you suppose that I — yes!' She threw her arms round her friend's plump waist. 'Of course — the back stairs. Send for my tailor.'

'Your tailor, Madame?' repeated the round-eyed Knesebeck. 'What should you want of the tailor?'

'A suit, dear fool. A page's suit. If I am to use their back stairs I must go habited as one of them, then I won't be noticed. My hair,' she pulled at it, 'is no disguise. I must braid it close to my head and wear a blonde wig to look like Hans or any of them. I'm thin, and have got thinner with pining for Philip when he went to fight the Danes. Thank goodness I *am* thin. If I had breasts like a cow's udders or the Schulenberg's, the Electoral Prince might wish to spend his nights with me instead of with her. So send for the tailor now that he may take my measurements.'

'But, Madame, will the tailor not think it rather — odd that Your Highness should demand he make you a boy's suit?'

'Not if I say it's for a masquerade. There are sure to be masques and balls and racketings for the return of the Electoral Prince. So do as you are bid. Send for the tailor. Let him think what he likes and — don't fuss!'

Soon after the news of Philip's visit to Hamburg, Sophia Dorothea was dismayed to hear from him that he had gone to Dresden, which would unavoidably delay his return to Hanover. The death from smallpox of the young Elector of Saxony brought his still younger brother and Philip's good friend, Frederick Augustus, to the Electorate.

The sudden accession to power of Philip's boon companion gave him hope that he would now recover some of his gambling debts due to him from this hitherto impecunious Prince, debts which were something in the region of thirty thousand crowns. Not a fortune but a windfall, unexpected as welcome at this time when all his heart was set on flight with his adored.

So to Dresden went Philip, and could hardly have wished for a more gratifying reception from Frederick Augustus. That the new Elector was madly infatuated with Aurora, Philip's sister, offered further hope of reimbursement, but not so speedily as he could have wished. With all the goodwill in the world, Frederick had more pressing commitments. The funeral and subsequent coronation festivities would have to be met besides sundry other debts to creditors, for Frederick had lived to the top of his bent, unwisely and too well.

One may believe he did not mourn his departed brother more than merest decency allowed. Within a week of the interment the Court of Dresden was the scene of nightly saturnalia in which Philip joined, in no haste, it seemed, to fly with his 'goddess' to 'some far distant corner of the earth'. He played high, drank deep and on one occasion made a fool of himself with disastrous result.

This, when at the Elector's festive board Philip, who in his cups could keep his head but could not hold his tongue, bragged to an hilarious company among whom were some of his fellow officers who had been with him at Steinkirk, of his various conquests with the Hanoverian ladies. The name of the princess was not mentioned, let that stand to his credit; but the English envoy, one Mr Stepney, a prudish elderly young man, also present at this orgy and evidently scandalised by Count Königsmarck's unrestrained divulgations, wrote to his king: 'I have no great opinion of that young spark.'

One other at this particularly riotous assemblage, who had come to Dresden to be in at the death of the late Elector and not out of the fun that followed it, was Monsieur de la Cittardie, scavenger of scandal. All ears and eyes for the vocal and active demonstrations of 'that young spark', Monsieur made mental notes of all he heard and saw of Philip's efforts to amuse the Elector.

The *leitmotif* of his anecdotes was unsparingly concerned with the Countess von Platen: the intimacies of her toilet, her diverse methods of seduction whereby she lured unwary youths to her card table and later to her alcove, were presented with highly garnished flavour. The litany exhausted he mounted on the table to give an impromptu of his reminiscences in bawdy song.

The applause was terrific; the Elector convulsed. The company held its aching sides, and when most of them were under the table, Philip came down from it, bowed to his host, now supine, bowed to the rest of them and took himself to bed.

De la Cittardie also took himself to bed. 'Really,' he reflected while his weary valet removed the paint from his face, the wig from his head and the teeth from his mouth, 'the young Swede has a wonderful mind.'

'Indeed, sir,' was the stifled yawn of agreement. 'Goodnight, sir. Sleep well.'

He did sleep well, and the next morning announced his intention of taking his leave of Dresden, having had a surfeit of the city's delights, and was on his way back to Paris via Monplaisir, where he could always be sure of a welcome.

La Platen, whose use for de la Cittardie was to draw from him, as from water in a well, a source of informative gossip, received, with gracious condescension, his request to attend upon Madame la Comtesse.

He was ushered to her salon to find there two other ladies: Schulenberg and Madame Weycke, the Platen's sister, drinking a concoction much in vogue among the English upper classes, known as 'tay' and which when offered to and accepted by the Frenchman with fulsome thanks, was declared to be 'delicious', but inly anathematised as *l'urine du chat.*

Bidden to tell of the celebrations he had witnessed during his visit to Dresden, he was delighted to oblige. He led up carefully to Philip's part in the entertainment at the recent banquet held by the new Elector.

'But, ladies, it was of the most amusing. We laughed — *c'était mourir de rire!* But…' He glanced aside, setting down his handle-less cup from which he had sipped. Disguising a grimace at the 'cat's pee', he leaned forward, his plump little hands on his plump little knees as, with some well-feigned reluctance, he said, 'One is most deeply ashamed, of course, *mesdames*,' he rolled up his eyes, 'to have to report all that Monsieur le Comte has said of you, *mesdames et Madame la Comtesse*.'

He got up to bow to all three of them in turn, which produced a chorus of: 'But we ask you to tell!' And from Clara, 'I *insist* that you tell.'

'Always, *mesdames*,' he was enjoying himself hugely, 'have I deplored the impoliteness of this Monsieur le Comte when he speaks with so — *pardon, mesdames*, that I say it — with so rude and big a mouth — of ladies as beautiful and sweet as yourselves, *mesdames*. It was —' more rolling and blinking of his eyes, to which his valet had supplied a redundancy of kohl that seeped a trifle, to be-smudge his rouged under-eye wrinkles, 'it was malicious, *mesdames,* without a doubt.'

'Malicious?' queried Clara. 'How malicious, and to whom did he allude so impolitely?'

'Of — of Mademoiselle Schulenberg, Madame,' was the hesitant reply to cause a stiffening of the Maypole in the whale-boned frame of her corsage.

'What had he to say of me?' she asked with a widening of those vapid blue eyes, so admired by George Louis.

'No, no, no, *mademoiselle!* I cannot myself bring to say of how he has disparaged the most beautiful, the sweetest...' More bows and blinkings.

'But surely,' she urged, 'you can tell what we are all dying to hear. How was I disparaged?'

'*Simplement, mademoiselle,* that, you are — too weighty, like — *pardon* — I have the grand shame to say it — like a — how you say — one cow. *Abominable,* yes?'

'Well, truly,' said Ermengarde, relieved it was no worse, 'I am so accustomed to being thus discussed by scoundrels at this court that I cannot take undue exception to the count's remarks concerning me. He was obviously drunk. And I am certainly overweight.'

'No, no! You,' de la Cittardie rhapsodically pronounced, 'have the size — the figure — of a goddess, that is for certain.'

'And what of me?' demanded Catherine, 'was I also "disparaged" by Königsmarck?'

'A little, madame, just a little. Only that *le Prince Electoral*, has — as he, *Monsieur le Comte* so rudely put it — more the fresh fish to fry than you, Madame.'

'Charming, I'm sure,' Catherine crimsoned, 'but that is old news, Monsieur. The prince has let all Hanover know that he found fresher fish to fry some years ago, which now…' She darted a venomous look at Schulenberg, who returned it with cow-like placidity. She was too well assured of her position as prime favourite to heed the malice of any man or woman in the Duchy. 'Which now,' repeated Catherine, furious that her spite had ricocheted without drawing blood, 'can be cried as *stinking* fish, since it grows stale!'

But this remark, as its predecessor, had no immediate effect upon Schulenberg and was entirely incomprehensible to de la Cittardie, whose command of German was virtually nil. He renewed his bows, having nothing more to say, until Clara broke in with, 'We have not yet heard what Königsmarck had to tell of me.'

'Of you, Madame?' Embarrassment was successfully feigned. 'I regret — *Non, non,* I cannot — I would the tongue of me cut out, Madame, that I am a mute — how you say? — dumb like an oyster — than offend the ear of Madame to recount what this cretin, this *animal si grossier* has to —'

'Cut the puffery,' snapped Clara, 'and come to the point!'

'Madame,' he spread his hands, ringed to the knuckles. 'I would,' another side-glance at those two who sat expectantly agog, 'I would entreat that I tell to Madame, *en privé* what I did hear of this ridiculous scandal.'

'If it is too bad to be spoken among friends,' she said lightly — but under the paint she paled — 'and rather than I should die of curiosity, then, my dears, leave me that I may hear this ridiculous scandal *en privé* and I promise to tell it to you later — if there is anything to tell!'

What later she had to tell was a highly expurgated version of the 'ridiculous scandal' de la Cittardie had told.

'Well? I'm waiting?' she commanded, when the ladies unwillingly had left. 'What had Königsmarck to say of me?'

That which Königsmarck had to say of her — 'I abhor, Madame la Comtesse, to give to you, *mais,* if you insist —'

'I do!'

'*Eh bien,* Madame, may I tell you in my own *langue?*'

'Go on, in French, then.'

And in French he went on to the effect that: Madame, of a truth — he suffered to say it — did bathe herself in the milk of the ass and gave to drink, in charity to the poor, the dirty milk of the bath in which she washed.

'Yes? And what more had he to tell of my toilette? I am enormously amused.' Her mouth was set in a squared hard line, the carmine of her lips red as a clown's against the greyish pallor that underlay the crude enamel of her cheeks.

'Pardon, Madame, of a surety one does not amuse oneself at these *fanfarons*. For example, one would wish to demand, at the point of the sword, satisfaction for defiling the name of a lady in such manner as to disgust one profoundly, is it not?'

'In what manner?' Her voice had a twang in it like the broken string of a lute. 'Speak, then. I attend.'

De la Cittardie spoke then, while the face of Madame assumed the grey of a cadaver on which paint in two grotesque blobs of scarlet was imposed.

He spared no detail of Königsmarck's revelations concerning Madame's most intimate relationship with Monsieur le Comte. The Elector had been most intrigued, and had laughed to kill himself when this Swede had made of the illustration dramatic, having mounted himself on the table. How he had dared, of these most shocking recounts, to liken Madame la Comtesse to a — no, no, he could not degrade himself to say it.

'Say it.'

He said it with relish: that Madame had truly insatiable demands, as of a she-dog for its he-dog. 'But —' shrugging his shoulders to his ears — 'one may believe he was more mad than drunk, for only one whose brain was of a malady the most severe could have uttered such abominable idiocies. And that he did repeat how the 'antics of love', as he named them, of Madame, did disgust to make him sick at the stomach. Pardon, Madame, that one repeats this — at Madame's request — but one has made of these remarks more delicacy than was uttered at the table of His Highness the Elector of Saxony and his entourage. Madame, without doubt, does understand one's shame in this repetition, of which much, not fit for the hearing of a most gracious lady has been eliminated?'

A smile was fixed on that red stretched mouth to answer him: 'Assuredly, monsieur, one is infinitely obliged for the delicacy with which you have eliminated much of these — idiocies. But one has heard enough to realise that despite the exuberance of youth, whether drunk or sober, the count must be reprimanded.'

'Madame,' de la Cittardie leaped to his feet in a fright, 'I spoke in confidence, yes? One would not wish one's name to be mentioned in this recount. It would place one in a slightly difficult position if it were known that one repeats what is heard at the table of the Elector of whom one is a guest, would it not?'

'It is, and your name will not be mentioned, Monsieur. But this Colonel of the Elector's bodyguard must be taught how he must not behave, nor slander the wife of Hanover's Lord Chancellor.'

Still seated, she held out two fingers for de la Cittardie to bend over and raise to his lips. He, too, was a trifle pale underneath his rouge. Madame's smile made him shudder. Had he said too much, although he had not told the half of it?

'You have rendered me a service which I shall not forget,' he heard her say in a thick choked voice, which none the less reassured him. He would not suffer any dolorous repercussions for indiscretion — he hoped. With a hand on his heart and his nose on his knees, he bowed himself out.

Long after he had left she sat dazedly staring. No sound passed her fallen lips save the deep drawn breaths that caused a spasmodic heaving of her bosom until: 'Ah-a-a-Ah!' A cry as of some wounded animal broke from her, to bring her woman running.

'Dear Countess, what have you?'

'Me?' That painted mouth struggled to mutter: 'I have been asleep and dreamed … an ugly dream.'

Sophia Dorothea was in disgrace with the Electress, and in somewhat less degree with her uncle, the Elector. In defiance of authority that she should occupy the State apartments in the Leine Schloss with her husband, now back from Flanders, she had not been there to welcome his return but had fled to Celle.

On her knees to her father she again petitioned him to arrange for a divorce or a legal separation. She reminded him of her husband's cruelty, both physical and mental. How he had so brutally attacked her that she bore the marks of his violence for weeks. How he flaunted his mistress before the Court of Hanover that all the courts of Europe must know of it.

'If you had any love for me,' she cried, 'you would not suffer me to be subjected to such ill treatment that I am an object, not of pity, but of contempt that I submit to this humiliation.'

Her mother, entirely sympathetic with her case, strove to induce the duke to free their daughter from her miserable marriage and, if to avoid scandal by divorce, then surely by some other means: that of legal separation.

All of which resulted in a choleric outbreak from the harassed Duke who had more on his mind than the fantods of Sophia Dorothea. He could not afford to quarrel with his brother of Hanover, his ally in the war against the Danes who still threatened Celle's territories. Moreover, these repeated demands for divorce — great heaven, divorce! What shame to bring upon him and his brother — he believed to be a mask for some disgraceful ulterior motive. He had heard rumours of an intimate association with that reprobate Swede whom he had dismissed from his service years ago for misbehaviour with this girl of his while she was still a child.

She, clutching his hand where she knelt at his feet, was saying, or rather screaming for all his gentlemen, pages and lackeys to hear, '*You* made me marry him — you and the Electress between you! And look what has come of it. Mutual loathing. He hates me as much as I hate him. It is a sin to live with a man you hate, a sin against God!'

'Blasphemy!' roared the duke, his face apoplectically red. 'I will not listen to your ravings. I know what is at bottom of this.

You may rage against your husband's infidelities but what of your own? Is your wifely honour stainless? Is it? *Is* it?'

'You —' She choked and stayed the epithetic inexcusable retort. 'You, to accuse me of — do you demean yourself to listen to court gossip?'

'I have eyes and ears.' Her father detached her fingers still convulsively clinging to his, and bade her roughly, 'Enough of this. Enough! Get up and get out. Back to Hanover and your duty as a wife. Go!'

She went — straight to the arms of her mother; but Éléonore could do no more than promise that she would persuade the duke to reconsider, at least, a temporary separation. Yet now, she said, was not the time for intervention on her behalf. 'Your father is in great distress. The Danish war has told on his resources. He is sorely tried, so don't, my darling, try him further. Go back to Hanover, placate the Electress, bear with your husband for just a little while longer, and then — we'll see what can be done. I will do my best for my dear one. You may rest assured of that.'

With which ambiguous comfort she was sent back whence she had come, to find that in her few days' absence Philip had returned.

And now, as always, letters were exchanged under cover of Knesebeck, for they dared not meet. His position in Hanover was invidious, in that he had accepted a commission in the Swedish army and had not yet resigned his service as Colonel of the Elector's Guards. Nor did he show himself in public. He was occupied with Hildebrand, his secretary, in arranging his affairs, struggling with debts, and warding off clamorous creditors. The princess, likewise, remained in seclusion on plea of illness; so, for several days, she and Philip were unable to communicate except in written words that, if intercepted, offered damning evidence of their intent. They knew they were closely watched; every movement reported to the lynx-eyed Electress, and la Platen. She, too, was making plans of her intent, resultant on the 'recount' from de la Cittardie of Philip's performance at Dresden.

Then, regardless of danger, on the first day of July 1694, when George Louis was gone to Berlin, Knesebeck smuggled Philip to the princess's apartment by the door of the corridor that led to the Rittersaal, Hall of the Knights. He went disguised as a purveyor of trinkets for Her Electoral Highness's approval; these, presumably, gifts for her attendants of which she would lay in a store for birthday or Christmas presents. All prudence forsaken, they prepared for flight. She would go to Wolfenbüttel where she would be certain of welcome from Duke Ulrich. He would not hesitate to aid and abet her bid for freedom. He had long harboured cankerous resentment against his cousin of Celle for having bereft his son of a wife and her fortune. It was the greater loss of a fortune rather than of a daughter-in-law that rankled, unforgiven.

From Wolfenbüttel the princess would escape to France, financially supported by Duke Ulrich. There Philip would join her. Louis, at enmity with Celle and Hanover, would gladly give sanctuary to a daughter of France by virtue of her mother's birth. The Sun King had a weakness for lovers, and: 'No matter what the risk may be,' she told Philip at this, their first meeting after his return, 'I am prepared to take it.'

'As am I,' was his assurance, 'to the death.'

'No, no!' She shuddered in his arms. 'No talk of death — unless we die together. Nothing can part us now. It is life that lies before us. Life eternal.'

If they realised their danger, they were past caring. She knew — apart from her flight with Königsmarck, which, as she hoped, would bring about eventual divorce — that she would also be guilty of treason.

Her escape to Wolfenbüttel, sworn ally of Denmark and Sweden, could only be regarded as an unpardonable breach of policy in the eyes of the Hanoverian Government, even more so than her flight to France, the enemy of Hanover and Celle against whom, for years, they had been intermittently at war.

But those two, love-blinded, were ready to face whatever consequence might follow. All was now prepared. What better opportunity than to take the final plunge, with George Louis in Berlin and expected back within the next few days?

Philip had it well in hand. 'Hildebrand has implicit instructions. Tomorrow, beloved, I will be waiting for you fifty yards from the postern gate with a pair of horses. You say you have a page's suit. How adorable to see you as a boy!'

'I shan't be seen by anyone but you.' She snuggled up to him. 'Down the back stairs and in a boy's wig I'll not be noticed, and if I am then it will only be thought that Hans or one of them is stealing out to go a-courting the innkeeper's girl. My pages are all lined up to have at her — she is the prettiest thing. Knesebeck and I have often passed her when out driving, and she standing at the door to wait for a sight of a foot-page. I am,' she whispered, out of breath from his stormy kiss, 'just the least alarmed. I remember what you told me of your brother — how his page was brought to bed of a baby on the table in the kitchen of an inn where they lay the night!'

Her laughter bubbled over; he kissed again to stifle it. 'If that were so, then how would I rejoice!'

'But not on a kitchen table. Now, love, you must leave me … until tomorrow.'

'Not yet, not now. How can I leave you now when for so long I have hungered for this … and this…'

And not until late in the night, when Knesebeck at the door reminded them that the changing guard would be more watchful than the sleepy sentries, did he leave her. But they and the confidante had overlooked another, more watchful than any of the guards.

She, whose love beyond all reason had turned to bitter hate, had one desire only: to be revenged for Philip's ridicule and defamation of her before the Court of Dresden. Possessed of hell's fury she determined that full penalty be paid by him who had publicly scorned her; and with more cunning and forethought than they who rushed headlong to their fate, she also laid her plans.

'You are sure you saw the count enter the palace by a side door, guided by a light in the window? You can swear to it?'

'Dear Countess, I can swear to it.' Doggedly the spy repeated and enlarged. 'My man has sent me word that the count went disguised as a pedlar. He is with the princess now — has not gone yet. My man, who followed him, keeps watch. It is their first meeting since the count's return.'

'And it shall be their last.'

Those drawn-back lips distorted her ravaged face that the spy, Mesbeck, in a cold sudden fear, likened to one of the gargoyles on the porch of the cathedral. 'You say he goes unarmed?'

'Madame, a purveyor of baubles carries no arms. It is a disguise he has often used in the past, and also that of an apothecary to gain access to Her Highness's apartment.'

'So!' For an instant her eyes were closed. 'Often used to gain … access. You were in attendance on your officer at the banquet of the Elector of Saxony on a certain occasion?'

'Yes, Madame.'

'I have heard an account of what took place that night. Can you repeat it to me that I may have corroboration?'

Wooden-faced, the spy gave his undiluted version of how Königsmarck had entertained the Elector and his guests with lewd words and gestures to illustrate Madame's methods of seduction.

'Was the name of the princess mentioned during this — entertainment?'

'No, Madame, but before the count and others had much to drink, Count Königsmarck did speak in highest terms of the beauty and virtue of the Electoral Princess, to which the Elector did warmly agree.'

'Her *virtue*!' A grating laugh escaped her as she tendered him a purse of gold. 'Your reward for faithful service. There is more to come if my orders are obeyed.'

'I thank you, gracious lady.' He slid the purse into his pouch, turned to go, and was recalled.

'Your men are in readiness?'

'Yes, Madame, they have their instructions, but —'

'But what?' like a whiplash she demanded. 'But me no buts. There is treason here of which the Elector must be at once informed.'

'Treason, dear Countess? May I entreat your ladyship that I and my men be not involved in —'

'Nothing that can injure you.' She held him with her eyes, mere slits in the whiteness of her face beneath the paint. 'Only in so far as you will be the means of exposing a traitor and thus serving your Elector and the Duchy. Go now. I have that to do which must be done before the count shall leave the palace.'

As the door closed behind him she rang a silver bell, and to the woman who answered her summons she said, 'Have this note —' she scrawled a message, sanded and sealed it, 'delivered to His Electoral Highness immediately.'

The Elector was ailing. He had been stricken with a tertian fever, and for the past week had been kept to his bed. Clara, in nominal attendance on the Electress, occupied a wing of the palace when not in residence at Monplaisir, and since Philip's return she had seen to it that she should be in waiting on Her Electoral Highness and in immediate communication with the duke to whose apartments she now hurried.

She found him still bed-ridden, but decidedly better, and partaking of a cup of chocolate before his valet settled him down for the night.

Rising from her curtsy: 'Dismiss your man,' she said, low-voiced. 'I have to speak with you.'

The tassel of his nightcap wobbled to the startled turn of his head as he bade his valet, 'Leave us,' and to her: 'But why,' he fretfully enquired, 'do you come at me with this?' He held out the note she had sent him. 'On what urgency am I aroused from what I had hoped to be a peaceful night, now that the fever has abated?'

'Dearest.' Taking the half empty cup, she placed it on a table to kneel beside him. 'It is of the utmost urgency, or I would not have disturbed you. It has come to my knowledge of a plot against you and Hanover at the instigation of that treacherous scoundrel, Königsmarck, and the Electoral Princess. I, who have only your interest and that of the Duchy at heart, have watched and waited for conclusive evidence of that which, time and again, I have warned you, but you would not believe me. You made light of it — or mistrusted my motive. Now you *must* believe. At this very moment Königsmarck is with the princess. He beds with her. No, wait — you must hear me out. I tell you truth and nothing but the truth. I'll swear to it, as

God shall be my judge. Hanover's honour and your son's honour, is at stake. Königsmarck and the princess plan for flight together. I have taken the precaution to intercept certain of their letters. They go, or rather she goes, to Wolfenbüttel tomorrow, thence to France where Königsmarck will join her. She seeks the aid of your enemies, France and Wolfenbüttel in her adultery, while he betrays your honour as Colonel of your Guards and receives a commission in the army of his king. This is espionage and treason, in that he cannot serve two masters, passing state and military secrets back and forth to Sweden with his woman — your heir apparent's wife!'

'My God!' was the horrified incredulous response to this. 'What do you tell me? What infamy! Treason — adultery! My trusted Colonel of the Guards and the princess — my niece — my son's wife? What scandal should it be known! In the palace with the princess, you say?'

'In her bedchamber. Highness, even now, as I have ascertained. My servants are more zealous in guarding your honour than is the traitor Königsmarck, who seeks to ruin your royal name and dignity and play you into Sweden's hand, which has been his aim since first he came to Hanover — your enemy's tool!'

'My God, my God,' was feebly reiterated from the shocked duke.

'But,' she went on, taking his thick paw in hers to chafe, 'there is yet time to stop a scandal that will resound throughout all Europe. Give orders — or I will, as from Your Highness — that Count Königsmarck be arrested on a charge of treason — now!'

'To have chosen such a time as this,' moaned the Elector, 'when my son is in Berlin.' The mottled dewlaps shook to the fall of his jaw. 'Ach, my love, how can I thank you for your devoted loyalty?' He released his hand to lay it on her bowed head as if in blessing.

She caught it to kiss and said, 'There is no time to waste in thanks. That which I do and have done is only my duty as a faithful subject of my lord and master. I go now to summon the men whom I have taken upon myself — with Your Highness's permission — to arrest Count Königsmarck as he leaves the palace. I knew this would be your wish.'

'Yes, yes! Arrest him. He shall be tried *in camera,* yes? Nothing —' those eyes, so like a pair of boiled gooseberries, pleadingly sought hers — 'nothing must be known of this outside my council chamber. Your husband, my chief minister, will see to it. Have the count arrested and kept in close confinement. The princess also must be guarded until she can give account of her treachery to her husband on his return. The case must be hushed up. You understand?' Slow painful tears slid from under his puffy eyelids and dripped mournfully down his nose. 'I am too old for this.'

His sight was dimmed. He did not see the ghastly grin of triumph that bared her teeth to answer: 'Yes, it will be … hushed up, I promise you!'

'So now we burn our boats. Oh, joy!' Sophia Dorothea threw her arms round her confidante to hug her. They were busy pulling open drawers to pack into one small bag the bare necessities required by the princess for her flight. 'No more uncertainties, no more sneaking up back stairs, no more spying once we are away. I hope I can ride cross-saddle in a page's suit … Don't look so glum, Lennie. I know we can't take you with us, but once we are settled in a home of our own you will come to me. What sort of night attire does a page wear? I can't wear a nightgown. I'll have to sleep in my shirt or — nothing!'

They laughed together, but Knesebeck's laughter had a sob in it. 'If only I could come with Your Highness. You can't dress yourself even as a woman, so how will you manage as a boy?'

'Philip will dress — or undress — me! Oh, Lennie, I'm so happy. But there's fear in too much happiness and — I'm afraid.'

'So am I,' said Lennie, more than ever glum. 'Suppose they find you gone and follow you? The Count will be arrested and you —'

'And I will be arrested with him. They can't keep us apart. We would sooner die, both of us, than be parted ... My poor Fritzi!' This to the spaniel at her feet. 'You'll take care of Fritzi, won't you, and bring him with you when you come to us? He knows there is something going on. He always knows when I go away, but I am sure he guesses that this is no ordinary going. Look at his eyes.' She stooped to the dog who sat miserably gazing up at her. 'All is well, my sweet,' she told him, kissing the satiny head. 'It won't be for long, then you will be with me again. I hope he won't pine too much. Boris, Philip's boarhound, will come with us, he is used to running at a horse's heels.'

'Won't you,' suggested Knesebeck, 'go to bed now? It is so late, past midnight, and you have a longer night before you tomorrow.'

'Yes, I'll to bed, but I doubt if I'll sleep. I'm too excited. And Lennie,' she took her friend's hands in hers, 'whatever happens, you must swear to it, should they ask you — as they are bound to do when they find me gone — that you left me sleeping as usual, at eleven o'clock — Oh, I was almost forgetting. I must take this. I'll wear it under my tunic.'

'This' was a miniature of Königsmarck which she kept locked in her bureau with his letters. 'I can't take his letters, there are too many for my one little bag. You must take care of them, Lennie, and bring them when you come. And see that Fritzi doesn't pine. He may be off his food for a day or two, but the children...' Her face crumpled. 'How can I leave them? I can't ... but I must. It is the choice of them or him or ... hell!'

She rushed to the door.

'Highness, where are you going?' Lennie was after her, but she was gone, down the corridor to the nurseries. The children were asleep in their respective rooms. She tiptoed to the night nursery where the child Sophie slept, guarded by a somnolent night nurse who rose to her feet in alarm, but seeing Her Serene Highness she bobbed and ... wondered.

'I wanted,' said Sophia Dorothea, 'to see the princess. I thought she had a slight cold today when I saw her.'

'The princess is well recovered, Serene Highness, if she had a cold,' was her answer, guarding surprise.

'I wanted to make sure,' murmured Sophia Dorothea. She leaned over the child, whose head was turned sideways on the pillow, her face, flushed with sleep, resting on her hand.

The mother bent over her, a prayer in her heart. 'God forgive me, and you, my darling ... will you ever forgive me?'

The child stirred and nestled closer in her pillows. The night nurse appeared in the doorway.

'Yes, she seems quite recovered from her cold.' She slid past the bobbing nurse to the adjoining room, where her son was fast asleep. Kneeling by his bedside she buried her face in the coverlet. He lay on his back, breathing heavily through his parted lips.

He ought not, she told herself, *to breathe through his mouth. I must ask the doctor to* — Then remembrance came to strike her. 'Oh, my boy,' she whispered, 'my son, my Georgie, how can I do this to you? How can I leave you?'

Between a second and a second his eyes opened, then his eyelids sank and from those lips came a murmur, 'Mama ... goo'night.'

A sob racked her body. Tears fell on the small hand thrown out on the silken sheet. She turned, and hiding her face from the nurse who had followed her, fled back to her apartments.

I can't ... I can't, was her heart's anguished cry, *but I must ... too late ... too late ... I am condemned.*

While all this was going on in and out of the princess's bedchamber, Philip, having left the outer door of the State apartments, felt his way along the lightless corridor, for the candles in their wall-brackets were extinguished at this hour. All thought of the perilous adventure on which he was about to embark — elopement with the Electoral Princess, and the consequences when their flight should be discovered — held no qualms for him, although he knew his whole life's future was at stake. Ruin, disgrace, all would be worth it to have her for his own. Divorce must surely follow; if not, then he would have her still, so long as love should last.

Whistling a little tune under his breath he went stepping softly as a cat, and like a cat he could see in the dark along this way he knew so well that led to the Rittersaal, Hall of the Knights, where as Colonel of the Guards he had so often been in attendance on the duke at State banquets.

The door at the left of the corridor opposite the entrance to the Rittersaal, and which Knesebeck had left unlocked earlier in the evening when she had admitted him in his disguise under the unsuspicious eyes of the halberdiers, with explanation for the purpose of his coming with his pack of trinkets — that door was now locked and bolted!

The tune he still whistled between his teeth died in the clutch at his heart. He must go back to her bedchamber and wait there till morning when he could effect his escape … *Not so easy as that, my friend,* he told himself. *There's no tree at her window here, in the main wing of the palace.* Besides, in broad daylight, he would surely be seen. What would a pedlar be doing in the princess's room all night? He would have to wait there all day until tomorrow night, when Knesebeck must take a message to Hildebrand and his servants, all of whom were sworn to secrecy and utterly trustworthy, to bring the horses and baggage to the appointed meeting-place beyond the postern gate. He must go as he was, in his disguise, and change to riding kit en route. Meantime — back again the way he had come.

All his senses sharpened, he was about to retrace his steps when in the heavy silence he thought he heard the sound of breathing, or could it be his own, quickened in the certainty of danger? He was not alone! And suddenly, in that weighted dark, he discerned the faintest glimmer, not of light, of steel, reflecting the probe of a moonbeam through the chink of a loosely drawn curtain.

Adder-swift he turned to meet the flash of a sword as two shadows from that pall of darkness came at him — to strike. He had been trapped!

In a second he had leaped aside and cursed himself that he had not worn his armoured uniform under his shabby fustian. He carried no weapon more than a small dagger concealed in his belt, but with this he lunged at the first of his assailants, who uttered a hoarse oath as Philip struck home; but even as he struck again at a second man, two more rushed at him. He was one against four, all armed! Yet he who, unhorsed, had held his own against half a dozen mounted Turks, was not to be daunted by four clumsy Germans who knew nothing of a duellist's skilled sword-play.

Using his small weapon to good purpose until it was wrenched from his hand, he received a vicious stab in his armpit, slipped but was up again to wrestle and fight with bare fists. His strength giving out from loss of blood, he swayed and felt the rasp of steel under his ribs striking deep and deeper and as, overpowered, he sank, he saw in the light of a candle held high, a woman's shape. Then, as his life in a scarlet stream flowed from him while recognition swam before his eyes, still seeing, his voice still speaking...

'You! Murderess!' he gasped. 'She-devil, kill me but ... spare her ... the princess ... is innocent.'

'Liar! You lie — hot from her bed, you lie! Mesbeck —' to one of those four who nursed a wounded arm — 'finish him! He is not done for yet ... Curs! Cowards all! ... You won't? Then I *will!*'

With a snarl as of an enraged beast she raised her foot to stamp those words from his mouth where the fresh blood gushed. His head fell back, and as he stared up into that face bent above his own she withdrew in terror at the look of loathing in those dying eyes.

'God in heaven!' Another of the four had approached her victim. 'It is the colonel!' And to her whose order from the Elector had been obeyed, 'you said to make only an arrest, and if he resisted to —'

'Quiet! Fools — you fools!' she screamed at them, the candle dropping grease from her shaking hand on to that dead face. 'I gave no order to kill — to arrest only, as commanded by the

Elector — but *should* he resist, then to attack in self-defence, but not to kill. When His Highness the Elector hears of this, you will be hanged — all four of you, unless you bear witness, every one, that the count may have died in his struggle to escape, fighting like a madman, and was taken with heart failure. The Elector's own dog died in just that way. Men die and dogs die, as he, the traitor —' she kicked at the fallen body — 'dies the dog's death that he deserves. You who have disobeyed the Elector's orders have overstepped your mark, but I can save you from the hangman's rope if you testify as I instruct you.'

She gave them word for word what must be told. 'And if you follow my instructions implicitly, His Electoral Highness will be satisfied that you are not to blame for the traitor's disappearance. When questioned by the council for allowing the count to escape, and which you will swear to on oath, you may be severely reprimanded, but the various wounds you have sustained will absolve you from undue negligence, and you will receive, each one, a thousand thalers from me for holding your tongues. This I promise you.'

A promise that sufficed to overcome their scruples. To save their necks and be possessed of what to them was a fortune they, to a man, agreed to obey.

'If your evidence is doubted or disproved, this —' she kicked at the body lying in its pool of blood — 'bears witness, if discovered, of murder. The count has fled, none knows where. He will be in Sweden by the time he could be traced. He cannot be arrested in his native land. He, the servant of the Elector, has betrayed him and Hanover and has passed his spying secrets to Sweden and his king. What you have done this night is to serve your Elector and the Duchy. Your consciences, and mine, are clear.' And ignoring the doubtful looks exchanged between those four, she commanded, 'Get to work now. There is no time to lose. Fetch water and cloths. Clean all stains away. You have yet two hours before dawn. But first — the body must be hidden — there.' She pointed to a chimney-breast where, the week before, workmen had been making some repairs. 'Remove enough bricks to take the corpse and wall it in. I see that one of you carries a battle-axe. Use it, with your swords and his dagger. Make all haste and the least noise. The body must be sealed in bricks and mortar. None but you four must know of this night's work. It will be hushed up — for ever.'

And none did know of that night's work, until many years later it was revealed to the world, not by one of those four sworn to secrecy but by an aged hag riddled with a foul disease, blind and helpless who, on her death bed, confessed to her part in the murder of Count Königsmarck in the year 1694. They thought that, in her delirium, she raved; but again, many years later, when further repairs were required to the walls of the Rittersaal, the skeleton of a man was discovered, identified by the ring on its finger and the remains of some hair on its head.

ENVOIE (1727)

ENVOIE

Over, Over, Hanover over
Haste and assist our Queen and our State
Haste over Hanover
Fast as you can over
Put in your claim
Before 'tis too late

To the old tune of *Lillibullero* it had been shouted in the streets of London, in every club and tavern frequented by the Whigs, who defied the wish of their dying queen, that her exiled half-brother, rightful heir to the Throne of Great Britain and Ireland, son of her dead father, James II, should succeed her. But the Whigs would have none of him who, although he refused to renounce his adherence to the Church of Rome, had sworn he would not enforce his Catholic Faith upon his Protestant subjects. On this main issue the country stood divided. The Tories, led by Bolingbroke, loyally supported the Stuart while in derisive unison they out-bawled the song of the Whigs.

The Crown's far too weighty
For shoulders of eighty,
She could not sustain such a trophy
Her hand, too, already
Has grown so unsteady
She can't hold a sceptre
So Providence kept her away

Poor old Dowager Sophie.

Alas, the suspense, after all these years, with the sceptre almost in her hand, the crown almost on her head, was too much for that ailing body and its spirit's strength to bear. By the narrowest margin, within less than three months before the death of Queen Anne, she, self-styled 'Heiress of Great Britain and Ireland' died of a seizure while walking in her orangery at Herrenhausen. So Providence did keep her away, poor old Dowager Sophie…

In the Castle of Ahlden — euphemistically named, for it was nothing of a castle, merely a moderate-sized country house — Sophia Dorothea, one-time Electoral Princess of Hanover — now a lifelong prisoner — heard that he, once her husband, had ascended the throne of Great Britain and Ireland.

Word came to her through her mother — the widowed Duchess of Celle, grudgingly permitted an occasional visit to her daughter — how this First George of the Hanoverian dynasty had entered his capital.

With scarcely one word of English in his mouth, no love for England in his heart — for, unlike his mother, he had cherished no hope of this kingdom nor desire to leave his native land as sovereign of a country in which he was so utterly a stranger — he had driven through the streets of London with his Schulenberg and a later mistress, Frau Kielmansegg, in state coaches behind him.

The Maypole, grown scraggy in her late middle age, was soon to wear the strawberry leaves as Duchess of Kendal. Kielmansegg, nicknamed 'the Elephant' on account of her gross overweight, would be raised to the peerage as Countess of Darlington. From these two favourites, vilified by Grub

Street hacks as 'ugly old trulls', King George the First refused to be parted; yet while the Tories at their first sight of him and his 'trulls' stayed ominously dumb — save for a few of the equally loyal, if less restrained, working classes who gave vent to their animadversion in hisses and boos — the Whigs, who had brought him there, yelled themselves hoarse with their greetings. But they, too, may have found it hard to stomach a pair of such unprepossessing German women as members of their British aristocracy, or even His Majesty himself: this bloated, beery leery little man, bowing and beaming from his gilded coach, his head topped with a white wig — an innovation not greatly admired, especially by those who could still remember the entry into London of another king, restored to them after years of Cromwellian dictatorship, his black hair flowing on his shoulders — their beloved King Charles. But this German George was here and they must all, Whig or Tory, make the best, or worst, of him; although staunch Jacobites and Scots growled among themselves that he wouldn't be here long. Their king over the water, with them behind him, would sooner or later come into his own...

In the dusk of a sunless day at her window overlooking the garden of the Schloss Ahlden, bounded on one side by a moat and on the other by the river Aller, the uncrowned queen of a mighty kingdom sat watching the mist slowly rise from the level marshland beyond her prison walls.

Her hair, now silver, framed a face where the sorrowing years had left their mark in faint coin-like lines on features, just a little blurred, that still bore traces of lost beauty.

It was more than thirty years since they had brought her there, disgraced, dishonoured after a long-drawn-out tribunal in the divorce court, by which a president and eight judges had found her guilty of potential treason and desertion of George Louis, Electoral Prince of Hanover, and persistent refusal of her matrimonial duties and cohabitation with the 'illustrious Prince, her husband'.

For want of sufficient evidence, and to avoid a further scandal that had already rocked the world, the Electoral Princess was not found guilty of adultery, since he with whom she had prepared for flight, and had exchanged certain incriminating letters, had vanished … none knew where.

Day after dreary day through all these lonely years she sat waiting and watching … for what? For deliverance from this unending prison life? For the return of him who was gone, dead, murdered …. who could tell? For surely if he lived he would have come to rescue her, entombed in this living death that might have been just bearable had she been allowed her children, even on such brief visits as those conceded to her mother.

Her mind went searching back.

When they had brought her here after that mockery of a trial, deprived of her royal title, and now named Duchess of Ahlden, she was, as ever, surrounded by spies; her ladies-in-waiting were wardresses, her halberdiers gaolers to watch her every move and to intercept her correspondence, lest she should attempt to escape or communicate with her son and daughter. But she knew there could be no escape, no contact with the outside world other than her drives through the village, always with her 'ladies' in attendance; or, although not allowed to enter the cottages of villagers, she took the poor under her care, sending food to and comforts for the sick; while the school children were permitted to come to her in the castle on fête days to receive prizes from her hands.

But of her own children — for whom, with all a mother's longing, she yearned —never a sight of them was granted. Nor of her faithful Knesebeck, her one and only friend, no sight of her whom they had also taken and flung into prison as an accomplice to the attempted flight of the princess with Count Königsmarck.

Mercilessly examined, Knesebeck denied on oath that there had been any adulterous association between the count and her mistress, but they did drag from her the admission of a few letters that might have been misconstrued as — indiscreet. An admission which caused her to be taken into custody and imprisoned for four years, until a miraculous means of freedom was offered when the roof of her cell collapsed. Then, possibly manoeuvred by her sister at Mainz and other friends, one in the guise of a tiler come to repair the roof and who, with a rope let down from the roof's cavity, enabled Knesebeck to escape at night undiscovered.

When far beyond pursuit she was received by the Duke of Wolfenbüttel. Later, the princess heard, with what thanksgiving, that her daughter, now Queen of Prussia, married to her cousin, Charlotte of Brandenburg's son, had taken Knesebeck into her service, where she remained till the day of her death.

And as the prisoner of Ahlden sat, as so often she would sit, at her window, she relived the years along her Via Dolorosa, for in her despairing loneliness the past became the present and there was no life but memory.

One incident, as of a golden thread in faded tapestry, recurred to haunt her with the baying of hounds and the echo of a hunting horn ... on such a day as this, when dusk had spread a bridge between evening and the nearing night, and a new sickle moon lay on her back above a solemn yew. What hunt could be heard in that grey sullen marshland, unless a stag from the distant forest had fled his pursuers to take refuge in the river? One she saw, how vividly, to set her pulses racing with the throb of her expectant heart. Who? Who could it be uprisen from the river's mist? Not he, for whom unceasingly she waited and for whose return she hoped, even when all hope had died in the wintered ashes of unforgotten hopelessness. No, not he whom she prayed to see and would never see again. And then … ah, God! Who was this young figure wading through the moat?

The last of the day illumined him where, his arms outstretched, his voice, a boy's cracked voice that rang the changes from a harsh distressing croak to a shrill treble, called to her: 'Mother! My own darling mother! Yes, it's I, your Georgie!'

Guards rushed out, splashing through the moat to seize and take him from her — if he had ever come, if it were not a dream within a dream, born of what might have been and now could never be. For that boy, her son, a man of middle age and Prince of Wales, was forbidden by the king, his father, ever to see her again, to bring bitter enmity between father and son that endured throughout their lives.

Then, superimposed upon that vision as of a mirage in a desert waste, came another, of a girl and boy in a green arbour's shade. His words, hot-spoken, in just so adolescent a young voice, mingled with the mournful cry of curlews circling the marsh…

'And then we'll be married. I am sixteen. In four years' time you will be sixteen, and I'll be twenty … I am going for a soldier … All my family are soldiers — and great lovers.'

From the darkening sky the crescent moon cast a path of silver light across the moat where shadows met and melted in the shrouding mist. High above the yew tree one ice-blue star shone out in limitless space. Somewhere in the distance an owl hooted; and soon there was no sound of bird nor beast, no breath in the cold still air...

When her women came they found her seated at her window. Her head had drooped a little sideways; and on her parted lips a smile seemed to linger in her eyes, upraised to that lone star. Her eyelids sank. They thought she slept...

Nor did she wake.

A NOTE TO THE READER

If you have enjoyed this novel enough to leave a review on **Amazon** and **Goodreads**, then we would be truly grateful.
Sapere Books

Sapere Books is an exciting new publisher of brilliant fiction and popular history.

To find out more about our latest releases and our monthly bargain books visit our website:
saperebooks.com